Merry Christmas
·CORONATION ST.·

Maggie Sullivan writes Northern family dramas, including the bestselling Coronation Street series, that have taken her into the bestseller lists and have garnered her legions of fans and readers around the globe.

Maggie was born and brought up in Manchester where the award-winning soap was compulsory family viewing, and she acquired a lifelong passion for its legendary characters. She won't admit to having a favourite but can't deny a soft spot for feisty, strong-willed Elsie Tanner who, despite hard times, always managed to have some fun.

Maggie has a love of travelling, is a freelance lecturer, and an active member of the Romantic Novelists' Association. Maggie lived in Canada for several years, but she now lives in London.

MAGGIE SULLIVAN

HarperCollins*Publishers*

HarperCollins*Publishers* Ltd
1 London Bridge Street,
London SE1 9GF

www.harpercollins.co.uk

HarperCollins*Publishers*
Macken House, 39/40 Mayor Street Upper,
Dublin 1, D01 C9W8

First published by HarperCollins*Publishers* Ltd 2024
1

Maggie Sullivan asserts the moral right to
be identified as the author of this work

A catalogue record for this book is available from the British Library

ISBN: 978-0-00-852609-2

This novel is entirely a work of fiction.
The names, characters and incidents portrayed in it are
the work of the author's imagination. Any resemblance to
actual persons, living or dead, events or localities is
entirely coincidental.

Set in Sabon by Palimpsest Book Production Ltd

Printed and bound in the UK using 100% Renewable Electricity
by CPI Group (UK) Ltd

This book contains FSC™ certified paper and other controlled
sources to ensure responsible forest management.

For more information visit: www.harpercollins.co.uk/green

To Helen Centre

Chapter 1

October 1943

Peggy Brown clenched her fists and desperately tried to control her breathing as she stood on the concrete steps and stared at the dull stone frontage of the Weatherfield Majestic Theatre. The pillars that had been painted to look like ancient Ionic columns really did look old on what was a grey October morning, although they were brightened by the shiny new posters, advertising the Christmas Pantomime which had been attached to them and were now flapping in the breeze.

There hadn't been a panto in Weatherfield since all the theatres had gone dark at the beginning of the war in 1939 but now, four years later, here was the local repertory company preparing to bring *Jack and the Beanstalk* to Weatherfield once more, in time for Christmas. Peggy had been thrilled when she had read in the *Weatherfield Gazette* that theatres had been allowed to open again because the authorities felt that they had, in fact, an important part to play as morale boosters and distractors to the besieged citizens of Britain.

She was excited, happy even, or as happy as she could be given that the war was still raging in Europe as well as in the Pacific and the Far East, so that it was impossible to avoid all the miseries and difficulties that that entailed. But her heart had skipped a beat when she had seen, in a separate advertisement, that the Weatherfield Repertory Theatre were inviting anybody who was interested in joining the company to sign up and attend auditions. It seemed they were specifically looking to recruit new, young members to replace those who were now involved in the war effort.

At seventeen, Peggy hoped she might be just the right age. She didn't know whether she had any big talent, but she had long since been drawn to the magic of the theatre and she read the invitation over again. Whenever things got particularly bad at home, with her drunken father constantly nagging at her to get a better-paid job, or worse, threatening to take his belt to her for one imagined misdemeanour or another, she had always been able to escape to one of her special secret places where she could sit quietly and get lost in her own fantasies. Then, the previous summer, she had been introduced to the theatre when she had joined a drama club that included tuition in singing and dancing which had opened in the next village, close to where she lived at the foot of the moors on the other side of Weatherfield. She really enjoyed it and did her best to attend regularly. It was only a shame that it was run by someone from their neighbourhood who her father referred to as 'an airy-fairy theatrical excuse for a man' whom he had no time for and he'd tried to forbid her to go.

'Not the sort of man you should be hanging around,' he'd told her. But Peggy had been entranced and secretly continued attending the weekly sessions, paying for them out of the little she earned at the local newsagents, though she felt sad when they put on a Christmas show for the parents and she couldn't persuade her mother to go. Somehow, her father had found out and he'd threatened to give them both a belting – but if he had thought that that was the way to 'drive such nonsense out of her head', as he saw it, he was very much mistaken. Peggy would not be put off. If anything, she had become even more determined than ever to pursue the possibility of working in the theatre more seriously, and so, when an opportunity arose, as it had done now, she couldn't wait to get involved and 'give it a go'. And now here she was, doing her best to control her nerves as she approached the theatre to attend for an audition. It was only a shame that the day had got off to a bad start, for before it had really begun her father, suspecting that she might be up to something, had done his best to spoil things – as he usually did whenever she tried to have a bit fun.

'And where are you going?' he'd bellowed, chasing after her when she'd tried to slip out of the front door, unnoticed.

'I'm going to meet up with some old school friends.' Peggy did her best to sound defiant as she edged through the doorway, hoping that he wouldn't challenge the lie she had agreed upon with her mother.

'What do you mean, meeting friends? Why aren't you going to work? I know it's not much of a job, but at least it *is* a job. Shouldn't you be down at the newsagents already, sorting out the morning papers or whatever it is that you do there?' he had screamed at her. 'Or have you lost your job and you're not telling me? I know you, you're a lazy bugger and you'll avoid work at all costs.'

Peggy wanted to laugh and throw 'pot calling the kettle black' at him, as she thought of the miserable pittance that he contributed to the kitty each week, but instead she tried to defend herself, even though she knew it was hopeless and she could never hope to win. 'I've already sorted the papers for the paper-boys and they gave me the rest of the day off,' she said instead, glad that at least that much was true.

Her father shook his head. 'I don't know why I ever agreed to letting you take on a job like that – and for what? A pittance. It's high time you got yourself a proper job and brought some real money into this house. If you want to keep living under my roof I can see I'm going to have to march you down to the munitions factory myself and get you started earning the kind of money that'll put some decent food on the table.' He'd banged his fist down on the hall table and Peggy had jumped. 'Never mind you skiving off with your fancy friends.'

Now Peggy shivered. She resented the amount of money she had already contributed to the household coffers, knowing that her father managed to convert most of it into alcohol that he poured down his throat without even noticing. But she didn't want to get into that argument, preferring to keep her thoughts to herself. It was true that she no longer brought in the steady wages she had once been able to command when she had worked as a machinist in the local raincoat factory, but since her accident involving one of the heavy-duty sewing machines, she had no wish to work again with any kind of machinery, and certainly not the kind that had been installed when the raincoats had been swapped to make government munitions. That was the last occasion she had felt the outline of her father's belt buckle on her back, blaming her, as if the accident had been on purpose, all while her mother looked on helplessly.

She wondered what would her father have said this morning had he known where she had really been heading to spend the day? But thankfully, she had managed to flee down the street without answering any further questions.

She had reached the top of the theatre steps now and was aware of someone approaching from the street on the opposite side as she struggled to open the heavy double doors. Looking up, she saw a girl of her own age, quickly climbing the steps, her glossy dark brown hair caught up in what looked like a series of sausage rolls. With a huge effort, Peggy managed to pull back one of the heavy doors at the entrance and she held it back, smiling as the girl with the sausage curls went through, not so much as swivelling her head in acknowledgement but sailing through without a glance in Peggy's direction.

'If you're here for the auditions, perhaps you could wait for me,' Peggy called after her. 'I'm not sure where to go,' stepping aside too late as the swinging door slammed into the backs of her legs. But the girl didn't seem to hear her and she hurried through the next set of internal doors and disappeared up a short flight of carpet-covered stairs.

Chapter 2

'Don't worry, I think you'll find the auditorium is well sign posted,' said a voice behind her and Peggy turned to see another young girl coming through the internal doors that led into a small foyer. She was wearing a striking hand-knitted sweater in what her mother always referred to as fire-engine red, her mousy hair cut in a fashionable bob.

'Are you here for the auditions too?' Peggy asked, letting out a sigh of relief that she was at least in the right place. She hadn't realized how tense she was.

'Yes,' the girl said, 'though I've worked with Lawrence before so I'm hoping he'll remember me and make it easy to get through. I hear the poor love's pretty desperate.'

'Poor love?' Peggy queried without thinking. 'You know him well?'

'I worked with him for a whole season. You do know he's the director and producer?' the girl asked.

'Yes, of course,' Peggy responded quickly, hoping she hadn't sounded stupid. 'He's quite well-known around these parts for his pantomimes. Before the war he came here every year and I would love to have the opportunity to work with him, have a chance to get to know him.'

The girl chuckled. 'You might regret saying that!'

'Why? The girls in my drama club wouldn't half be jealous.' Peggy looked at her but all the other girl said was, 'Well, there's a good chance that you'll get what you wish for. I believe there are so many of the old gang from the rep company now committed to some kind of war work, or they've joined the forces, or have gone off to till the land somewhere, that I wasn't surprised to hear he's having trouble trying to put a whole new team together.'

'Oh dear,' Peggy said.

'It's not necessarily, "oh dear" at all. It could mean that new people like you might get a chance you wouldn't normally get – and it won't even matter if they're any good or not.'

'Still, I suppose he might cut down on the cast numbers in general if he really can't find enough people,' Peggy said with her usual pessimism.

'I don't think so,' the girl said. 'Lawrence likes to develop crowd scenes, wherever possible, even if they aren't written into the original script. He always told us that having lots of business going on, on stage, helps to keep the audience engaged. It gives them more to look at, adds a sort of extra layer of interest.' She stared at Peggy for a moment. 'Are you any good?' she then asked, unabashed. 'Are you likely to be offered a part?'

'I hope so, but I really don't know.' Peggy blushed. 'That's for the director to say, isn't it? I've never done anything like this before, professionally.'

The girl shrugged. 'Then there's no point in worrying about it. As I say, he's desperate – only he doesn't always do what you expect. If he does take you on, I would watch him if I were you. He can be particularly tough with first-timers.

'What do you mean? Isn't he good to work with?' Peggy suddenly felt anxious.

The girl gave Peggy a conspiratorial smile. 'You might just get lucky,' she said and she laughed as she held out her hand. 'I'm Denise, by the way, Denise Morgan.' She glanced around and frowned. 'I don't see any signs to the auditorium, do you? It seems as if someone has removed them all.' She sounded incredulous. 'Now that really is an "oh dear!" It's as bad as being stuck in one of the country lanes in the dark. But at least I do know my way around in here, so if you come with me I'll show you where the auditions are usually held. I'm sure one thing that won't have moved is the stage. And what's your name?'

'Err, it's Peggy,' she said.

Denise led the way through the auditorium as if she and Peggy were part of the paying audience. Most of the house lights as well as the footlights were on and Peggy blinked in the unexpected brightness. A man and a woman were sitting in the middle of the third row in the stalls, each scribbling notes in a notepad that was securely fastened on to a clipboard. Another young woman was playing the piano, banging hard on the keys as if the extra pressure would help to drown out the noise of the tap shoes of the small group who were singing their hearts out while hoofing away at what looked like a well-rehearsed song-and-dance routine.

'Thank you, we'll be in touch!' the man shouted mid-song and clapped his hands in a form of dismissal. The woman next to him stood up and, catching sight of Peggy and Denise, called out, 'Name?' as she moved along the row, through the upturned seats, while beckoning them to come closer.

'I've worked at the rep with Lawrence before,' Denise informed her as she drew close and the woman glanced up.

'So, you know the routine? You remember where to go?' she said, pointing her clipboard in the general direction of the stairs at the side of the stage that led to the wings. Denise nodded. 'I'll show Peggy, if you like,' she said confidently.

The woman waved them both away. 'You can use the large dressing room if you need to change,' she said, going back to her seat. 'We're running a bit late but we'll be calling you shortly. You can leave your sheet music with me; I'll make sure the pianist gets it.'

'Sheet music?' Peggy sounded alarmed as Denise handed hers over. 'I don't have any sheet music. I didn't know we had to . . .'

The woman shrugged. 'It's not a must, you can just tell me what you're going to sing.' She nodded her head as she wrote 'We'll Meet Again' next to Peggy's name. 'Don't worry, I'm sure the accompanist will know that already,' and she gestured a sign of dismissal with her clipboard in the direction of the dressing room.

Peggy had only ever experienced one previous audition and that had been when she had been asked to show what she could do before being allowed to join the drama club, although it was unlikely that anyone would be refused entry into the club on the strength of their performance at the audition. However, the teacher had said that it would be helpful for them to experience exactly what was involved, in case they ever wished to take their drama work seriously to the next level of performance.

'It's important,' the teacher had said, 'for you to know what to expect should you ever be called upon to attend a real audition with a job dependent on it at the other end,' and Peggy had taken her words seriously. She had never forgotten the feelings she had experienced on that day but they were nothing compared with the feelings she was experiencing now: standing with her own accompanist in a full-size theatre in front of a real, professional director with a job dependent on her performance.

She had no costume to change into, although she had brought her tap shoes with her, second-hand ones that her mother had found in a Salvation Army charity shop. The only problem was that they were black and she had hoped for red ones, but she knew she should be grateful and she had shined them up properly. She slipped them on in the dressing room, delighted that they made her look and feel like a real dancer, only pinching a little. She tied the satin bows as loosely as she could and hoped they wouldn't come loose as she followed Denise through the rabbit warren of corridors that took them under the stage, behind the scenery, and into the wings where Denise had said they should wait.

Denise was called first and Peggy watched, peeping out from in between the scenery as the girl strode out confidently and proceeded to perform two songs and an intricate little dance. She only seemed to be partway through when the director clapped his hands and called, 'Thank you!' Denise stopped, a look of surprise on her face. 'You've been with us before, Denise, haven't you?' Lawrence Vine asked and Denise nodded enthusiastically. 'Yes, I have,' she said. 'I was in the chorus for your production of—' But he didn't let her finish. 'Then that will be all for now, thank you,' Lawrence said. 'Make sure we have all your contact details. Next!'

Peggy stepped out of the wings onto the empty stage when her name was called, wishing she could look half as confident as her new friend. She looked out at the rows and rows of red velvet seats that were empty now and did her best to imagine what it might feel like to be playing to a full house. She took a deep breath and then stumbled towards the front of the stage, desperately trying to remember the opening words of the Vera Lynn song, 'We'll Meet Again', she had chosen to sing. She could clearly hear the piano and she recognized her cue to come in, but to her horror, when she opened her mouth no sound came out. The pianist was kind enough to say nothing as she replayed the introductory bars one more time, pressing heavily on the last key to give Peggy her final cue, as if that would make any difference. She made another attempt to start but noticed that the director was tapping on his clipboard for her to stop.

'I-I'm really sorry,' Peggy said, looking out at her audience of two. 'I'll start again, if I may.'

'I think you better had,' he said.

'Perhaps you should pause completely for a moment,' the woman beside him said. She stood up and clasped her hands to her rib cage. 'Now, why don't you take a deep breath, like this . . .' She demonstrated, her ribs lifting her hands away from her chest. 'And try again,' she said on a long outward breath. Peggy did as the woman had suggested and this time a reasonably sweet note came out that she was able to sustain for several seconds. The pianist picked up the melody and she completed the rest without further incident. At the end of the song Peggy stood still, her breath coming in short gasps, and she didn't dare to move until the director called out, 'I believe you have prepared a short dance routine for us?'

'Yes, I have,' Peggy said. 'It's the sailor's hornpipe.' Before she could ask if they had the correct music, the pianist struck up the opening chords that she recognized and Peggy took up her position, feet splayed, arms carefully folded aloft. She was concentrating so hard, trying to remember the initial sequences, that she missed the opening steps and looked as if she was about to fall over her own feet. But then they miraculously disentangled and Peggy then was off, legs pumping up and down, arms rolling forwards then backwards, head tilting, but it was some beats before she was able to fully pick up the rhythm and relax into any kind of passable performance and her only concern was whether she had managed to save the day.

Chapter 3

The letter that would decide her fate was promised for the next morning and although she had hardly dared to hope, Peggy made certain she was up in time, just in case the theatre people had indeed sent out the audition results right away. She was prepared to snatch any letter she might receive from the postman's hand before it had time to hit the mat, ready to squirrel it away to her room – and to her amazement, there *was* one letter that morning and it was addressed to her. Not wanting to wait until she was upstairs, she checked to make sure that she was alone, struggling to contain her excitement when she saw the repertory company's seal on the back of the envelope. But her hands were shaking so much she was hardly able to tear it open. She scanned through it as quickly as she could, immediately registering that it had been signed by Lawrence Vine, the director himself. She stopped only when she came to the phrase she hadn't dared to look for at first, 'We are pleased to offer you . . .' Then she gasped and continued skimming through while doing her best to pick out any other relevant words. Through watery eyes she managed to see the words, 'singing, dancing' and 'chorus' and read what she thought was a reporting time for later in the morning of that day. But she only paused long enough to absorb the final line: 'Please report to the theatre in good time for first rehearsals to begin promptly . . .' and she couldn't help a slight squeal escaping.

Peggy had thought that the audition had not gone well; as she told her mother, her nerves had got the better of her, making her dance as if she had two left feet, and although she had been flattered when Lawrence kept telling her how pretty she was and that her svelte figure and long slim legs looked as if they were made for dancing, she really had not expected to be chosen, particularly as the other judge had been keen to bring her back to reality, telling her that she would have to be prepared to do some serious work on her voice projection if she was to get anywhere with a stage career.

When she heard heavy shoes clattering down the

wooden staircase she immediately hid the letter behind her back but she was relieved to see it was her mother and she rushed towards her, embracing her in a hug.

'Oh, Mam! You must look at this! Can you believe it?' She shoved the letter under her mother's nose and all but sang out the words, not hearing her father's footsteps follow his wife's down the stairs and she was alarmed when he snatched the letter out of her hand. He caught hold of her arms, his fingers painfully sinking into the flesh. Lifting her off her feet, he spun her around, not planting her back firmly on the ground until her face was only inches from his own.

'What's all this, then?' He spat the words out at her and she had to wipe away the saliva that landed on her cheeks. 'You little liar!' he shouted. 'Out with your friends yesterday, were you? Then what's this about you attending auditions, eh? And all this nonsense about rehearsals? You've been sneaking off behind my back to that fancy drama place you're so fond of, haven't you? Go on! Admit it!'

With a mixture of hatred and fear, Peggy watched him reach for his belt, feeling the bile rising in her throat. She was too old for this. How much longer could she let it go on? Why did her father feel he still had the right to treat her like a child? It had been bad enough when she *had* been a helpless child,

21

and it was always worse when he had been drinking, but now it was time she stood up to him and put a stop to it. She had never been sure whether she had enough talent to try for a career on the stage but the letter had finally given her the ammunition she needed. Silently, she hung her head for a moment or two, desperately wanting to speak, yet knowing that if she did she wouldn't be able to keep the giveaway trembling note from her voice and she couldn't afford to show weakness. She was gathering her thoughts when, to her surprise, she heard her mother speak up.

'No, Henry,' she said, her voice unusually cold and hard. 'There's no need for that.' She indicated the belt and made a tentative movement towards him but stopped short of actually touching his hand. Peggy stared at the belt that he had failed to unhook, surprised at her mother's boldness. 'Why can't you leave the girl alone?' her mother asked. 'You should be pleased she's been offered a job and one that she'd really love to do.'

'Call that a job? In a bloomin' pantomime?' Henry Brown sneered. 'That's kid's stuff, for kid's money. What we need is a decent wage coming into this house now that I can no longer do it myself.' He paused and wheezed out an exaggerated chesty cough. Both Peggy and her mother looked at him incredulously as he turned to Peggy, wagging his finger in her face. 'Well, let me tell you something for nothing, you won't be doing a job like that off my back. If you think you can carry on living under this roof with your crazy ideas, then all I can say is you've got another think coming, cos I shan't be keeping you.'

Peggy gasped, only too aware that the boot had been on the other foot, and that it was she who had been providing him with beer money.

'Go and see how far your stupid dreams get you when you need to put a roof over your head and food on the table. I guarantee you won't be able to look after yourself for more than five minutes and then you'll be sorry you didn't grab the chance to take on a proper job like one of them going begging in the munitions factory. And don't think you can come back here to sponge off me. I won't be taken for a fool. I've already been too soft and now I want you gone. Get out of my sight and away from here – you're a drain on this family. And I'm warning you: once you set foot outside this house there'll be no coming back. And from now on, no one from this family will have owt to do with you.' He turned to his wife, advancing towards her menacingly. 'Do you hear what I say, woman? And I mean no one!'

His voice had risen and as Peggy automatically took a step back towards the staircase, she noticed her young brother, Colin, coming down the stairs. He stopped before he reached the bottom and hovered uncertainly, looking as if he really wanted to run back up to his bedroom. But before anyone else had a chance to move, Peggy's mother scooped the eight-year-old off the final step and into her arms, cradling him close to her chest, well out of reach of his father. It was as though he was a babe in arms again and, not surprisingly, the boy struggled to be free. Not that Henry seemed to notice; he was too busy still glaring at Peggy.

'I'm telling you, I want you out of my sight!' He was shouting again, almost at screaming pitch now, and he made another move to release his belt, swearing as he was unsuccessful. 'You and your blooming fancy ideas. I'd get out now, while you still can, if I were you! You're neither use nor bloody ornament around here, and ain't that the truth?' He threw the letter onto the floor in disgust, stamping on it and grinding it down onto the floorboards with his heavy work boots. Peggy let out the breath she had been holding, and as he stepped away, bent down to retrieve what was left of the white vellum, relieved that the immediate danger from the metal-buckled belt seemed to be over.

'Don't worry, I'm going!' She managed to squeeze out the words though her breath was tight. But she would get to the theatre on time – come what may, she wasn't going to be late on her first day. She stuffed the crumpled paper back into her pocket then fled up the stairs to the safety of her room.

Chapter 4

There was a tentative knock before she even had time to close the door and Peggy shrank back in a momentary panic, breathing hard. To her relief, it was her mother's face that peered in. The two hugged silently until her mother pulled away, smoothing her greying hair with one hand and patting the pink candlewick cover with the other so that they could both sit down on the bed.

'Why does he always have to do this?' Peggy no longer tried to hide her tears. 'He treats me like I'm still a child when I'm seventeen now. It doesn't make any sense.'

'No, it doesn't,' her mother agreed, 'but I honestly think he responds automatically nowadays. He doesn't stop to think what he's doing and why. If he feels he's being challenged in any way, he just hits out and reacts. It's like he has to show who's boss.'

'Well, I've had enough of having to live with his reactions, if that's what they are! After all these years I shouldn't still be worrying about what kind of a mood he might be in when he gets up or whether he'll talk to me without snapping my head off when I get home from work. I'm fed up tiptoeing around him. I can't do it anymore – no, I don't *want* to do it anymore.'

There was a short pause then Peggy looked directly at her mother. 'I'm sorry, Mam, but I think he's gone too far. It's time I left and found somewhere of my own, even if it's just a room somewhere.' Peggy had at first fleetingly entertained the idea that she might be able to live at home if she was offered a job in the theatre, but she knew now that that would be impossible. 'In fact, maybe he's doing me a favour by turfing me out of here. I might be better off moving closer to the theatre, perhaps even sharing with someone. I'll make new friends at the theatre and I'm sure the rep company must have lists of people with rooms to rent and they'll be cheap, too.'

'Yes, I agree,' her mother said, wiping her eyes. She looked as if she was trying her best to put on a cheerful face. 'You'll be better off being with other people, especially those that you're working with,' she said, though she couldn't stop herself snuffling into a freshly laundered white handkerchief. 'I just worry that if you're not earning much you won't be able to manage – and I won't be able to help you out.'

'You don't have to concern yourself with things like that, Mam. It doesn't matter how much, or how little, I earn – I'll make do and I'll manage, I promise you. And what's more, I'll make sure I can save a bit, however small, each week so that every now and then I can send a little something for you and Colin.' She set her face into a frown. 'Just you watch, I'll prove him wrong!' Then she grinned as she wagged her finger. 'But it will only be for you two, mind. I don't want to hear that he's used it to buy more stuff to pour down his throat, giving you nowt.' She hated the thought of her father getting hold of her money somehow, no matter how small an amount, and she worried that her mother would be too soft if he challenged her. She jerked her thumb in the direction of the door, as if expecting her father to come crashing through at any moment. 'You have to promise me that won't happen,' she begged. 'He mustn't get anything.' She certainly did not want him using any of her hard-earned cash as his beer money, even though she knew he did that now.

'Oh, you mustn't worry about us,' her mother began. 'Don't even think about it—'

'But I do think of it,' Peggy cut in. 'I can't help thinking about what he might do if he no longer has me to use as a punchbag. What if he turns on Colin?'

Her mother looked shocked for a moment, as though the thought had never occurred to her.

Peggy looked up directly and was aware of her mother's hand covering her own. Tears were sliding down the older woman's cheeks but she didn't say anything.

'You know, I've never understood why he feels the need to treat me like a wicked child all the time,' Peggy said, scrutinizing her mother's face. 'And then I ask myself if it's me he hates or whether there's something about the theatre that he objects to. It certainly seems that way at times, but whenever I've brought it up before you've always dismissed the idea, haven't you? I know, whenever I've asked you questions before, you've never really answered them, have you?' Peggy whispered.

It took several moments, then her mother shook her head. 'That's because I don't really know the answers.' Then she added, 'But I'm happy to tell you what little I know.'

'Why don't we go back to the beginning right now and you can tell me, even if I've heard some of it before. Please?' Peggy pleaded.

Her mother sighed. 'Well, what I know is that his mother ran off with someone when he was very young and never came back. I've always wondered if maybe that had something to do with the kind of man he became.' She shrugged. 'I can only guess, though, I don't really know, but he grew up not really liking women very much. Of course, as he's grown older he's tried to drown his sorrows and I reckon that his moods nowadays are to be more associated with his excessive drinking. He didn't use to drink so much when we first got married, but that has definitely got worse over the years and very much worse recently.' She paused while she blew her nose.

'And the bit about him hating the theatre?' Peggy prompted. 'Where did that come from, do you think?'

Her mother shrugged. 'Who knows? All I can tell you is that his mother ran off with one of the workers she met at a local carnival one year – from what I gather she was completely besotted with him.'

Peggy sat forward eagerly. This was something she had never heard before, but her mother held out her hands, palms up, in a helpless gesture and shook her head without saying anything more. Peggy let the silence hang, then she said sadly, 'I see. So maybe the best thing really is for me to leave.' She put her arms around her mother's shoulders, as the older woman began to sob. 'I hate the thought of leaving you like this,' Peggy said.

Her mother blew her nose and patted her daughter's hand. 'It will probably be for the best. It's important for you to go off and live your life, Peggy. We'll manage. We always have.' She squeezed Peggy's hand. 'And much as I hate to admit it, you'll be far safer out of the house.'

Peggy got up and began to pack a small, battered suitcase with her scant belongings. Her mind was in turmoil as she realized for the first time since the letter had arrived exactly what it would mean to strike out on her own, to no longer have a family or a home to come back to. She felt scared, but she knew she had to make a clean break; she had no choice – for, once she left, there was no going back. She lifted her chin and set her face into a mask of determination as she clicked shut the locks on her case. She would be leaving behind the two people she loved most in the world but there was no other way for her now. She hugged her mother and went slowly down the stairs. And, as she slammed the front door behind her, she realized just how angry she was with her father for taking all the pleasure out of what should have been a very special day for her.

Chapter 5

Arriving alone at the theatre with her old battered suitcase on that first day of rehearsals felt very different to Peggy from attending a short audition. There seemed to be so many people rushing back and forth, gaily greeting each other, and she stood for a few moments on the steps, trying to take it all in. She was finally here, had made it despite her father, and what happened next was now entirely up to her.

In the foyer there were signs indicating that the Male dressing room was to the right and the Female dressing room was to the left, but first Peggy peered inside the auditorium, surprised to find the stage was already buzzing with people gathering. She shut the doors quickly and followed the arrows that had been put up down several flights of stairs that led deep into the rabbit warren of corridors and rooms that underpinned the building and she hoped she wouldn't get lost in the maze of narrow passages that threaded back and forth underground. If she had thought the front of house was impressive, she was now equally impressed by the myriad of hallways that allowed actors, unseen by the audience, to criss-cross from one side of the stage to the other without interfering with the action on the stage above. It would be a good place to be in the event of an air raid, Peggy mused, although she shuddered as she thought of there being dozens of people crammed into the small spaces, all having to share the stale air.

Signs declaring No Smoking hung from the ceiling, and some had been pasted onto the walls; given the narrowness of the passages Peggy could see why they were necessary. But from the nicotine-stained paintwork and the lingering smell of stale tobacco that hung in the air throughout the entire underground labyrinth, it was obvious that not everyone abided by the rules.

The passages were dimly lit, which only added to the hazardous nature of the whole area and Peggy had to tread carefully and keep close to the wall to steer clear of the stagehands who were bringing up some old scenery flats from the basement below. She tried to imagine what it would be like down there on performance nights, with everyone rushing back to the dressing rooms for their costume changes, colliding in the corridors, while all announcements over the Tannoy were drowned out by the music emanating from the orchestra pit.

The deeper she got, the more Peggy became aware of the murmur of conversation that seemed to be growing louder, and as she rounded a corner she finally came upon the room labelled Ladies Dressing Room where the noise was coming from. Outside there were rows of hooks with costumes hanging from them, some already labelled with the names of the actors and actresses who would be wearing them.

She pushed the door open gingerly and was immediately greeted by a wave of hot, rancid air. Shocked to see the number of occupants who were crowded into the small room, she was knocked back by what was the result of too many sweaty bodies being crammed into a tiny space. But no one else seemed to notice. They were all eagerly chattering, only pausing momentarily as Peggy entered.

There weren't enough chairs for everyone to sit down and those who had been lucky enough to have grabbed one sat facing what looked like a row of small dressing tables, each with a set of small drawers. The cheap plywood tabletops were littered with hairbrushes, combs, pads of cotton wool and different colours and sizes of pansticks of make-up that looked and smelled as if they were in various stages of decay and melting greasily; some countertops even had overflowing ashtrays. A mirror surrounded by starkly lit lightbulbs was propped up on each of the tables, although it seemed that every second one of the bulbs had either been deliberately extinguished or was not working. Peggy had seen pictures of illuminated make-up tables like those featured in her favourite women's magazines and had always thought they looked very glamorous, but now she was near enough to touch one she was disappointed to find that, close to, they actually looked cheap and flimsy.

In fact, the whole room looked as if it was a throwback to the Victorian era and would have benefited not only from an update but from a coat of paint. She wondered if Daphne Dawson, the star of the show, was sharing this room with the rest of the cast or whether she had at least got a dressing room that was more befitting her leading status and she looked around to see if she could spot her, but she was distracted when she heard a voice shout, 'Peggy! Darling!' and she was delighted to see Denise, on the other side of the room, jump up and then rush over to hug her.

'I was wondering if you'd got through the audition. I'm so pleased to see you!' Denise seemed genuinely thrilled.

'Yes, I got the letter today and I'm really, really excited,' Peggy said, not wanting to tell her new friend the whole story. 'I could hardly believe it! I still have to keep pinching myself at the thought of me working with the great Lawrence Vine.'

Denise raised her eyebrows and made a sort of snorting sound. 'It's certainly good to be working again, and I'm happy enough to be working with Lawrence, though I don't know that I'd say he was *great*.'

'He is in my eyes.' Peggy blushed.

'It's not as though he's world-famous or anything,' Denise said. 'Let's just say . . . he's well-known in the profession.' She hesitated, as though she was choosing her words carefully. 'Maybe those who work with him in the business have a different view of him; I mean, we all see a different side of people at work than at home.'

Peggy felt momentarily deflated. 'Well, all I can tell you is that he's very popular around here,' she insisted. 'Everyone looks forward to the panto season in these parts and I don't know anyone who wasn't thrilled when they heard he was coming back this year.' She hesitated not wanting to add, except perhaps her father. But she did finish with, 'I, for one, think it's an honour to be working with him, don't you?'

'Let's just say that I've worked with him before so I'm used to his little ways and I don't get too many surprises. The thing is, not everyone loves him and not everyone is as much in awe of him as he likes to think,' Denise said cautiously. 'But then, you must remember that we're only talking pantomimes here, not William Shakespeare. It's just that he has a bit of a reputation in the entertainment world and you have to be prepared for the fact that he doesn't always live up to expectations. All I can say, darling, is that I hope he lives up to yours,' she finished with a grin.

There was a moment of tension as Peggy stared at Denise, trying to make sense of her words, then she leaned forward and hugged her new friend and quickly changed the subject. 'I always wondered if it was true that actors really did call each other darling,' she said.

'Of course they do,' Denise said lightly. 'Especially when they can't remember someone's name, isn't that right, ladies?' She looked around at the group of girls who now almost surrounded them, each trying to catch a glimpse of themselves in the nearest mirror.

'It certainly is,' one of them said, 'although they're not always quite so pleasant and polite to each other when they're scrambling for a spot where they can apply their make-up and there's hardly enough room to sit down.'

'Then no one's anyone's darling,' another girl said, 'and they don't give a damn what anyone's name is.' Several other girls laughed at that and nodded in agreement but before anyone could comment further they were interrupted by the sound of someone running along the corridor, panting and not stopping until they reached the dressing-room door. Then a young boy's voice called out, 'Opening chorus on stage in five minutes please! Opening chorus and beginners, please!'

'Who's that?' Peggy asked in surprise. Denise sighed. 'That is an example of what life in the theatre has been reduced to recently. There used to be a perfectly good Tannoy system down here before the war but it seems they've gone back to using child labour,' she said. Several people tittered. 'Honestly, it's back to the bad old days. Probably had to show willing to give up something for the war effort.' She stood up, preparing to leave, and so did most of the girls. 'I suppose it gives some young lad employment, gets him onto the first rung of the ladder so that he can say he's got a job in the theatre.' Denise gave a wry smile.

'Beats scrabbling up chimneys,' someone else quipped and everyone laughed.

Then everyone seemed to move at once and Peggy felt as if she had been caught up in a maelstrom as she was almost knocked off her feet. She didn't know which way to go and, having lost sight of Denise momentarily, was relieved when she heard her friend's voice. 'Stick with me, Peggy, love,' she heard Denise call out and felt a tug on her jacket. She grabbed hold of Denise's outstretched hand and followed her as she led the way upstairs.

The final flight of steps led directly into the wings and Peggy realized that she had surfaced on the Prompt side of the stage where many of the other cast members were already milling about. She peered into the tiny cubicle, wondering what it might be like to have to sit on a stool in such cramped quarters, night after night, with only the beam of a torch guiding the way through the script. There was certainly no room for anything else.

As the entire company gathered together on the stage, Peggy was surprised by the large number of cast and stagehands who were involved in the production. The stage manager called aside the stagehands, lighting technicians and props manager and very soon the whole stage had come alive. The footlights and spotlights were being tested and the stage was being marked out so that the first essential pieces of props and furniture could be strategically placed. Large two by four flats that looked as if they had been freshly painted with background scenery were being hauled across the stage in readiness for later that day when they would be put together like an oversized jigsaw according to the set designer's blueprint.

Peggy watched from the wings as the musicians filed into the pit that was half hidden by the front apron of the stage. She couldn't see if the conductor was on his rostrum yet, wielding his baton, though she thought he probably wasn't as she could hear the individual instruments still tuning up.

Then everyone seemed to stiffen and when Peggy heard a voice she recognized she felt a strange fluttering in her stomach as Lawrence Vine himself stepped forward and held his hands up for silence.

'Welcome to the Weatherfield Rep,' he said, 'and to our new version of the old favourite *Jack and the Beanstalk*. Now, we have a lot of work to get through in a short space of time and, as you can see, some of the backroom boys have already started. Next, we need all the supporting actors to come forward onto the stage, please, so that we can begin blocking out the opening scene. Everyone needs to know where they should be starting from and where they should be going to by the end of the scene.'

There was a lot of uneasy shifting of feet and self-conscious giggling, but Peggy was struck by the respect his deeply resonant voice commanded. She had noticed it when she had first met him at the previous day's auditions and it was even more apparent now in the large auditorium where it sounded as if it was being carried effortlessly to the back of the gods. Peggy thought of her own voice, sure it would carry no further than the front row of the stalls, and she admired how easily he was able to project above the hubbub, making himself heard in all corners of the theatre without having to shout. He held up his arms once more for silence and, once again, everyone complied. He certainly has an awesome, almost intimidating, presence, Peggy thought. It wasn't that he was big or muscular but he had a certain aura of authority and when he followed up his orders with an encouraging pat on the bottom, mostly of the young women as they passed by, they smiled and nobody complained.

Peggy studied his face and had to acknowledge that he was good-looking, with a film star's sort of style, and she had to admire how the sharp cut of his clothes outlining his lithe figure somehow enhanced his good looks and the way he sleeked back his blond hair to accentuate his unusually low hairline sent a frisson down her spine.

As people around her began milling about, Peggy stepped out of the melee to the edge of the stage and peered at the upturned seats of the almost empty auditorium where, in a few short weeks, a Weatherfield audience would pay for the privilege of sitting. She took a deep breath and felt a brief surge of excitement. She closed her eyes tightly, as if to hold on to the image. This was what she had been dreaming about for so long. If only her mother could see her now, she would truly understand that this was where Peggy needed to be. But the excitement was short-lived, for when she opened her eyes again she couldn't help noticing how much the crimson upholstery had faded, how worn the velvet – and how badly the once magnificently sculpted auditorium required a fresh coat of paint. She looked down at her feet, shocked to see that, close to, even the stage itself was in need of some repair and didn't look as grand or as magical as it had always appeared when viewed from the auditorium. She had been too nervous on the day of her audition to notice such things, but today she had got close enough to see there was nothing glamorous about the stage itself and that the floor was actually made-up from odd, not to say old, planks of wood that didn't match. And all she could think of was not wanting to have to dance barefoot.

It was not even as smart-looking as the only other stage she knew, which was in the local school where the drama club met. She had never expected that one to feel special, but she was disappointed to find that a professional stage didn't look any better.

Maybe some of the magic would be recaptured when all the scenery and lighting were in place and Jack's beans could be seen to be growing as high into the sky as the flies would allow, but for now she felt quite let down. She heaved a sigh as she reflected on what a day of contrasts it had been and she thought about Charles Dickens' famous line that she had once recited at a school concert: 'It was the best of times, it was the worst of times', for that seemed to succinctly summarize her feelings. What should have been the most exciting day of her life had actually been a disappointing one, beginning with the row that had sparked when she had received the letter of acceptance. Maybe she was judging too soon, but it was difficult to accept that the reality of the theatre she had so far experienced did not match up to the theatre of her dreams.

Chapter 6

Lawrence rapped with his pen on the clipboard he was carrying and called them all to order and for a moment Peggy thought she was back at the drama club. 'Ladies and gentlemen, boys and girls, this is where the hard work begins – here, now. And it *will* be hard I can assure you. First, a brief reminder what *Jack and the Beanstalk* is all about in case you haven't read the script thoroughly or you got hold of a different version of the story.

'Basically, apart from the few who are playing specifically named characters like the bean seller or the Giant, the rest of you are all supposed to be townspeople, friends of Jack Spriggins the poor, young boy who lives in a farm cottage with his widowed mother and a dairy cow. You will be pleased to know there will not be a real cow in this production.' He paused, as if waiting for the inevitable titter, and several people obliged. At the end there was much shuffling of feet, coughing and throat-clearing but the noises died away as his sharp gaze swept across the stage, missing no one.

Lawrence's manner had begun by being chatty and friendly but Peggy quickly detected what she could only describe as a steely edge to his voice, and from the look in his eye as he surveyed the large group as a whole, it was clear he expected his wishes to be carried out to the letter and that there was no room for discussion, interpretation or anyone lagging behind.

'Now,' he said after a moment's silence, 'I'm going to ask you to get together in small groups and for each of you to identify a specific character for yourself within that group. You might decide to be a shopkeeper or the schoolteacher's daughter – I don't care, so long as the character is clear enough to you so that when you have to come together in small groups between songs you won't just be standing about. When you're supposed to pretend to chat together, I want you to be *actually* chatting together animatedly. Not loud enough for the content to be heard, of course, but in such a way as to look convincing to the audience.'

Lawrence then paused and introduced the man who had been standing next to him as his assistant director, Jimmy Caulfield. 'I'm afraid I won't be with you for what's left of the morning,' Lawrence said, 'but I will be handing over the reins to my right-hand man who will take you through your paces.' He nodded to his deputy. 'Jimmy will stand in for me whenever I'm not available,' Lawrence said, 'like now, when I have other actors to deal with and I know he'll make sure you're working hard.' He glanced in the direction of his second-in-command. 'Be nice to him – though not too nice!' And he flashed a smile which Peggy noticed the deputy did not return. Then, as Lawrence left the stage, the large group quickly broke up, everyone looking to connect with someone they wanted to work with.

Jimmy Caulfield's style was very different, although he still managed to keep them working hard and after Lawrence's departure he took centre stage where, in somewhat gentler tones, he issued his own instructions. 'You have five minutes to get yourselves into groups,' he said, his manner non-threatening by contrast to Lawrence's. 'Introduce yourselves within your group and ask any questions you need so that you can begin to get to know each other. By the time we break, you should know at least three things about the other person that you could pass on if you had to introduce them to the audience. After that, we'll move on to some group gelling exercises that I'll explain and later we'll finish with some improvisations where you'll develop small scenarios for your characters. No scripts, just you having to ad lib.'

Several of the younger people looked horrified when he said this but he just smiled, not unpleasantly. 'I may as well tell you now that by the time we meet up again this afternoon, I expect you'll no longer be just a stage full of strangers but you'll already be thinking like ensemble actors, collaborative colleagues if not yet actual friends. I'm relying on the more seasoned actors among you to take the lead in these exercises and to show those of you who are new to the whole experience how to pool your skills and support each other.'

Peggy was grateful when Denise asked if she would like to join the group she was putting together, and immediately introduced her to two young men Peggy had never seen before, although it transpired that Rob Hill and Rick Waters had also been at the auditions the previous day and they seemed to remember her although Peggy didn't recall seeing them. Rob had a limp from having polio as a child and Rick wore thick glasses; Peggy wondered if they hadn't passed the medical for the army call-up. The two boys were friends who travelled about in rep and they always tried to get work together. Peggy shook hands with them warmly, though she couldn't help thinking that her father would have looked at them suspiciously and written them off as being 'too bloomin' theatrical for their own good', a phrase she had never understood and he had never bothered to explain.

Denise said there was another, slightly older girl she wanted to ask to join them, someone she had worked with before, and when she grasped hold of the girl's arm in order to steer her across the stage, Peggy instantly recognized her as the young woman she had seen on the theatre steps on the morning of the audition. Peggy made no reference to it and was surprised to hear that she and Denise were well-acquainted. 'This is Nora Johns, everyone,' Denise said, bringing Nora forward, 'and I can tell you, before anyone asks, that we first met in the chorus of a previous panto directed by Lawrence and we got to know him pretty well.' The two girls exchanged a knowing look, though Peggy was not quite sure what they were trying to say.

'My real name's Eleanor Johnstone,' the newcomer said, 'though I think I'll stick with Nora Johns from now on. After doing two different productions as Nora, it's beginning to grow on me, though I still forget sometimes.' She turned, 'And you are?' she asked, scrutinizing Peggy's face.

'Margaret de Vere,' Peggy said, 'though I still answer to Peggy Brown so often that I sometimes forget I'm supposed to be Margaret.' She laughed uneasily, thinking how pretentious the new name sounded, wondering if she would ever feel comfortable enough to use it all the time. It was a name she had randomly picked out for herself on the day she had decided to follow her dream because she'd thought it sounded much more sophisticated and grown-up than the name her parents had given her. But so far she still felt somewhat bashful about introducing herself as Margaret even though Peggy Brown reminded her, in an uncomfortable way, of the life she had left behind. She rolled the words Margaret de Vere around silently in her mouth and even said them softly out loud, though she giggled with embarrassment when she saw Nora looking at her strangely. 'No, I'm not really going mad,' she said, clearing her throat. 'I'm still trying to get used to my new name. I'm not really sure I like it but it does help to put a healthy distance between me and my family.' She lowered her gaze and said softly, 'My – my father doesn't agree with me being here.'

There was silence for a few moments then Nora said gaily, 'I know what you mean, but don't get rid of the old one just yet. I've always said that the day my name goes up in lights in front of the theatre is the day I'll permanently become Nora,' she said dreamily.

'Yes, I often wonder what it would be like to have my name in lights. And I do think that would help me to remember.' Peggy gave a self-conscious giggle.

'I believe names can be really important in lots of ways,' Nora said. 'Choose the right one and it can help catapult your career.'

'Nora's the understudy for the principal boy,' Denise explained with a certain pride as if she had been a party to the decision. 'If that's not a potential catapult, then I don't know what is.'

'Really?' Peggy's eyes grew wide. 'That must be a huge step up! Daphne Dawson's the star of the show, isn't she?'

Nora nodded. 'Unfortunately I can't claim that since becoming her understudy my career has gone anywhere, at least not yet, though I keep telling myself I've still got plenty of time for things to happen – not that I wish Daphne any ill,' Nora added quickly. 'The problem is that I can't be sure whether or not getting the step-up to understudy had anything to do with the fact that I'd changed my name to Nora Johns.' She laughed.

'Do you work with Daphne a lot? Do you two rehearse together?' Peggy was eager to know. 'I was wondering only this morning what the chances were of seeing Daphne here today,' Peggy said. She glanced around as though fully expecting the star to appear, but Nora quickly put her right. ''Fraid not,' Nora said. 'I don't get to work with her any more than you do. You'll see her eventually, of course, but not at this stage of the proceedings. She usually rehearses her own scenes and all her own songs and dances with Lawrence, or with the voice coach and the choreographer, while we get stuck with Jimmy, Lawrence's assistant. Not that he isn't very good,' she added hastily. 'Don't get me wrong, he's a good egg all round, but, surprise, surprise, we won't be getting together with any of the stars until later on, much closer to opening night.'

'That's true,' Denise chipped in, 'but I can tell you that you'd not get much of a chance to talk to her even if she were to appear here at the rehearsal, right now. My experience of her is that she pretty much keeps to herself. She's not one to mix much with the hoi polloi, isn't that right, Nora?'

But Peggy had stopped listening; all she could think about was how it would feel to actually meet the star and how lucky she was to know and to be working with her understudy. It briefly flashed through her mind to wonder how Nora had got to such an elevated position, though she quickly banished such thoughts. She had read stories about understudies becoming famous overnight if the star was suddenly taken ill or had had an accident. That must be something, surely, that Nora must dream about.

All the small groups having been assembled, they spent what was left of the morning swapping personal details and developing their individual characters as Lawrence had instructed. Rob suggested he and Peggy should play a husband and wife team, farmworkers living on Jack Spriggins's farm, so that when they were pretending to chat together animatedly between songs they could be making up stories about their fictional livestock and why they've come to the village fair.

It wasn't until they finally broke for lunch, after what seemed like hours of hard work, that Peggy was able to turn her mind to something other than Jack and his beanstalk and she realized how much she had enjoyed the morning. It had been fun being immersed in the fantasy of another world, but when she heard Jimmy announce that they should all be back at two o'clock sharp, she was abruptly brought back to the present. They hadn't been given long for the break and, as they had been asked to make sure to give their local address in to the office, most people drifted away in order to check on their digs. Peggy, having forgotten about Lawrence's request, realized then that she didn't actually have anywhere to go. She made her way to the office to see if they knew of any rooms where she might board but everyone seemed to have disappeared and the office was locked up.

'Problem?'

Peggy jerked her head up when she heard Lawrence's voice in the foyer and she felt a bloom rush to her cheeks.

'I . . . I didn't realize we were supposed to organize our own digs before we came,' she stammered. 'I was wondering if there might be a list somewhere of places to rent, near here, but the office seems to be closed.' She could feel her eyelids begin to prickle and fought to hold back the tears.

'Hmm,' she thought she heard him say as she added softly, 'I don't have anywhere to go.'

To her relief, Lawrence laughed at the same time as he wagged his finger at her.

'Who didn't read their acceptance letter properly?' he joked. 'Maybe you're in the wrong pantomime.'

Peggy didn't feel like smiling. She was thinking guiltily of the piece of paper she had snatched up from the floor after her father's tirade.

'You are one of the new girls, I take it? Forgive me,' he said as an aside, 'I'm afraid I don't remember everyone's names – at least until opening night.' He put his hand on her arm in a soothing gesture. 'We always tell people to make their own accommodation arrangements, but as a last resort you could come and share my digs. You're in luck, because I've got far more room than I need.' He winked at her and nudged his elbow into her ribs as he whispered the words, while his gaze unashamedly appraised her figure.

Peggy was shocked and didn't know what to say, then he grinned at her in such a way that she couldn't work out if he was teasing or not as he scrutinized her face.

Peggy caught her breath and had to look away as she felt the blush rushing up from her neck, but Lawrence continued to grin, his hand reaching up to cup her chin as he added, 'There's really no need to look so anxious.'

She froze, still unsure what might be an appropriate response but she said nothing. She sucked in her lower lip, could feel it begin to quiver. She hoped Lawrence wouldn't notice as she bit down hard and shook her head. Now Lawrence put his arms around Peggy's shoulders and pulled her towards him in a semi-hug and, with a look on his face that she still wasn't sure how to interpret, he said, 'Don't worry, I'm sure we won't have to resort to that, because, as it happens, I do know someone who lives near here who might be able to help. She's offered digs to company members in the past, including me. She doesn't take people regularly anymore but she has said that we can always try her "in emergencies". It would seem to me that this could be described as one of those emergencies and, as she's not far from here, you could go and see her.'

He released his hold to leaf through the papers that were attached to his clipboard and tore off a strip from the bottom of one of them. Peggy looked down at the name and address as he handed it to her: Mrs Elsie Tanner, 11 Coronation Street, it read.

'Why not give her a try?' Lawrence said. 'She's a good sort and I'm sure she'll accommodate you if she can.' He looked at his watch. 'You've just about got time to get back if you go now. The stage doorman will be able to point you in the right direction, and if you're quick, you could still be back in time for the first run-through.'

'Thanks very much, I'll do that.' Peggy felt a rush of genuine gratitude although she tried not to look at him directly as she offered a smile of thanks.

'Let me know how you get on.' Lawrence beamed at her, placing his arm around her once more.

'I will,' she said, carefully twisting out of his grasp. Satisfied that she had forced him to remove his arm from around her shoulders, she turned to go back down the stairs to the dressing room to retrieve her suitcase. As she did so, she was astonished to feel his hand lingering unnecessarily on her bottom as he leaned forward and patted her from behind.

Chapter 7

Elsie Tanner looked puzzled when she opened the door and saw Peggy standing on the step, suitcase in hand. 'You're after some digs, you say? Who told you to come here? Where did you get my name?' She scratched her head and reassigned several hairpins before Peggy could reply. 'I haven't rented a room out since the last time the panto was here – and that was before the war.'

'No, I realize that,' Peggy said. 'That's what I'm trying to explain. Actually, it was the panto director who gave me your address when he realized I hadn't sorted out any digs. I didn't know I had to and that got me into trouble. Apparently I should have done that before coming to work here at the Majestic though I'm not sure when.' She laughed. 'He was trying to be helpful as I seemed to be the only one who had nowhere to stay.' Peggy flashed the slip of paper that the director had given her and to her relief saw a spark of recognition in Elsie's eyes when she read Lawrence Vine's name.

'Course I remember Lawrence Vine,' Elsie said, her eyebrows twitching as her eyes suddenly sparkled. 'He's stayed here himself more than once, and he never stopped telling me how lucky I was. But I'm afraid my circumstances have changed somewhat since he was last here so I've had to forego the pleasure.' She chuckled and opened the door wider. 'Why don't you come in and see what's on offer for yourself?'

'Oh, no! I couldn't do that. I didn't mean to bother you. I'm sorry if it's not a convenient time.' Peggy backed off the step.

'It's no bother,' Elsie insisted. 'I don't mind having visitors. I'm always ready to snatch a break. Besides, you won't be able to stop for too long as I'm off out soon. But there's nothing says you can't come in for a minute before I go. Then you'll be able to report back to him firsthand about the changes. But come on in for now. I've got a fresh brew on the go and you look like you could do with a cup of summat hot.' She stood back as if to underline her invitation and so, without further protest, Peggy stepped gingerly into the dark hallway.

'I'd heard about the panto coming to town this year,' Elsie said as she led the way into the living room which had been brightened by some very lively looking wallpaper, 'but I gave it no real thought other than that I might want to take my oldest for a birthday treat. Our Linda will be four come January and I reckon she'd like it – if I can get her to sit still long enough. Our Dennis, on the other hand, is much too young, so I'd have to get someone to mind him.' She gave a throaty cough and led the way into the back room. 'As you can see,' she said, 'my circumstances have changed somewhat since the rep were last in town.'

Peggy managed to hide her surprise as she followed Elsie and immediately saw the maidens full of freshly washed nappies and baby clothes that were standing guard around the fireplace, even though the fire was not lit. Peggy wanted to laugh. It was not the kind of place where she would normally have asked for board and lodgings. It was no wonder Elsie Tanner had been surprised. Lawrence obviously didn't know. A thought crossed Peggy's mind about what it might be like to have to live in such close quarters with someone else's children but she quickly dismissed it. It had been hard enough with her own family, and then having to leave them. A sudden lump rose up in her throat as she thought of her young brother, Colin. She was about to say something about him but stopped, realizing that she couldn't trust her voice not to betray her if she tried to say his name. She was wishing she hadn't come here and wondered if she might be able to beat a hasty retreat, but Elsie had slipped a cigarette out of a fresh pack of five Woodbines and was offering the packet to her visitor.

Peggy shook her head. 'I don't, thanks,' she said. Elsie lit one for herself, then waved her hands about in a general gesture of hospitality, even though there wasn't a flat surface to sit on that wasn't covered with at least one pile of children's clothes. Elsie hastily cleared the stacks from two of the kitchen chairs and, taking a couple of thick pot cups from the dresser, poured out the well-stewed tea. She retrieved a milk bottle from the outside window ledge and sniffed it approvingly before adding a splash to each of the cups. 'He didn't stay that long but he was an interesting tenant, Lawrence Vine, I'll say that. What's he like as a boss?' Elsie asked.

'Too early to say, we haven't really got going yet, but he seems nice enough,' Peggy replied. 'It's my first proper job in the theatre and it still feels a bit like being at school.'

Elsie giggled. 'Do you know, when he first came to stop here, I thought he was going to ask me to call him Mr Vine like he was a teacher, cos he could be right bossy, like he had to be in charge of everything – and that doesn't suit me. Though there was a lot about him that did suit . . .' Elsie closed her eyes for a moment and chuckled at the memory, not sure how much she should tell Peggy. 'Thank goodness he got over that and pretty soon he calmed down and wasn't mithered what I called him. Not that it mattered much – we managed to have a bit of fun after that, if you know what I mean.' She looked up and sighed but her lips were curled into a smile. 'It was a shame he was only here a brief while and he didn't come to stop here again after that. I quite missed him, though it did turn out to be for the best cos I had a lot of other things going on in my life at the time.' She waved her hand vaguely in the air as if to indicate everything in the whole room. 'He was nice enough to have as a fixed-term lodger but that was all, if you know what I mean. He seemed to be an interesting chap at first, although I could never quite figure him out. I suppose, in that sense, being his landlady didn't help. Seemed best not to get too close. Not that he was my type, anyway, a man like that. Too theatrical for my liking. Very full of himself, full of his own importance; thought he was the answer to every girl's prayers. Maybe he was. Some girls liked to believe nonsense, like he was offering them a shortcut to Hollywood, but not this girl, he never fooled me.' Elsie lowered her voice even though there was no one else in the room. 'I must say I like my men a bit . . . stronger looking, if you know what I mean. The kind of man a girl wants to be seen with, yet . . .' she struggled for the words, 'yes, someone more subtle, with hidden depths. You know, like Clark Gable.' She lowered her eyelids and peered out from underneath, giving an imitation of what she thought of as a hot and sultry Gable-style look. The kind of look he'd given Scarlett O'Hara in *Gone with the Wind*.

Peggy knew what Elsie meant, although she preferred the more sensitive type. But as she hadn't yet been courted by a steady boyfriend she couldn't be positive about what kind of man she would settle for. She only knew that he had to be good-looking.

Elsie indicated a photograph in a small silver-coloured frame on the mantelpiece. It showed a tall young man in naval uniform, beaming at the camera. 'Believe it or not, I thought my husband looked like a film star when I first met him,' she said. 'But you don't want to be hearing about my love life when it's a room you're after!' Elsie laughed. 'Try as I might, I can't think of anyone else round here that might have a spare room.'

'Ah well, never mind,' Peggy sighed. 'But now I'm afraid I have to be getting back as we're about to start some serious rehearsing. And I can see you're busy. It's really not a very fair thing for me to be asking about at this moment. Thanks very much for the tea,' Peggy finished. She drained her cup and somewhat reluctantly got up to leave. 'I'm sorry if I've wasted your time,' she apologized but Elsie put her hand on Peggy's arm.

'You don't have to be in such a rush,' Elsie said. 'Cos I've been thinking, and you know, I think I might be able to find a way to help you. You're pretty desperate, right?'

'I suppose I am,' Peggy said, fighting back the tears that had suddenly welled.

'There might be a way that I can offer you a room here,' Elsie said. 'We might be able to work something out.'

Peggy raised her eyebrows but Elsie was deep in thought.

'The kids could move into my room and sleep with me. Then you could have Linda's room, all to yourself.'

Without thinking Peggy sat down abruptly on the arm of one of the easy chairs, knocking over a pile of clothes and almost landing on the floor on top of them.

Elsie helped her to her feet but didn't even attempt to pick up the washing. 'Where there's a will,' Elsie said and she made a triumphant gesture. A broad smile lit up her face and for the first time that day that made Peggy smile too.

'I couldn't ask you to do that,' she began, a sceptical note back in her voice.

'Why not? I'm not all heart, you know, so you don't have to worry on that score. There'd be summat in it for me too.' Elsie gave a chesty laugh.

'Of course,' Peggy said hastily. 'For starters, how much would you charge me?'

Elsie thought for a moment then gave Peggy her considered reply. 'I think that's a fair price, don't you?' Elsie said. Peggy let out her breath and nodded, pleased that it was within her means.

'Would that be for bed and breakfast?' Peggy thought she had better clarify.

'Yes, I'll do you a breakfast and I might be able to throw in the odd supper as well if you know you're going to be in late. Otherwise you can take pot luck and fend for yourself.'

Peggy let out a huge sigh of relief. She didn't want to appear too eager for she still had reservations about sharing her home with a baby and a toddler, but she didn't have to think about it for long before she gratefully accepted Elsie's offer.

Chapter 8

By the time Peggy got back to the theatre the first run-through was already underway and they were working with Lawrence himself on what he called blocking, a marking out of the basic moves across the set. Knowing now about the layout of the labyrinth underneath the stage, Peggy did her best to slip in unnoticed through the corridor that fed into the back of the stage and she milled with the rest of the chorus who were standing in their groups working on what Denise had called their 'let's-pretend-to-be-involved-in-animated-conversation' routine. She took up her place in Denise's group next to Rob and was delighted that she was quickly able to be absorbed.

'Where've you been?' Nora hissed, managing to maintain a false smile on her widely spread lips as she remained in character. 'Don't you know directors hate it when people are late?'

'I-I'm sorry,' Peggy stammered, not sure why she felt the need to apologize to Nora when it was Lawrence who had sent her out on her quest in the first place.

'You must be some kind of teacher's pet that he's not picked on you to shout at,' Nora said, 'cos he's been in a foul mood since dinner time and he's already had a go at just about everyone else.' She gave Peggy a look the girl couldn't read.

'Maybe he didn't notice.' Peggy shrugged as she looked across to where the director was indeed chastising several people in the other small groups.

'Huh! He'll have noticed, all right,' Denise joined in. 'Not much gets past our Lawrence.'

'But he's the reason I'm late!' Peggy thought she had better explain. 'What have I missed? Anything important?'

'Quite a lot, I'm sorry to say.' Nora didn't sound a bit sorry.

'Actually, he was going at such a rate of knots it was hard even for us to keep up with him sometimes,' Denise said.

'All I know is that he managed to block out most of the first act and part of the second within half an hour,' Nora said.

'He *has* done *Jack and the Beanstalk* before,' Denise mitigated.

'Then he gave us the usual pep talk about working hard and keeping focused cos there's a lot to learn and not a lot of time to learn it in,' Nora added.

'After that he went on and on,' Denise waved her hand in the air indicating an unending line, 'about learning the words and music as fast as we can.'

'How fast is fast?' Peggy asked jokingly, wondering what kind of miracle she might be expected to pull off.

Nora shrugged. 'Act one and two by the end of the week,' she said. 'Fast enough?'

Peggy's face registered shock. 'Are you serious?'

'That's what they all say, but now's not the time to be worrying about that, Peggy,' Denise said. 'It's not unusual for directors to panic when there's no need. My advice is to grab hold of a script at the end and then you can mark it up; make a note of all the major moves while you still remember them. That's what I do, and I think most of us do.' She indicated some stapled booklets piled on a table that had been left in the wings. 'But, for now, you'd best be getting back into character cos he's watching and you can share my song sheet till the next break.'

Peggy felt an elbow in her ribs and her cheeks flushed bright pink at the thought of Lawrence watching her closely. But as she took on the persona of Rob's peasant wife once more, arguing with her country yokel husband, Peggy felt her excitement overtake her nerves for the first time and she dismissed all other thoughts, concentrating on the task in hand.

Peggy watched attentively as Lawrence went over everyone's start position once more and briefly went through the initial moves and steps that would be required during the opening crowd scene. She was impressed by how quickly he had managed to convey the bustle and busyness of the daily market that they were portraying in the village square. He outlined the route that Jack would take in order to lead his cow to market and it was interesting to see how it all seemed to fall into place even after so short a time.

'This is where Jack will stop,' Lawrence declared marking a spot for each of the animals' legs on the floor boards with chalk. He pointed to one of the other actors. 'And this is where your shop is going to be, where Jack will swap his cow for your magic beans while the rest of you, the crowds of villagers and country folk, will gather about them witnessing the scene.'

Jack was not yet on the set and no one was expecting to see the actual cow so early in the proceedings, so an ironic cheer went up and everyone burst into applause when the oversized pantomime animal suddenly appeared in the wings. It reared on its hind legs then got back on all fours and clumsily attempted to weave its way across the stage. Unfortunately, the two actors inside the stretched animal cover would have benefited from more practice at walking in sync as they seemed unable to sort out the timing of the movements of the front legs from the back legs and they both kept falling over. The rest of the chorus couldn't help laughing at what seemed like a pantomime in itself but Lawrence was not pleased at having to halt the proceedings while they tried to untangle themselves.

'Phew! I'm sorry for whoever's inside that cow's costume, it must be stifling in there, but I'm glad to be able to grab a minute's breather,' Peggy said when an emergency break was called to sort out the rather forlorn-looking animal. 'I'm sorry for the poor cow getting his feet all muddled up like that, but I know how he feels.' She massaged her side which felt as if it had seized up with cramp though she couldn't help laughing. 'I keep getting my feet mixed up with some of those dance sequences. I was beginning to worry that I actually had two left feet and I'm grateful to the cow for giving me a minute to sort them out.'

'I suppose this kind of dancing is much harder than what she's used to?' Nora said pointedly. She seemed to be talking as though Peggy wasn't there, although Peggy tried not to let her feelings show on her face. She looked at Nora sharply and took a deep breath before responding, not wanting to sound too defensive but before she could reply Denise said directly to Peggy in a more kindly tone, 'Lawrence must have thought you could do it, or you wouldn't have passed the audition.'

'Not necessarily,' Nora persisted. 'I was reading in the *Herald* only the other day that there's a great shortage of people taking up jobs in service and entertainment. They don't see that type of work as important and would rather sign up for some kind of essential war work.'

Peggy clenched her jaw and blinked rapidly. 'My teacher at drama club thought I'd be OK, she encouraged me to apply,' Peggy said eventually, though she was unable to keep the defensive tone out of her voice completely. 'No matter how hard the dances were at the club I always got them right in the end. It's just that some of the steps we've done today are new to me, and they aren't half difficult,' she said, although even as she uttered the words, she regretted having made such an admission.

'It's bound to feel strange at first if you're not used to such dancing and some of the routines *are* complicated. But if you're finding them so hard why don't you sort of stand behind me and Rick and then you can follow us?' Denise suggested.

'It's only that I've never done them before,' Peggy mumbled.

'I understand, and I'm sure it would help if you watch me and do what I do,' Denise said. 'You won't be able to remember all of the sequences yet, even we can't do that! No one can expect to pick them up so quickly. But if you can concentrate on getting the actual steps right first the rest will follow, I'm sure. And there'll be lots more opportunities to practise – and if you grab hold of a script when we have the next break you can mark it up and make a note of the major moves.'

At that moment the piano struck up again, the impromptu break over, and as everyone on stage began to move again, Peggy concentrated on not tripping over her own feet as she did her best to imitate Denise's dance movements.

When a shrill-toned bell rang it drowned out even the deeper bass notes of the piano and everyone stopped dancing immediately; the dancers froze in their positions and looked up in alarm. But Lawrence merely threw up his arms and called out, 'It's all right, folks. No need to panic. It's not an air-raid warning, it's time for a scheduled break,' and there was an audible sigh of relief followed by a low murmuring. Lawrence continued to hold his arms aloft as he twisted around, making sure they were all listening. 'We're going to take a pause and for the next hour this stage will only be available to the choreographer and the main leads. The rest of you will have one whole hour to yourselves to do as you wish. You can continue to rehearse wherever and whatever you please.

The announcement was greeted with sighs of relief and expressions of delight as everyone began talking at once. 'The dance rehearsal studio downstairs is available for anyone who wants it,' Lawrence said, and there were general groans. 'But that's up to you. 'I'll be back here on stage in just over one hour's time and I'll expect the rest of you to be back here with me in no more than,' he consulted his watch, 'sixty-three minutes to be precise.' A comment that raised a smile. Peggy wasn't sure how best to fill the time but first she went over to the wings and helped herself to one of the scripts as Denise had suggested. She began to leaf through until she heard a man's voice say, 'That should certainly help you learn the songs by the end of the week,' and she looked up to see Jimmy Caulfield, Lawrence's assistant, smiling down at her.

'I thought I'd mark up the moves Lawrence has been talking about.' Peggy felt the need to explain and could feel the blood rush to her cheeks.

'You're one of the new girls,' Jimmy Caulfield said, making it sound like a statement rather than a question and Peggy looked away, continuing to redden. 'I don't think we got to meet at the auditions.'

'No, we didn't,' Peggy replied.

He extended his hand, a warm smile on his face. 'Welcome to the Weatherfield Rep.'

'Thanks, and it was nice working with you today. I enjoyed the session you did this morning.' She immediately felt embarrassed, wondering why she had said it.

'Your first professional show?' Jimmy asked and Peggy nodded. 'Well, I wish you good luck, then. I'll save the "break a leg" until opening night.'

'I should hope so,' another man's voice cut in, 'but talking of luck, did you have any this morning?'

Peggy swung around in surprise when she recognized Lawrence's voice behind her and before she could move he threw his arm across her shoulders, briefly pulling her towards him. She wasn't sure how to react but seeing the expression on Jimmy's face did her best to duck out of Lawrence's grasp without saying a word.

'She had nowhere to stay,' Lawrence explained to Jimmy, 'and I sent her to that woman on Coronation Street, the one with the flaming red hair, you know the one I mean. I think you stayed there once if I'm not mistaken.'

Jimmy nodded. 'A long time ago,' he said.

'Well, did you have any luck?' Lawrence addressed Peggy again.

'Yes, I did, thank you,' she replied. 'And thanks for the recommendation. Elsie said to say hello.'

'Elsie, yes, that's her name,' Lawrence said. 'A lovely girl. Lively, quite a character. I reckon she could have been on the stage herself. And she's had quite a life, as I recall, been married a while, though she can't be much older than you.'

'No, I don't think she is,' Peggy laughed, interested in his observations, 'and she already has two kids.'

'Two? I'd only heard about one, though if I remember rightly her husband was away in the navy. I suppose he was due some leave,' he said and he chuckled.

Peggy squirmed uncomfortably at his innuendo, but she made no comment.

'As I say, quite a girl!' Lawrence said, then he turned to Jimmy. 'Glad to see you're welcoming new members of the cast,' he said, and he patted Peggy on the back as he walked away, calling up to those still left on the stage, 'OK, time to clear the stage, please. Everybody out except the main leads.'

Peggy hadn't expected to see Daphne Dawson until much later in the rehearsal schedule and her eyes widened in amazement when she was nearly knocked off her feet as a very pretty young woman came rushing on to the stage, coming to a sudden stop as she caught Peggy's shoulder.

'I'm so sorry!' she exclaimed, putting up her hands. 'All my fault – I hope I didn't hurt you.' Peggy looked up and gasped, astonished to realize that she was within touching distance of the show's main lead. Now she could see for herself that Daphne Dawson really was as gorgeous close up as she looked from the distance of the auditorium and couldn't help staring at the young star, overawed by her striking good looks. She had never before been so close to anyone famous. Daphne had a perfect complexion and her alert brown eyes looked as if they missed nothing, but for the moment, all eyes turned towards her as she bounced across the stage. True to pantomime tradition, the principal boy at the rep was being played by a very attractive young woman who was only a few years older than Peggy. Daphne Dawson had been a popular choice when it had been announced that she would star as Jack Spriggins, the unfortunate young man who sold his cow for magic beans instead of money.

She was dressed in a close-fitting leotard that flattered her lithe, willowy figure and seemed to emphasize the length of her slender legs. She strode confidently across to the edge of the stage and gave an exaggerated bow in the general direction of the auditorium where Lawrence and Jimmy were now standing, and with a flick of the wrist she doffed her imaginary hat in deference.

Before Peggy could really register what was happening, she saw Nora come rushing across the stage to greet Daphne, eager to show off, and as the two embraced and exchanged pleasantries Peggy had to admit that she envied the ease with which Nora approached the star and the warm way that Daphne responded. The two hugged – and over Daphne's shoulder Nora's eyes seemed to flash a warning. Peggy wasn't sure how to read the message, but she couldn't help feeling like an outsider in an exclusive club and she took a step back. When Lawrence stepped on to the stage to clear it for the final time, Peggy noticed that Nora didn't leave and retreated only as far as the wings.

I can see that I've got a long way to go, she thought, if I'm to amount to anything in the entertainment world, and she wondered how Nora had managed to become an understudy to the star.

Chapter 9

Peggy left the auditorium reluctantly, the image of Daphne striding confidently across the stage still vivid in her mind. She felt as if she had been touched by magic having stood so close to the young leading actress and it stirred her memories from childhood of her longing to go on the stage. She closed her eyes, trying to imagine what it might feel like to be cheered on by a packed audience and called back for more. She had had a tiny taste of it when she had performed at the drama club but her acting dreams had always been dismissed by her father in particular as never amounting to anything and if she had one goal in life above all others, it was to prove her father wrong.

Peggy hadn't yet seen the dance studio and so as the stage rehearsal broke up and everyone dispersed, Peggy followed some of the other chorus dancers down into the labyrinth where Lawrence had said it was located, next door to the dressing rooms. It was an impressive room with a barre attached on three sides and a wall-to-wall, floor-to-ceiling mirror on the fourth side. One of the young men put a record on the small gramophone that stood in the corner and he wound it up so that the rest could carry out their individual series of exercises at the barre. Peggy found a space behind the others and took up a position towards the back of the room so she could copy the movements the others seemed to have remembered.

When she thought no one was watching, she looked up to catch glimpses of her image in the mirrored wall. She was trying to gauge how closely her figure resembled Daphne's and she kept changing position so she could view her rather angular frame from different angles. She glanced approvingly at her slender body, gratified to think that Daphne's long legs might actually be thinner than her own and dismissed the idea that she was too skinny to be a real dancer as her father had always claimed. She knew her face was not as pretty as Daphne's but given the distance of the stage to the audience that didn't seem so important and she could easily convince herself it didn't really matter.

When the gramophone began to whine as the mechanism wound down, an older woman from the group went over to play the slightly out-of-tune piano that stood at the front while the others came into the centre of the room to practise an endless variety of jumps and leaps and some of the more intricate sequences they had been taught earlier in the day.

After half an hour the pianist gave up and the small dance troupe left together, not seeming to notice that they were leaving Peggy alone. But she was grateful to be able to practise the dance steps she had been assigned and to retrace the different arrangements and movements she had memorized from the morning's routines.

The chorus filed back onto the stage for the last session of the day and when the final bell rang to indicate the end of the session they were all looking exhausted. Lawrence and the dance coach had barely let them rest throughout the afternoon, and any spare moments between the numbers had been taken up by the voice coach who was eager to run through the remainder of the newly written score before the session was over. By the end of the day Peggy's head was buzzing and she wondered how much of the words and music she had actually absorbed. Would she still remember it all the next day? She was pulling on a fleecy top to keep her overworked muscles warm and stop them from seizing up when she heard a now familiar voice and turned to see Lawrence Vine striding across the stage in her direction. He was clutching the clipboard that Denise had labelled his talisman. It had been blank at the start of the day but now Peggy could see that it was filled with diagrams, rough sketches and hastily scribbled notes.

'I presume you'll be going back to Elsie's,' Lawrence said. 'I'm glad things worked out well.' Peggy nodded, wondering what he wanted and how long he would detain her. She was longing to put her feet up.

'She's going to a lot of trouble to accommodate me,' Peggy said. 'But we were able to work things out. She's offered me a room that I can have to myself for the duration of the run and the use of her kitchen . . .' She tailed off because a look crossed his face that said he didn't need to know the details. Peggy could only look down at her feet, noticing for the first time how scuffed her dancing shoes were, almost threadbare where they had rubbed together at the heel.

'I know you came back partway through the afternoon,' Lawrence said, 'and that meant you missed some important instructions I gave out at the beginning of the session.

'Oh, I . . .' she started to say. Then she felt her cheeks redden because she wasn't sure if she should tell him that Denise and Nora had helped to bring her up to scratch.

'I'm sorry I was a bit late getting back,' she mumbled, instead.

He took a deep breath which sounded more like a sigh as he exhaled slowly. 'I don't normally spend valuable time going over things again,' he said, 'but as it was the first session . . .'

Peggy frowned, wondering what he was going to say, but he pulled a pencil from behind his ear and scribbled a few more notes.

'Of course, the rest of the show depends on starting off with the right moves and everyone being in the right place at the right time. We can't afford to have you being out of step with the rest of the company from day one, now can we?'

'No, no, and I'm sorry if I was floundering a bit, though I did my best to follow—' Peggy thought she must try to defend herself, but he cut across her. 'Yes, and that's what caused some of the problems. It only takes one person to start a false move and the whole thing is thrown out of sync. That's why I need original thinkers, not copycats.' He snapped out this last and Peggy raised her eyebrows in astonishment. 'That's why I ask each member of the chorus to be creative and develop a role for themselves. That way we can give an old, familiar story a spark of freshness.' His tone changed, as though he was slipping into one of his well-rehearsed speeches. He shook his head and gave an exaggerated sigh. 'But it looks as if I had better go over the beginning of the session with you. As it's our first day, I'll give you an extra hour, just this once. I think it might be worth it in the long run.'

Peggy looked at him in surprise. He gave her a sideways glance and there was an oddly enigmatic smile on his face. Putting his finger under her chin he lifted her face at an angle that she couldn't avoid his eyes, saying, 'Why don't you and me have an extra session together?

'I tell you what,' he said, finally looking away, 'why don't we take a break and come back here in an hour? I can take you through your moves so I can be sure you know what you're doing and you won't be starting off on the wrong foot, not knowing your jetes from your plies.' He gave a short laugh at his own attempt at a joke. Then he put his arms out, hands on her shoulders, and pulled her towards him. Lowering his voice he said, 'And let me tell you that that is not an offer I make to everybody.'

Peggy was startled. It sounded so overly dramatic. 'Thank you,' she thought she had better say, though her mind was racing as she tried to decide if he was hinting at some ulterior motive. He didn't look as if he expected an answer. Lawrence dropped his arms and looked at his watch. 'Then I'll see you back here later,' he said, and before she could say anything he patted her on the bottom in the same irritating way as he had before, as if she was a small child, but before she could protest, he was gone.

Chapter 10

After Elsie had closed the door on Peggy, following their agreement, she wondered, briefly, if she had done the right thing renting out Linda's room like that and she hoped the toddler wouldn't cause a fuss. Elsie normally prided herself on being able to persuade people to see her point of view, but she knew she would have to tread carefully if she was to sell this idea to her daughter. Though she was sure Linda would love the idea of sleeping in her mother's bed for a few weeks – that would be like a treat – she might not be so keen at the thought of not being able to go into her own bedroom without special permission. But, from Elsie's point of view, the bottom line was that she couldn't really afford to turn away the extra income, however little it was. Of course, she'd been managing well enough on Arnold's pay that she received regularly from the navy, but there was no harm in having a few extra bob to play with each month; with rationing and shortages and two little 'uns to worry about, that always came in handy.

'You never know when you might need it,' she told herself. 'Or when there might be some special treat available under the counter at the corner shop.' Besides, she'd felt sorry for Peggy. The lass didn't look as if she had two ha'pennies to rub together and she had nowhere else to go, and Elsie hated the thought that someone less scrupulous might try to take advantage of her. Their discussion had been brief and to the point and Peggy had been delighted to accept the offer; and she had not hung about after they had agreed terms but had rushed to get back to the theatre for the first run through of the script with the director.

Elsie stood looking for some time at the old battered suitcase Peggy had left at the bottom of the stairs and it flashed through her mind that she might take it upstairs. She even went so far as to lift it up by the makeshift handle that had replaced the original strap, but she stopped short of actually moving it. 'Start as you mean to go on, girl,' she said firmly out loud, 'and that doesn't include unnecessary pampering. She'll have to get used to fetching and carrying for herself.' And Elsie had decided all that was required at this time was for her to make up the bed and make some room in the bedroom cupboard for Peggy's clothes, although from the size and weight of the suitcase it seemed not much space would be needed.

As it turned out, Linda was not the problem for Elsie. The little girl was thrilled to have the new lodger in her house, but what Elsie hadn't reckoned on when she had accepted Peggy into her home was the stir the young actress would cause among her neighbours in Coronation Street. Naturally enough, Elsie had wasted no time in telling her friends in the bar of the Rovers Return.

'You mean it's someone from the panto?' Dot Todd, Elsie's neighbour from number 9 wanted to know when Elsie first mentioned Peggy's name. 'Is she one of them young theatrical lassies?'

'She is indeed,' Elsie said, almost proudly, not realizing it would take no time at all for everyone to be talking enthusiastically about having a young actress in the street; and so Peggy Brown became an instant celebrity before they had even met her.

'I didn't think anyone from the theatre would want to come and stop in Coronation Street.' Ena Sharples, the caretaker from the Mission of Glad Tidings, sounded off in her usual brusque way. 'I'd have thought they'd want to be nearer to the theatre.'

'Ooh! I don't think that matters,' Minnie Caldwell said, for once disagreeing with her friend, 'and it's not that far away. I think it's very exciting and an honour for us to have one of them lodging in Weatherfield.'

'Why shouldn't they come here? It's still walkable.' Elsie was goaded to respond. 'There was some what stayed here before the war, so why not now? Now that the blitz is over.'

'It's not Daphne Dawson by any chance?' Martha Longhurst nudged her friend Minnie.

'If that's the case then I shall have to get my autograph book out,' Dot Todd said.

Minnie's eyes widened. 'Is it one of the stars?'

Before Elsie could respond, Mrs Sharples gave a sardonic laugh, putting an immediate dampener on the speculation. 'It's hardly going to be the star of the show, now, is it?' she said. 'Daphne Dawson, indeed! Coming to Coronation Street! I'm amazed any young actress found her way here. What's brought her looking for Elsie Tanner in Coronation Street, that's what I'd like to know?'

Elsie ignored the sarcasm. 'Of course you're right, Mrs Sharples,' she said. 'It's hardly going to be one of the stars,' and she gave a brief smile in Mrs Sharples' direction. 'It's actually a lass from the chorus and her name's Peggy, she said, although I think she goes by Margaret as her stage name.'

She gave a shrug. 'She must have found my name on some accommodations list from the Majestic. Though from years ago,' she added quickly, not wanting to rake up any collective memories by mentioning Lawrence Vine's name. 'Apparently, it's her first professional stage job and she didn't know where to look for places to stay. No one told her until today that she had to find her own digs.' Elsie thought she'd better play Peggy's role down before the conversation got out of hand. 'But you could still get her autograph, Dot. You never know, she might get famous one of these days.'

'Well, it looks like she's already getting to be well-known in these parts,' Minnie Caldwell said.

'And she'll be known even better as soon as she sets foot inside the Rovers, won't she?' Martha Longhurst added with a chuckle.

'It's all very exciting – I certainly feel as if I know her already,' Dot said.

'Steady on,' Albert Tatlock said, sounding a note of caution. 'I'd like to actually meet this person before I'd agree to say that.' Albert was a veteran of the First World War who lived on Coronation Street with his wife, Bessie, and their ten-year-old daughter, Beattie.

'Well, I look forward to meeting her. You'll be bringing her in soon, I hope, Mrs Tanner?' Minnie Caldwell said.

'Won't it be a bother having a lodger, Elsie? You know what I mean. I hope she won't cramp your style,' Dot asked with a chuckle and she gave Elsie a wink.

'I'm sure Mrs Tanner is more canny than that,' Ena Sharples jumped in, uncharacteristically defending her neighbour before Elsie had a chance to say anything.

'When are you going to bring her to the Rovers? I'm sure we all can't wait to meet her.' Mrs Caldwell was insistent.

'Yes, when are you going to bring her in?' Martha Longhurst backed up her request.

'Give us a chance!' Elsie held her hands up. 'She's not even spent a night in the house,' she said with a laugh. 'Let her find her feet. But as she doesn't know anyone round here I'm sure she'll be pleased to meet you all once she's settled down.'

'I don't know about anyone else, but I certainly intend to go to see the show as soon as it opens,' Mrs Caldwell said. 'I love panto and it's been too many years we've had to do without it.'

'Me too,' Martha said. 'I'm looking forward to going to the theatre again soon.' She turned to look at Ena Sharples. 'How about you, Ena?' she asked.

'I'm making no promises,' Mrs Sharples said. 'I've a lot of harmonium practice to fit in between now and Christmas and that has to come first; before *Jack and the Beanstalk*, that's for sure!'

'We could all go together. I think we should have a Coronation Street outing to the Majestic for the whole street,' Dot suggested.

'I don't suppose this Peggy or Margaret or whatever her name is has got any of them free tickets, has she? You know, them compliments ones?' Albert Tatlock said, a chirpy look passing across his face.

Several of the ladies opened their eyes wide at that suggestion and looked eagerly towards Elsie.

'Then we could definitely have a street outing,' Mr Tatlock said, but Elsie made a wiping gesture with her hands as though to erase the idea from people's minds. 'The last time I asked anyone for one of those I was firmly put in my place,' Elsie said. 'I was told, in no uncertain terms, that if all the cast and stagehands got only one free ticket each there'd be no one in the theatre who'd paid for the seats. No paying customers, no money to pay wages. No wages, no show, is what I was told, so I didn't ask again.'

There were titters of, 'that's true', 'I never thought of it like that', and they all went quiet.

'Oh well, I suppose we can forget that idea, and those of us who want to go will have to shell out for our own tickets,' Dot Todd said. 'I see from the posters that they'll be doing three shows a day in the week running up to Christmas, and the morning shows are usually a bit cheaper.' She shrugged. 'But what about the Christmas party that we keep talking about? We've been promising ourselves we'd have one this year. If we're not having an outing we could at least start planning for a party?'

'Ooh, now that sounds like a good idea, Dot,' Minnie Caldwell said. 'What do you think, Martha?' and she leaned across to her friend sitting on the other side of Mrs Sharples.

'Now that *is* a good idea,' Martha Longhurst said. 'I'm sure if we put our heads together we could soon organize that.'

'Long overdue,' Ena Sharples said, shaking her head. 'We can have it at the Mission. I'll see what Christmas music I've got so we can have a jolly good sing-song. We've done nowt like that since the war began.'

'There's no need for that, Mrs Sharples. I think it might be more appropriate to hold it here where folk could let their hair down and relax. We'll be decorating the bar in any case, making it as festive as we can.'

Nobody else spoke at the sound of the new voice and they all looked up to see that Annie Walker, the Rovers' landlady, had taken her place behind the bar, and was beaming at everyone.

'Now that sounds like a good idea.' Dot was the first one to speak with Elsie soon jumping in to back her up.

Mrs Sharples opened her mouth as if she was about to object, turning to Minnie and Martha for support but Dot Todd spoke up again quickly. 'That sounds good to me, Mrs Walker,' she said, looking around the room, 'and if we're all agreed, I'd be happy to come and talk to you about it so we can set the wheels in motion and begin to plan for some Christmas fun.'

It didn't take much for Elsie to persuade Peggy to join her for a drink in the Rovers and she used it as an excuse to have a night out too. 'Fancy coming down to the local?' Elsie suggested when she thought her lodger looked a bit low. 'My babysitter said she'd stop by for an hour or so if you feel like an outing.' Peggy gave an indifferent shrug.

'I thought you might like to meet a few of the neighbours,' Elsie persisted, 'I know they're all dying to meet you.'

'Really?' Peggy looked at Elsie in disbelief, though she raised her eyebrows and immediately perked up.

'Don't you know most people think that anyone who has anything to do with the stage or the cinema has a romantic air to them?'

Peggy's brow furrowed. 'Really?'

'Yes, really. Who's your favourite film star?'

Peggy shrugged. 'I don't have one. I was never

allowed to go to the pictures. Do you have a favourite?'

Elsie laughed. 'You should have a look at my bedroom walls sometime. They're plastered with pictures of Clark Gable. He's my absolute favourite and best. I'd go anywhere if I thought there was a chance of meeting him.'

'Now I know you're kidding,' Peggy said.

'Course I am!' Elsie laughed. 'I don't think he's ever been to England. And anyway, I'm not seriously suggesting anyone at the Rovers wants any pin-up pictures of you, but I bet some might ask you for your autograph.'

Now Peggy burst out laughing. 'Why on earth would they want that?'

'Just in case you do get famous some day; but don't let that thought go to your head,' Elsie added quickly trying to keep her voice light. 'Seriously, though, they're all dying to meet you, you'll see. And once the show starts you won't have much time for socializing. You'll be working most nights.'

'And mornings, and afternoons,' Peggy added.

'That's true. I'd forgotten you do three shows a day in the run-up to Christmas,' Elsie said. 'You'd better try and enjoy yourself before the hard work really starts.

Chapter 11

As Elsie had predicted, from the moment Peggy walked into the pub and was introduced, everyone wanted to shake the actress by the hand and they all rushed to tell her how delighted they were to meet her. Except for Minnie Caldwell; she insisted on reaching out and clutching Peggy's arm for what seemed like an age before she was willing to let go.

'I hope you don't mind,' she said, looking Peggy up and down, 'but I've never met a real live actress before. I mean, not to speak to, personally.' Minnie's eyes were shining as she spoke, and she looked as if she was quite overwhelmed by the occasion. It made Peggy want to giggle but she managed to control it.

Elsie, on the other hand, didn't hold back, she laughed out loud. 'Oh, Mrs Caldwell, you are a one! She's only flesh and blood like the rest of us. See?' And she lifted Minnie's fingers from Peggy's arm and placed them on her own. 'And I hope you realize that there'll be no need to curtsy,' she giggled. 'Just think, if you're going to treat her like royalty you'll only end up turning her head. Isn't that right, Peggy, love,' she called out.

To Elsie's relief, Peggy seemed to be taking it all in good part and when she introduced her to Annie Walker, the pub's landlady, Peggy managed to fill her hands with glasses so that she could only nod her acknowledgement and make no further attempt to shake hands.

When Elsie was satisfied that she had introduced Peggy to her most important friends and neighbours and that she had a full glass in hand, she was happy to leave her animatedly chatting away to them while she took the opportunity to stretch her legs. When they had arrived earlier, Elsie had seen two new faces sitting at the bar and she was curious to find out who they were. But they weren't there now and she wondered what had happened to them.

Guided by the laughter and noises that sounded like a darts match in the snug she decided to check on the progress of the game.

'Either in or out,' a sharp voice snapped at her as

she held open the door while she peered into the smoke-filled room. Elsie withdrew only to find she had backed into someone whose fingers were wrapped about two pints of beer, precariously balanced one in each hand. She apologized as she watched the head of the foaming ale tip out of the glass and dribble onto his shoes. But it was his face that had really caught her interest as she glanced about her, for it was one of the young men she had seen at the bar earlier. Close to, she could see he was very good-looking and she loved his neatly trimmed, Gable-like moustache.

'Sorry if my mate was short with you,' he said. 'He can get like that by the end of a game, especially if he's not winning.'

'I hope he doesn't lose often,' Elsie said, 'but you needn't worry, it takes a lot more than that to scare me off,' she said, putting on her boldest front.

'This should cheer him up,' the young man said, and he went over to his friend to hand him the glass that still had a head of beer on it. He put his own glass down on the nearest table.

'I'm Ned, by the way,' he said, 'and that's my mate, Vinnie.' Elsie was about to cautiously offer her hand but she withdrew it quickly when Vinnie not only didn't offer his in return but ignored her. Despite her brave words it was all she could do not to shudder as Vinnie sank lower in his chair, his eyes glowering as they focused on the dartboard. His jet black hair fell forwards onto his face, untidily covering his forehead and brows and hung halfway down to his shoulders. It gave his face an overall threatening look and it was all Elsie could do not to shiver. 'I'm Elsie,' she said, smiling as she faced the neatly trimmed Ned. He looked to be very interesting, but it was the scowling image of Vinnie that she was unable to shake out of her head.

'Good to meet you, Elsie,' Ned responded. 'And I'm not like him.' He jerked his thumb towards Vinnie but then leaned away out of earshot of his friend and gave her a pleasant smile.

'I'm glad to hear it,' Elsie said.

'And to prove it, let me buy you a drink.'

'Thanks very much. That's very kind,' Elsie said. 'I'll have a gin and tonic please, if you insist.'

Vinnie made no attempt to communicate with her while Ned went to the bar and very soon the game began again and he returned to it in earnest, determined, from the look on his face, to reverse the previous scores.

'I've not seen you around here before,' Elsie said when Ned came back with a large gin and a bottle of tonic. 'What brings you to Weatherfield and to the Rovers in particular?'

'Business,' said Ned. 'We're checking out the area,

Vinnie and me, hoping to start a new business. And do I take it from that you're a regular?'

'For my sins. Born and bred Weatherfield, Rovers Return's my local. Means I can pop out for an hour while one of the neighbours keeps an eye on my kids.'

'Kids? You look far too young for that.'

'Flatterer!' Elsie touched her hand to the French pleat in her hair and gave him a sideways glance like the heroine might give in any one of her favourite films. But their conversation was interrupted by a loud shout and she looked up to see Vinnie pumping the air and yelling, 'Yes!' over and over.

'I see what you mean about Vinnie,' Elsie said, for he had obviously just been announced the winner and, as he grabbed his jacket and went back to the bar for the loser to buy him a drink, he was all smiles and generally looked much happier than he had been earlier in the evening. But Elsie still felt wary of him and did her best to keep out of his way.

Ned, on the other hand, had proved to be a chatty companion and the two of them remained in the snug with enough to talk about until Elsie looked at the clock and realized she would have to leave. 'I'm sorry I can't stay longer,' Elsie said, when Ned offered to get in one more round. 'But I've got to get home for the babysitter and I must pick up my lodger on the way out to make sure she gets home in one piece. It's her first night out here and I can't have her getting lost on the way. Besides, I know she doesn't want to stay out too late as she has an early start in the morning.'

'If we can't stop any longer tonight, how's about coming out for a drink with me on Friday?' Ned said. 'We can meet here and we could always go on somewhere else if you like. There must be other pubs near here that I'll need to get to know if I come to work in the area.' He grinned.

'That sounds like a good idea, thanks,' Elsie said. 'And it looks like Vinnie's waving at you. What's he trying to say?'

Ned looked up. 'It means he's ready to go,' he said, 'and I'd better jump to it if I want his good mood to last.'

Elsie watched as the two lads left and she stopped at the tables by the bar to collect Peggy, who seemed to be already basking in her newly acquired celebrity status. 'Have you come to show me the way home?' Peggy burst into giggles when she saw Elsie. 'I'm actually very glad,' she whispered behind her hand, followed by more giggles. 'The trouble is, I'm not really used to drinking,' she said, and this time she hiccuped. 'But these kind people seem to think I'm famous for some reason, though I keep telling them I'm not.' She hiccuped again and Elsie stared at her, wondering if she would at least be able to walk home under her own steam.

'We can talk about it when we get home,' Elsie said, thinking about what she might say that would stop her lodger making a fool of herself like this – and also stop her in her tracks before she got too many big ideas.

'I bet you're pleased you came out tonight, Peggy,' Ida Barlow said. 'Hope you've enjoyed yourself.'

'Oh yes, I have, thanks to you lot,' Peggy responded. 'I really have,' she said to Elsie. 'Everyone's been so generous.'

'I can see that for myself.' Elsie smothered a smile.

'It's been lovely to meet you. And I'm so pleased you're all coming to see the show,' Peggy said.

'And what about you, Elsie?' Albert Tatlock asked. 'You looked as if you were having a good time too.' Elsie stared at him for a moment, not sure how to reply. But she merely shrugged and said, 'Yes, I did, thanks,' as graciously as she could.

'No one we know?' Ida asked. 'At least, not anyone I've seen before.

'Me neither,' most of the others murmured.

'No, they're new to the neighbourhood,' Elsie said, 'though they might be moving into the area.'

'Well, I'd watch out for them if I were you,' Albert Tatlock spoke up. 'Especially the one with the long dark hair. He could be dangerous.'

Elsie stared at him. She was alarmed by the warning although she didn't want to admit it, and she had no intention of owning up to the fact that Vinnie had left her feeling extremely uncomfortable. 'Do you know them, then?' she asked as lightly as she could, but Albert shook his head.

'I can't say I know either of them myself, but I did hear a story about the dark one.'

'Oh?' Elsie was curious.

'Did you see him limping as he walked out?' Albert asked.

'I noticed that,' Mrs Sharples butted in, 'and I did wonder. Is there a reason?'

'There's certainly a story,' Albert said, 'though I'm not sure how true it is.'

'Go on,' Elsie encouraged him, really curious now.

'Rumour has it that, rather than signing up for the army, he literally shot himself in the foot.'

There was a loud gasp as they all tried to take in what Mr Tatlock had said and then he added, 'Only he didn't do a very good job of it.' They all stared at him, aghast.

Elsie shivered. 'Maybe that's why he gave me the creeps,' she admitted reluctantly, and Albert Tatlock said, 'Mmm. I'd make sure to keep my eye on him, that's all.'

Chapter 12

'What are you still doing here at this hour?' It was assistant director Jimmy Caulfield who Peggy met by the front doors as she was leaving the theatre and she pulled up short, wondering why he made it sound like an accusation.

'I know it's late and they want to lock up but I've just had a special session with Lawrence. He's been helping me with my dancing,' she explained. 'I've been finding it difficult to get the sequences right in some of the routines and he said he'd help me.' She tried to keep the boastful note of pride out of her voice that the director should offer her individual coaching, but she could see from Jimmy's face she hadn't entirely succeeded.

'Did he indeed?' Jimmy sounded surprised. 'I do hope you've not been spreading that information about,' he added.

Peggy frowned. 'Why? What do you mean?'

'I mean I've heard you're rather fond of sharing things,' he said, 'things that are best kept to oneself.'

'Sharing things? Such as what?' Her cheeks began to flame, though she was genuinely puzzled.

'Such as telling everyone that Lawrence helped to find you digs. In Coronation Street, I believe it was.' He paused.

'Yes, it was,' Peggy said quickly, 'and what's wrong with—?'

'Are you going home, now? Maybe we could walk together as I go in that direction. I'm staying not far from the Rovers Return. You must know the pub on Coronation Street? We can talk as we go.'

Peggy nodded, though she was unsure what he was getting at. 'What's wrong with telling people about Lawrence helping me find digs?' Peggy asked as Jimmy matched his pace to hers. 'I didn't know we had to find our own places to stay and I had nowhere to go when I first arrived. I was very grateful when Lawrence gave me Elsie Tanner's address and I may have mentioned it to a few of the people in the group I was dancing with.'

Jimmy looked uncomfortable. 'Hmm. I suppose

you've never worked in a professional theatre company before?'

Peggy shook her head and felt her throat tighten with anxiety, wondering what he was going to say.

'It's just that you need to understand that people in our world may react differently to what you're used to and I would hate to see you getting hurt.'

'How different?' she asked her brow furrowed.

'Well, for instance, it might have been all right when you were at school to boast about being teacher's pet, but in the theatre it's a whole different ball game,' he said. 'Actors are always wary if they see someone sucking up to the director,' he said, 'which is how they would see it. They would be wondering what you were going to get out of it at the end of the day; that kind of behaviour can get you a bad reputation.'

Peggy wasn't sure she understood and suddenly she wanted to cry.

'What do you think he might offer to help you with next?' Jimmy asked. 'Because he will, you know, and all I'm saying is that it might be an idea to be prepared so that you don't think you owe him something for doing you a favour and ending up paying too high a price.'

Peggy was puzzled. Jimmy seemed to be talking in riddles. She wondered what he would say if he knew that Lawrence had promised to give her an

Equity wild card and had encouraged her to build up her professional working hours so that she would eventually be able to join the actors' union in her own right after the war. Even though the rules had been relaxed during the war, he had assured her that it would make it easier for her to get a job in the future and she had decided not to mention it to anyone as she knew there were several others in the company with an eye to the future who desperately wanted a card.

'He's already told me he wants me to be an assistant stage manager in charge of props,' she said instead, scanning Jimmy's face as she spoke.

'He made it sound like a promotion, I suppose?'

'Well, yes, he did as a matter of fact.'

'Hm, and you've already told him you'd be delighted to take it on?'

'Yes, of course.'

'Peggy, every one of the actors in a rep company like ours takes on extra jobs. Haven't your friends told you that yet? You ask anyone in the chorus. They're not only actors, or singers, or dancers. You'll find them sitting in the prompt corner, taking charge of the book, or they might be responsible for props or for helping out wardrobe. Without a distribution of such jobs the company couldn't function. And the lower down you are in the pecking order, the more jobs you'll be expected to take on. You'll get no extra money – you check your contract. You need to be aware he's not doing you any favours because the point is that you owe him nothing in return. So don't let him take advantage of you and trick you into thinking that you do.'

Peggy was shocked at his words, still not sure she understood what he was getting at and she wondered if the role of understudy was considered to be one of those 'extra little jobs' too? Maybe it wasn't as special as she had once thought.

'I've seen you dancing with Denise and Nora, and Rob, the fellow I believe she's stepping out with; you could do worse than take a lesson from their book. They're probably about the same age as you but they've been in the business long enough to know their way around. Follow their lead and stick close to what they do. I think you'll find that the more you can blend into the group the better – don't try and make yourself stand out as special or you'll end up getting everyone's backs up. There are a lot of people, very full of their own importance, who believe themselves to be special and you don't want to be upsetting them. If they think you're getting too close to Lawrence they'll jump to one conclusion.'

'And what's that?'

'That he's grooming you for the casting couch.' He fixed her with a firm gaze until she had to look away.

'You do know what that is?' Jimmy asked tentatively. Peggy's cheeks flushed and she shook her head.

Jimmy looked at her directly, as though he were imparting bad news. 'It's long been known that there are some directors who will only give the plum roles to actresses who are willing to sleep with them,' he said. He had lowered his voice so that Peggy had to strain to make out his words, and what she heard made her gasp. Is that what Lawrence was expecting? Was that what her friends had been hinting at? No wonder they kept trying to warn her.

But Peggy was confused. Denise had told her to do things to make her stand out in a crowd so that she would be noticed and here was Jimmy advising her to blend in and almost make herself invisible. She had been floating on a high after her session with Lawrence, having taken it as a compliment that he had picked her out for special attention. She had even boasted about it, and yet here was Jimmy pricking her balloon. At first she had been brought down to earth with a bump by Jimmy's words but now she wasn't sure she believed in his interpretation of them. But she couldn't dismiss them completely. She had been flattered by the interest Lawrence seemed to have taken in her, flattered that he had treated her differently, but she couldn't help shuddering now when she thought of how Lawrence had behaved when they had been alone together in the dance studio, He had taken every opportunity to be close to her, finding any excuse to be constantly touching her. Is that what Jimmy was referring to? Was that – and more – the price she would have to pay for such individual attention? She refused to believe it. Lawrence wasn't like that. Or was she being naïve? Now she came to think about it she had noticed that while he patted some part of the anatomy of almost all the newcomers to the chorus, she had never seen him touch Denise or Nora in that way; and he never even stood close to them when they were with Rob and Rick.

Peggy realized she had reached home and they parted with a brief wave at the end of the street. Peggy had thought she was doing so well, but now, the more she thought about Jimmy's words, the more she wondered if she had made a mistake.

Chapter 13

Elsie had no wish to take any responsibility for her lodger and she had told Peggy right from the start that she would not try to be a substitute mother or to interfere in her life in any way. But despite her declared intentions she couldn't help worrying about Peggy and wondering whether she really knew how to handle someone like Lawrence, who was so obviously a man of the world. Elsie stood in front of the mirror in the hallway of her house, painting a bright vermilion onto her lips. While the babysitter was already entertaining Linda in the sitting room, she waited for her neighbour Ida Barlow to collect her so they could have an hour or so out at Jackson's chippy on Victoria Street. She looked at her reflection again. She was pleased to see the maturity of the face that smiled back at her. Sometimes she found it difficult to believe she was only a year older than Peggy, for she had already had to handle so many things that life had thrown at her.

'Honestly, you'd think she was a child, fresh out of school, the way she behaves,' Elsie confided in Ida when they were finally settled in Jackson's, ready for an evening of gossip, beginning with Peggy. 'She's really very sweet but so inexperienced. I can't imagine what they make of her down at the theatre,' Elsie said.

'I was wondering how the two of you were getting along together,' Ida said, 'only I wasn't sure I should ask. I sometimes see her in the street with a young man and I wondered if it was something serious. Someone she'd met at the theatre, perhaps? And I got to thinking about how well she was settling in.'

'I think she's settling well enough. Oh, and I do know about the fella,' Elsie said. 'Peggy said he's the assistant director of the show and he's in digs himself, somewhere nearby. He seems to fancy her and I know he likes to walk her home sometimes though she doesn't seem particularly keen on him. But it's very early days.'

'She's not asked to bring him into the house?'

'Good heavens!' Elsie paused with a chip hovering

on the end of her fork. 'I've not encouraged *that*. We rub along well enough, Peggy and me, but not that well that I have to stand in for her mother. That's exactly the kind of stuff I don't want to get involved in, though I do try to keep a general eye on things. But that's because she does seem to have come from a strict home and I worry she could go off the rails with her new-found freedom if she thinks I don't care at all.'

'I suppose naïvete will get her so far – though I know there's always the danger that genuine innocence could lead her into deeper waters than she might expect,' Ida said with a shrug.

'I did try to warn her about men like Lawrence,' Elsie said, 'but I'm not sure she fully understood all the implications of the casting couch. But I certainly don't have the time or the patience to play nursemaid and spell it out for her.'

'I should imagine it must be quite a contrast for her, coming from her parents' home, where it sounds like she didn't have much freedom, to a relaxed house like yours.'

Elsie had an astonished look on her face as she replied. 'Ida Barlow, what are you suggesting?' Elsie said, and when the words finally exploded it was with a part exclamation, part laugh. Ida gasped and covered her mouth with her hand as she realized what she had said. 'Oh, goodness! No offence intended,' she said, adding quickly, 'but I'm sure you know what I mean.'

'Don't worry. None taken,' Elsie said with a grin. 'I know you're my best friend, really. Though I can see how it could go to her head realizing she has no one hovering over her, watching her every move. But it's high time she learned how to look out for herself,' Elsie said and Ida agreed. 'Besides,' Elsie went on, 'I've got my own things to worry about,' and she held up her hands and began to inspect her recently painted fingernails.

'Worry about? Or be pleasantly preoccupied with?' Ida wanted to know.

'A bit of both, I suppose.'

'That's good to hear,' Ida said, 'because that was going to be my next question. How are you getting along with your new young man, if you don't mind me asking? I couldn't help noticing.'

'I don't mind you asking; no one who lives on Coronation Street can get away with much as we all know, but I'm not sure I'd call him my young man. We've only stepped out together a couple of times.'

'That's as may be, but whenever I've seen him I'd say that he's shining a torch for you whether you like it or not; he's difficult to ignore, I shouldn't wonder.'

Elsie patted her hair down with a self-conscious gesture. 'Oh, but I'm not trying to ignore him. If anything, I find it rather flattering,' she said, a coy look flashing across her face.

'Are his intentions honourable at least?' Ida joked. 'How much do you know about him?'

'Not much, really,' Elsie had to confess. 'Only that he doesn't come from these parts, but he wants to set up a business here, in Weatherfield, or perhaps in Manchester itself with his friend Vinnie.'

'Do you two ladies happen to be talking about your new friend Ned, by any chance?' A man's voice chimed in to their conversation. 'I had a drink with him only last week.' Elsie looked up to see Albert Tatlock had come into Jackson's and had to walk past their table to reach the counter to order his takeaway supper.

'Cooker's playing up, so Bessie sent me for fish and chips for our tea.'

'We've had a grand feed,' Elsie said, pushing her plate away. 'We *were* talking about Ned, as a matter of fact,' Elsie said, wondering where this might be leading. 'He's been in the Rovers several times, I believe.'

'It wasn't that I was eavesdropping, or anything,' Mr Tatlock murmured, a guilty look on his face.

'Don't worry, I believe you,' Elsie said.

'Though thousands wouldn't,' Ida muttered, adding, 'Do you perhaps know more about him than we do?'

'It just so happens that I was talking to a pal of mine the other night,' Mr Tatlock said. 'He's not from round here so you won't know him, but he seemed to know Ned quite well.'

'Oh!' Elsie said, her face expressionless. She'd had several local residents try to shock her with stories about Ned recently, though she mostly didn't believe them. But she liked Mr Tatlock and she was prepared to listen to what he had to say. She waited for him to continue.

'I've told you before about his friend, haven't I?' he said eventually.

'About Vinnie? Yes, you have,' Elsie prompted.

'Well, it seems that him and Ned are looking at going into business together.'

'We knew that, but what kind of business?' Ida asked before Elsie could open her mouth.

'Ah well, that's the thing. It sounds more like monkey business to me.' He slapped his hand down on the table and made the plates jump.

Elsie did her best to look unconcerned but Ida leaned forwards, looking at him eagerly. 'Go on, Mr Tatlock,' she encouraged him.

'From what my pal told me, it seems your Ned Travis is an illegal bookie,' he said looking pleased with himself. It was all Elsie could do not to accuse him of making it up, but somehow she managed to hold on to her usually fiery temper.

'It seems he's been running card tables in a disused warehouse on the other side of Weatherfield,' Mr Tatlock went on, 'and he and Vinnie are looking to expand the business.' Elsie really didn't want to believe what she was hearing and her first reaction was to call him a liar. But she held back.

'I know, it sounds like American gangsters have come to Weatherfield.' Mr Tatlock actually chuckled. Elsie stared at him, though she had seen enough films to almost agree with him. She couldn't deny that the cloak-and-dagger aspect of his revelation had almost a romantic ring to it, but she still wasn't sure whether or not to believe him.

'What did you make of that?' Ida asked Elsie as they strolled home together from Jackson's. It was a clear, crisp night outside, in contrast to the warm atmosphere of the chippy. Once the door had swung shut behind them it was pitch-black, with not a pinprick of telltale light giving away the location of any of the local people or their houses. Thanks to the local residents like Albert Tatlock and Ena Sharples who were air-raid wardens, the blackout was being strictly maintained, in a concerted effort to keep them all safe. Only the occasional bicycle bell piercing the air revealed that there were others out and about on the street.

'It's a good job my feet know their own way home

without me having to guide them, cos I'm not sure I could guide them anywhere in this darkness,' Elsie said with a giggle, temporarily ignoring Ida's question.

'And thank goodness for once I can't hear any wretched planes flying overhead,' Ida said, 'or see any fires on the skyline.'

'You can feel it's autumn, though, and I'm not sure if I'm glad or sorry about that.' Elsie shivered and pulled her coat more tightly about her, securing the belt that was tied about her slim waist with an extra knot. Silence fell between them for a few moments before Elsie responded, 'What do I make of what?'

'About what Albert Tatlock had to say about Ned Travis.'

Elsie shrugged, not thinking that Ida wouldn't be able to see her response in the dark. 'Frankly, I don't know what to make of a lot of the stuff Albert Tatlock says,' Elsie said eventually. 'And I'm usually inclined to take most of it with a good old-fashioned pinch of salt.'

'Me too,' Ida agreed. 'But does he know Ned? Where do you think he got his information from?'

'Goodness only knows,' Elsie said and the two joined in laughter.

'I don't think he means any harm by it,' Ida said. 'He just wants to be involved in the conversation. I do try to give him the benefit of the doubt.'

'I know, and so do I. But we've said before that Ned's friend Vinnie always looks a bit dubious. He could pass for a gangster any day of the week. I've said as much myself, several times. But I certainly don't think the same of Ned,' Elsie said, wondering if she should tell Ida she had agreed to go out to the pictures again with Ned the following week and that she had had no qualms about accepting his invitation. It didn't really matter to her what Albert Tatlock had thought about him, because for some reason she found herself drawn to him and she considered him to be a rather good-looking young man. And although she wouldn't admit it to Ida, there was something strangely romantic about the notion that she could be stepping out with a would-be gangster who looked as though he had come straight out of one of her favourite films. When Mr Tatlock had been talking about Ned possibly being involved with illegal gambling, she had immediately conjured up the image of a basement warehouse. The whole thing had rather a romantic angle to it that, she had to admit, did have a certain appeal.

She had probably seen too many films, but all she could picture was a speakeasy where you had to whisper a secret password to the guard on the main entrance and again to the guard at the basement door that led directly into a smoke-filled room full of card players and gamblers. In her mind, she styled the owner after Humphrey Bogart or Jimmy Cagney, someone who might have had a burning cigarette hanging from his lips, which forced him to mumble unintelligibly out of the side of his mouth. She pictured herself sashaying into the club on Ned's arm in a slinky, close-fitting outfit and her scarlet high-heeled shoes. She found such cloak-and-dagger scenes to be titillating, with a certain romantic flavour to them, and as far as she was concerned the thought of being involved with such a man made her want to smile. She suddenly felt ashamed, as if by having such thoughts she was condoning illegal activities, and she covered her mouth with her hand to hide her embarrassment, remembering only as she did so that Ida would not have been able to see her.

'Well, I don't see owt wrong with Ned,' Ida said, touching Elsie's arm as they stopped outside number 11, 'so don't you mind Albert Tatlock.'

'Don't worry, I won't,' Elsie said, though she couldn't help wondering if perhaps there had been some truth in what he had been saying.

Chapter 14

Peggy had been confused at first. Once rehearsals were up and running and she was attending them regularly, she realized that it was all very well having a stage name but she wasn't quite sure how Margaret de Vere should behave. She wondered whether she should stick with Peggy, whose personality and character she knew best, and forget Margaret, which seemed pretentious anyway. She hovered between following Denise's advice to make herself different, so that she would stand out from the crowd and be noticed or to listen to Jimmy and try to blend in more with the others in the chorus, making herself almost invisible. At least that way she wouldn't annoy the others in her group by attracting too much attention. In the end, Jimmy won. Or at least, his suggested approach won, for she had been trying to avoid Jimmy himself recently. He always seemed to be hanging about after rehearsals had ended for the day, wanting her to go for a drink or offering to walk her home. He seemed to be interested in chasing after her whereas she didn't really have much time for him. But she knew she couldn't afford to dismiss him completely, not if she really wanted to make new friends and Jimmy might also be able to help her to deal with Lawrence.

As the days wore on, Peggy was surprised to find that despite her shaky start she was beginning to settle into her new daily routines, and was feeling much more confident about what she was doing. She was only sad to find that, as she settled down, some of the magic sparkle that had first drawn her to the theatre seemed to have disappeared and the initial frisson she had felt when she first took her place on the stage had already begun to wear off. She didn't want to admit it, but she was dismayed to find that the reality of her life was far removed from how she had always dreamed it would be. She felt almost like a traitor when she confessed this to Elsie one morning when they were eating an unusually late but companionable breakfast together.

'It's much harder work than I had ever imagined it would be,' Peggy said, spreading a small square of margarine on to a slice of dry toast that still looked unappetizing. 'And I don't think I ever considered how difficult it would be having to learn so many new things all at once. I thought it would be exhilarating, going over and over the words of the same songs and dancing the same steps until I really knew them. It didn't occur to me that going over the same sequences time and time again could get very tiresome.'

'I suppose it's the only way you can learn though; practice and more practice,' Elsie sympathized. 'They must become automatic eventually.'

'Yes, I suppose they do, but before you reach that stage they become as boring as when we had to do the times tables at school,' Peggy said, 'and I never did see the point of that.'

Elsie shrugged. 'But this is different. It has to be like that while you're learning if everything is going to come together and run smoothly in the end. You've got to be sure of what you're doing so you can do it in your sleep without having to think. I mean, you haven't got that much rehearsal time to put the whole thing together, have you?'

'No, I suppose not,' Peggy said. 'I do understand the need for practising, when I think about it in my head – it's just that I never really thought before about how it might feel to be actually doing it.'

'Maybe you should try to concentrate on how

lovely it will all look and sound in the end,' Elsie suggested. 'That will make the hard work worthwhile, won't it? How far have you got? Do you do it scene by scene?'

Peggy sighed. 'Actually, I suppose I'm not doing too badly, if I stop and think about it. I've learned the words to a lot of the songs already, nearly all of us have – we sort of have a bit of a competition to see who knows the most. And I've even begun to master a large number of the dance steps and the overall movements about the stage.'

Elsie chuckled. 'So you're not the worst in the group. You're no longer being pulled up by the dance teacher?'

Peggy reddened. 'Well . . .' she admitted, 'let's just say, not as much as I was, though she does still nag at me sometimes when I forget some of the lengthier sequences of the harder routines. But I like to think I'm improving. In fact, I decided to stretch myself. I haven't told anyone but I'm trying to learn some of the other parts and the songs as well.'

'Gosh, that's brave. Do you really need to do that?'

'No, but I thought it might help me untangle some of my own more difficult sequences in the dancing. I stayed behind the other day to watch Daphne Dawson, the principal boy, go through her routines. Lawrence usually works with her at the end of the day and we're not supposed to watch her but I sneaked in at the back of the stage with Nora. She's Daphne's understudy so she's allowed to watch. Then I went to the dance studio to see how much I could remember. Nora had gone home and there was no one else about but I wanted to see if I could do Daphne's stuff. I mean, it's something I would have to do if I was ever offered an understudy role.'

'Yes, of course,' Elsie said. 'And could you do it?'

'I did remember quite a bit, but some of it was very tricky. I sort of kept tripping up on some of the moves which were quite complicated. I can see that I would need a lot of special coaching if I ever had to dance any of Daphne's part.'

Elsie looked thoughtful as she stood up and unhooked two thick pot cups from the kitchen cabinet. 'Drink?' she asked, pouring some coffee essence into them without waiting for a reply as the kettle began to whistle on the stove. She held one out to Peggy and poured in some hot water.

'Thanks,' Peggy said gratefully and stirred the mixture. 'You never know what you can do till you try, eh?' she said. 'I'd like to think I could do it if I had to. Though I'm not sure I'd want to be offered an understudy role now that I know more about it and I can see how difficult it is. The worst part is that you get no extra pay.'

Elsie stared at her in surprise. 'Really?'

'Yes, really, and believe me, it involves a load of

extra hard work. You don't get to be a star in this business by being a slouch, I can tell you. I felt quite worn out!'

'I'm not surprised,' Elsie said. 'Has Lawrence not offered you any more individual sessions? Wouldn't he be able to help if push came to shove and you had to do extra work?'

Peggy shook her head. 'He hasn't offered me any more extra sessions.'

'Then he must think you're improving,' Elsie responded cheerily.

'I think he's been far too busy with a load of other things to worry about, than having to think about me,' Peggy said. 'Honestly, most people have no idea how much goes on behind the scenes before a production actually gets on to the stage. They certainly don't know what goes on in the build-up, like during rehearsals, and in set building. I must admit I had no idea about any of that stuff before I came here.'

'I thought you'd been to a drama club?' Elsie sounded surprised.

'I had, but preparing for a performance at that level is nothing like working on stage professionally. It's really like chalk and cheese. We didn't rehearse so often for a start, or for such long hours; we never had to rehearse so hard because, at the end of the day, we were only performing for our friends and families so it wasn't totally disastrous if one of us was out of step occasionally or made a mistake.'

'Did you think that once you were a professional then it would all happen by magic?' Elsie asked, clicking her fingers, her eyes widening as if a whole magical scene had instantly opened up in front of her.

Peggy laughed. 'I suppose I did really, if I thought about it at all. But theatre does that to you, or it did to me, and it was nice being under a spell like that, pretending you could sprinkle everything with magical stardust.'

'I can see why you need to believe in the magic of it all,' Elsie said. 'I suppose the audience needs to hold onto the magical elements too. I'll try not to think about all the practical realities when I come to see the show,' Elsie laughed, 'I'd hate to spoil it for Linda, hate her to lose the magic of the stage at her age.'

Peggy's hand flew to her mouth. 'I'm sorry,' she said. 'I hope I haven't spoiled it all for you. And Linda can't afford to lose it yet, she's far too young. I apologize, I didn't mean to spoil it for you, either. I suppose I shouldn't really talk about things like that, it's just that I've been amazed to find out about the amount of work that goes into a professional show, like designing and building the set, for starters. I was watching the carpenters the other day making different bits of the scenery and then fitting it all together like a giant jigsaw puzzle. And I haven't told you yet that we've all been given additional admin jobs to do apart from being on stage.'

'Like what?' Elsie was curious.

'Like for example, I've been told I'm to be in charge of props.' Peggy tried not to allow a boastful tone to creep into her voice as she said that, as if she was secretly pleased to have been given such a responsible job. Jimmy had tried to downplay its importance, making light of nearly all of the ASM jobs he was handing out.

'*I'm afraid none of them result in additional pay or even raise your status.*' That was how Jimmy had begun his little speech but everyone in the theatre understood by that time the extra workload actors had to take on for very little pay once they were part of a company. 'Don't let the audience seduce you, not everyone can be a star,' he had said with a sigh.

'I hadn't really thought much about props before, I'd sort of taken for granted that things would be automatically in the place they ought to be until it was pointed out to me that important items on stage don't just appear and disappear on their own. Someone is actually responsible for putting them there and taking them away again, so it's quite an important position,' Peggy said. 'I'm quite enjoying it, though it makes me realize I'm glad I'm not responsible for pulling the whole show together. There are so many people involved at so many different levels that I'm amazed the director and the productions manager can coordinate everything on show nights.'

'I suppose they rely on everyone pulling their weight and doing their bit.' Elsie suddenly giggled. 'I remember a couple of years back, when we tried to put on a bit of a show for everyone in Coronation Street over Christmas. Ena Sharples, bless her, assumed the mantle of director without waiting to be asked and she didn't know what she was doing. Nobody had wanted her in that position in the first place but we didn't know how to tell her. It could have ended really nastily because we all sort of went on strike and refused to do anything she wanted.' Elsie smiled at the memory. 'Not the merriest of Christmases as I recall.'

'I don't think anyone would dare go on strike against Lawrence,' Peggy said and she shuddered at the thought.

'Well! If you enjoy doing it, that's fine. What does being in charge of props actually involve?' Elsie wanted to know. 'Is it a big job?

'I didn't realize how big,' Peggy said, and she tried to explain how much of a headache it could be if any of the items went missing or were out of place at the crucial moment in the script when an actor needed them.

'I not only have to make sure that they're in place but that they're removed when they're no longer required. One day everything stopped because I'd forgotten to replace the magic beans in the shop-keeper's till. That meant he had nothing to exchange for Jack's cow when he tried to sell it on market day. I had no idea that I'd forgotten to replace them until I heard Lawrence screaming about "that bloody useless props girl!" I'd forgotten to replace them after the previous day's rehearsal of that scene – and believe me, I found out the hard way what it sounds like when Lawrence isn't pleased.'

Peggy was staring off into space as she thought back to the scene. She was trying to laugh it off now, though it had been humiliating at the time. And if she was going to succeed in this cutthroat business she would need the goodwill of people like Lawrence. She had to find a way to work with him and to keep him happy. She needed to take advantage of whatever it was he had to offer, while not allowing him to exploit her and take advantage of her innocence and inexperience. 'I'd love to be able to talk to my mam about some of these things,' she heard herself say. 'For one, I know she'd love it, and better still, she'd know what I should do.' Peggy had a vision of her mother talking to her about it, advising her, helping her to prioritize, offering practical advice, when without warning, she was flooded with images and overwhelmed by a wave of homesickness.

She had always been able to confide in her mother so long as her father wasn't on the scene and she wished she could talk to her now. She didn't want to admit, even to herself, how much she was missing her home and her family, more than she ever imagined she would. Elsie always did her best to be nice and was often able to offer some sensible advice but it wasn't the same as being able to talk to her mam. She felt angry at her father for having ordered her out of the house. She closed her eyes tightly. Maybe she had been away long enough and she could try to go back at least for a visit? If she timed it right, she could no doubt avoid her father and she thought only of how wonderful it would be to see her mother and her brother Colin again, for she missed them both so much. Thinking about Colin she remembered she had dreamt of him the previous night, and on several occasions before that. She hated the thought that he was growing up without her.

'Won't your family come to see the show once it opens? At least you would see them then.' Peggy realized that Elsie was talking to her.

'I certainly hope so,' Peggy replied. 'I've put my name down for two tickets so I can get them as soon as they go on sale. But the thing is, I'm not sure I want to wait that long to see them. I was thinking just now that I might make a trip home fairly soon. What do you think?'

'I think that sounds like a good idea,' Elsie said.

'Until the actual performances start I could go of an evening, couldn't I? I could get the bus from the centre of town.'

'Good idea!' Elsie agreed. 'Get some extra support in during the countdown to opening night.'

Chapter 15

As Peggy settled down in Weatherfield she gradually grew accustomed to Elsie's ways and she gratefully accepted her landlady's invitations to join her at the Rovers for a drink. Elsie proved to be a useful companion, making sure as she did that Peggy met a number of her friends among the local residents. To Peggy's surprise, the next time they were in the Rovers together Elsie even introduced her to Ned Travis, the new young man she was obviously sweet on. Ned immediately grinned and put out his hand, unlike his mate Vinnie who just stared at her from the other side of the table as if he'd never seen a young girl before.

Things settled down in the theatre too and Peggy

felt more comfortable as her social life generally began to improve. She was regularly asked to join Nora, Denise, Rick and Rob, her little group who danced together in the chorus, whenever they got together beyond rehearsal times, particularly if they were going out for a drink. They all lived within easy walking distance of Coronation Street and Nora and Denise took it in turns to invite Peggy to join them in one of their many visits to the cinema. They also asked her to join them when they visited each other's houses in the evening after work.

'May as well make the most of any free time we get right now,' Nora said, 'because let me tell you, once the show opens we won't have a minute to call our own. We'll be working morning noon and night and we won't remember what it means to have time to ourselves.'

'I'm only sorry I can't invite you to visit me at Elsie's, only my room isn't big enough. You couldn't swing a cat, never mind squeeze in the five of us, sitting down,' Peggy said. 'I suppose we could all sit downstairs if Elsie isn't home, but I can't rely on that, and I can't expect her to go out so that I can entertain. Don't get me wrong, Elsie's very sociable generally, but I don't know how she'd feel about having a houseful of strangers downstairs while she's otherwise engaged upstairs, if you know what I mean. I usually disappear to my room if she brings anyone home. After all, it's her house and I do try to give her some privacy.'

'There's really no need to worry,' Nora reassured her, 'my landlady has said she doesn't mind me having friends in.'

'And neither does mine,' Denise agreed.

Peggy was relieved. She didn't feel too guilty, for she knew that Denise was lodging in one of the bigger terraced houses a few streets away where she had a room to herself that was big enough for them to gather together comfortably whenever they wanted. They had already spent several pleasurable evenings mulling over the events of the day and gossiping about the rest of the company. Peggy was finally learning to relax with the people she now saw as her friends; it was only when Jimmy's name came into the conversation that she felt anxious, for she still wasn't sure how she should deal with him. Sometimes she thought she liked him, but at other times she couldn't help regarding him as a bit of a nuisance. She didn't know how much to say about him to the others as he was, after all, Lawrence's second-in-command and she didn't want to speak out of turn. But the others had noticed.

'Can I ask why you're always so down on Jimmy Caulfield?' Nora asked Peggy one night when they had settled down with a cup of coffee and biscuits from what Denise called her secret stash. Peggy looked at her astonished. 'I-I didn't think it showed,' she said.

Denise laughed. 'I'm afraid it does, and I'm sure he'll have noticed if no one else has.'

Peggy squirmed uncomfortably. 'Oh dear. I'd hate to upset him, but I suppose it's because I feel as though he's constantly watching what I'm doing. I know he means well, but sometimes it feels more like he's pestering me,' she said. There was no fire in the old-fashioned grate in Denise's room and Peggy shivered as she tightened her grip on the blanket Denise had offered her to stave off the chill of the evening. 'He pops up when I'm least expecting it and keeps asking me to step out with him. So far, I've managed to avoid actually saying yes, but I'm not sure how much longer I can keep doing that. He won't take no for an answer.'

The others looked surprised. 'Why do you want to keep putting him off? What's wrong with him?' Denise wanted to know. 'I think he's rather cute and he obviously likes you. I'd go if he kept asking me.'

'Me too,' Nora agreed. 'He's perfectly presentable and he can be a lot of fun, you know, if you'd give him a chance. Why don't you give it a whirl?' she said. 'I think he deserves an opportunity at least. You've got nothing to lose and you never know where it could lead. It's not as though he's creepy or anything; he's not like Lawrence – he's the one you want to watch out for! You don't want to be doing any favours for him, you don't know what he might be expecting in return.' Denise laughed and Nora shuddered. Then Peggy laughed too, but their remarks did make her stop and think. She had been warned before about Lawrence, but maybe she wasn't being fair about Jimmy. Perhaps she had made a hasty judgement and she wondered if she should give the situation some serious thought. Perhaps she should accept more graciously the next time he offered to walk her home, and she wouldn't automatically refuse his next invitation to the cinema, particularly if it was a film she wanted to see.

Peggy took time out the following day to go to the dance studio so that she could work through some of the more difficult routines. She was usually on her own at that time of day and most people seemed to have the moves down pat by now, so she was surprised to find some of the older, regular members of the chorus were there, and they seemed to be working on some steps she hadn't seen before.

'Sorry to have disturbed you . . .' Peggy backed out of the door immediately and was surprised when they called her back in. 'Don't go, it's very helpful that you're here right now,' one of the group called after her. 'It's Jean, Jean Atkinson in case you don't remember.' Peggy didn't remember and reluctantly went back when the woman called out to her again.

'Why don't you come in and meet the rest of my group? We never get time to do that on stage.'

'I was just going to go through some of my steps,' Peggy said hesitantly. 'But I can come back later, I don't need to disturb you now.'

'You're not disturbing us. These rooms are for everyone, although not many people seem to use them.' Jean smiled but Peggy caught a patronising note to her voice as she ushered Peggy into the room. Peggy smiled back although there was something about Jean Atkinson that she didn't quite trust.

'You usually come in here for some extra sessions with Lawrence, don't you?' Jean said. 'So maybe it's us who are disturbing you.' She feigned an innocent look.

Peggy felt the blood rush to her cheeks.

'No, I haven't seen him today and we have nothing booked in for this afternoon,' Peggy felt obliged to say, 'so please do stay. I've just come to try out some of the more complex routines that are still tripping me up.' Peggy wasn't sure why she felt the need to explain.

'Well then, this might be perfectly serendipitous timing,' Jean said, 'because Lawrence has told us about some changes he wants to make and we can now pass them on to you.' Her smile broadened. The rest of the group murmured their agreement and gathered around Jean. 'He said he wants us to practise them in time for the next rehearsal. So that's what we've been doing.' The rest of the group were nodding.

'It's the scene when the townspeople are coming to the market, the one when Jack comes to the village square hoping to sell his cow.'

'Yes, I know the one you mean,' Peggy said, her interest piqued.

'Well, he intends to make some last-minute changes and he's given us some notes on it. We could let you have a copy so you can practise. They need to be added to your script notes.' Jean produced some extra sheets of paper and handed them to Peggy. 'I think you'll find there's a new scene that has a few solo lines just for you.'

'For me? Really?' Peggy was thrilled.

'The only thing is you'll have to make sure you know it all in time for tomorrow morning's rehearsal.'

'I'm sure I can do that,' Peggy said, though her face fell.

'Good!' Jean said. 'And if you're not in a rush now, we could go through the movements with you and make sure you know exactly what to do. You'll know the tune of the song already, so all you'd have to do would be to learn a few extra words. You follow the usual cue. Come on, let's go through it now and I'll show you what you have to do, then you won't even have to bother Lawrence with it.'

'That would be really very kind of you. I'm sure I could do that if you don't mind showing me.' Peggy suddenly felt inspired and couldn't wait to get going, delighted to have the opportunity. She would show Lawrence what she was capable of.

'Here, let me show you the new steps, it's not complicated,' Jean said and Peggy fell into line beside her and practised it over and over again after Jean had left. Determined not to let herself down, Peggy was up half the night going over the new dance steps and practising the moves in her bedroom. And when she finally climbed into bed, exhausted, she was still singing to herself – softly, so as not to wake Elsie or the children.

The next morning she was dying to see the others in her group, wondering what they thought of the new lines, but she overslept and arrived at the theatre later than she had intended so there was no time for idle chatter.

Peggy did her best to control her breathing, eager to show off in front of Lawrence, and as the rehearsal had already started by the time she got there she had to concentrate hard so as not to miss her musical cue. As soon as she recognized it, Peggy peeled away from the group and, stepping forward, danced across the stage from the back towards the footlights at the front. At the same time she was singing the new words to what she understood to be her new solo as loudly as she could, projecting her voice to the seats at the back of the gods as she had been taught; but she was surprised to realize that she was not singing solo. On the contrary, everyone else was singing too, but they were drowning her out, singing the original words. Then, above all the cacophony she heard a deep voice boom into a microphone, 'Fee Fi Fo Fum, I smell the blood of an Englishman!' as the rest of the group danced all the old steps and moves, treading on Peggy's toes, criss-crossing the stage so that the whole thing began in mayhem and confusion and descended into chaos.

At first there was anger as the chorus members' paths crossed and they bumped into one another, almost knocking Peggy off her feet but this was quickly followed by laughter prompted by Jean, which the rest of the group couldn't help but join in as they realized what was happening. It soon became clear that the whole thing was nothing more than a prank. Peggy stopped in her tracks, as did the rest of her small group and eventually the whole scene ground to a halt. Most people were laughing by now. Only Lawrence was not amused. He was furious, while Peggy stared down at her feet in dismay.

'What the heck do you think you're playing at, wasting our time like this?' Lawrence screamed at Peggy. She stood still, mystified.

'Don't take it out on Peggy.' It was Jimmy who cut across the stage and confronted Lawrence. 'I don't think any of it is her fault.'

Lawrence looked at him and frowned, looking ready to shout.

'You know how these things go,' Jimmy persisted, spreading his palms to the sky.

Lawrence hesitated, allowing a moment for Jimmy to continue. 'Everyone's a victim of a practical joke at least once in their stage life, aren't they? I'm sure it won't happen to Peggy again.'

Peggy caught her breath and stared at Jimmy, and then at Lawrence. She still felt humiliated, although Jimmy's words had somehow taken the immediate sting out of the situation. Peggy was breathing hard as she turned and ran from the stage with tears streaming down her face.

Peggy sat in the empty dressing room, the loudness of her sobs increasing as she tried to make sense of what had just happened. She wondered how on earth she was going to redeem herself. She could hear, once more, the laughter ringing in her ears, see the scowl of disapproval on Lawrence's face and feel the sense of ridicule of the rest of the cast as she replayed the scene in her head. She could never forgive Jean. How could she ever face her and the rest of the company again? Had anyone else been in on the joke? Denise?

Nora? Surely they wouldn't have humiliated her like that? But how easily she had been duped, how vain was she that she had been so willing to believe that Lawrence would really have been prepared to offer her some solo part, no matter how small? She would have to resign, leave the company. She could see no other way out. No matter what Jimmy said, she could never live it down.

There was a hesitant knock on the dressing room door and before she could say anything the door opened revealing Jimmy Caulfield. For once she felt relieved to see his familiarly comforting face. 'Can I come in? he said, his voice tentative as he stepped inside. Peggy hastily swiped her handkerchief across her eyes although she realized it was useless to pretend when it was so obvious that she had been crying.

'I don't know what to do,' Peggy wailed, 'how will I ever be able to show my face up there again?'

'Of course you will.' Jimmy came and sat on the bench beside her, and Peggy was grateful that he was trying to avoid looking up into the illuminated mirror. She didn't even object when he put his arm across her shoulders by way of consolation 'Do you think you're the first person to be the victim of a prank like that?'

Peggy stared up at him incredulously. 'What must Lawrence think of me?'

Jimmy shrugged. 'He might have sounded angry in the heat of the moment because once he's in full flow in rehearsal mode he hates interruptions, but believe me, he's seen it all before. We all have. There's always someone amongst the newcomers that gets picked on for a lark.'

'Really? But why me? Who have I hurt? Am I such an awful person that I need to be punished like that?' She turned to him seeking an answer and was disappointed when none was forthcoming.

'Of course you're not,' he said eventually. 'That's what I'm trying to say. Tell me what happened, from the beginning. Though I'm not asking you to name names at any stage, even if you know them. You must understand that.'

Peggy hesitantly sobbed out her story while Jimmy listened patiently. 'OK,' he said, eventually. 'Believe me when I tell you it's a familiar enough story, although as practical jokes go this was a pretty good one.'

'But Lawrence was so angry!' Peggy wailed.

'I know, but you have to tell him you're sorry for the chaos caused and that you were the victim of a giant hoax. He might not let on at first, but he'll understand that. He'll know you didn't mean to sabotage the rehearsal on purpose but it won't do any harm to tell him that yourself. Tell him you'll be more wary from now on, not quite so gullible, and might possibly be a bit more humble so that you won't let it happen again. The only thing is to not point the finger or snitch on anyone in particular, much as you might want to. It's really not a good idea to identify who played the joke on you. If they come forward, all well and good, though I don't imagine they will, whoever was behind it. But nobody will ever force you to tell. Believe me, I've seen it before, it's almost a part of Weatherfield theatre tradition. And let me assure you the whole thing will be swept aside and forgotten in a few days.'

Peggy wasn't sure she believed him, though he did sound convincing. 'What you need to do is to get back on stage as quickly as possible, as if nothing has happened. You know they always tell a rider to do that when they've fallen off a horse?' he said and, almost against her will, for the first time that day Peggy actually laughed.

Chapter 16

Peggy was grateful to Jimmy for saving the day, and at least a scrap of her dignity in front of the rest of the company, although she hated the idea that he had, at that moment, seen her at her most vulnerable. But he had managed to bring a certain sense of calm to the scene, which was welcome following all the madness that had been dumped on the stage, and he had somehow coolly handled what could have developed into an impossible situation. As she sat in the dressing room, Peggy began to realize that her friends were right: Jimmy had a lot to offer and the fact that he seemed to like her a lot more than she liked him at this point might well work in her favour. The more she thought about it, the more she accepted that maybe she had been wrong in not giving him a chance.

She was grateful that he had at least grasped hold of the situation and understood what was happening and she decided it might be wise to follow his advice and return as quickly as she could and apologize to Lawrence without actually blaming anyone for what she would call the misadventure. It hurt her not to be able to voice her grudge against Jean when it had clearly been all her doing, but she understood that, when working in such restrained conditions, tempers would heal more quickly if she didn't point the finger of blame at anyone in particular and she knew Jean was hardly likely to come forward of her own volition. Much to her surprise she found that, even by the end of the afternoon, the events of the morning were second-hand news, and the more peripheral members of the company, such as the set builders and backstage helpers – and even some of the cast – were no longer focusing on what had been the major talking point of the morning.

The more she pondered the incident, the more she appreciated the speed with which Jimmy had spoken up on her behalf when Lawrence was at his angriest and she accepted that she really had been too hard on him before. She began to think that, as her friends had suggested, she should perhaps view him more kindly, and she even thought that in the future she might consider stepping out with him if he were to ask her again. But the incident still loomed large in her mind and she knew she wouldn't be able to forget it as quickly as everyone else seemed to have done. Even as she made her way home at the end of the day Peggy had difficulty picturing herself trying to explain to Elsie what had happened and she realized it would take a lot longer for her own shame and embarrassment to subside. But she knew Elsie could on occasion be very warm and understanding and she hoped this would be one of those days when Elsie was in a sympathetic mood.

Peggy was reliving the events of the day, her mind filled with all the different ways that Elsie might respond when she heard Peggy's story, so she was taken by surprise when she crossed the threshold of number 11 to find that Elsie's first words were, 'There's a letter waiting for you,' as she thrust a slim envelope into Peggy's hands. 'It's not a bill or owt, you can see that it's handwritten on a plain white paper envelope, so I reckoned it must be summat personal,' Elsie said, beaming as if she had written it herself.

'Who is it from?' Peggy asked without thinking, when Elsie waved the slim envelope in front of her.

'How should I know?' Elsie sounded affronted. 'I haven't opened it! I told you, it's addressed to you and it doesn't have a return address on it.'

Peggy turned it over and instantly recognized her mother's handwriting. She didn't say anything but quickly excused herself as she rushed upstairs so she could read it in private.

She had been thinking of home so much recently that Peggy had actually sent a short note to her mother assuring her she was well and enjoying her new life. She had added a few words about Elsie and her room in the house and had included her new address in the hope that her mother might respond some time, although she hadn't expected to hear from her so soon. She had suggested her mother might like to bring Colin to see the panto-mime as it was her first professional show but even as she had written the words she had wondered if she was perhaps being too hopeful. Peggy ripped open the envelope and sprawled across her bed to read it. She hastily scanned the single thin sheet of lined paper, taking in the signature at the bottom of the page that confirmed her conjecture, and when her eyes fixed on the words, 'Really sorry' and 'maybe next time' she stopped reading and screwed up her face. It was some time later when she heard the front door bang shut that she realized she must have fallen asleep reading the scant words over and over. She sat up with a start, the letter still in her hand. She reread it, this time making sure she didn't miss any of the words though it took a few moments for her to digest fully that not only would her mother and Colin not be coming to the Majestic Theatre at Christmas to see the show but that she should not be thinking of visiting home over the holiday as she would not be welcome.

Peggy stopped reading, feeling shocked, even though she knew those were not really her mother's words; it was her father who was barring Peggy from going back to her own home and her mother, sadly, didn't have the clout or the courage to contradict him. Peggy took a deep breath as she considered the implications of what her mother had written. She knew her father was angry with her and he had always warned her that once she moved out of the house it would be for good, but she had sincerely believed that when the time came he would relent and be prepared to allow her back for a visit, if only for Christmas. She found it difficult to accept the idea of being thrown out of her own home forever. It was particularly difficult not to be able to go home on Christmas Day, for that was the one day of the year when the Majestic Theatre, and indeed all theatres, would be dark, and she would not be working; the one day of the year when almost everyone she knew in the company would be going home. Whether her mother realized it or not, her father's ban would virtually be condemning her to spend Christmas alone. She hadn't thought that even he could be so cruel.

Peggy went into the bathroom to splash cold water on her face in an attempt to reduce the puffiness in her cheeks and the red rims around her eyes before she went back downstairs. She stuffed the letter into her pocket.

Elsie was standing by the mirror, pulling strange faces as she carefully painted her full lips with bright red lipstick.

'I thought I might sneak off to the Rovers for an hour, if it's all the same to you,' Elsie said. 'That is, if you don't mind stopping in with the kids for an hour.' She hesitated, then turned and gave Peggy a warm smile. 'And I've said I would have a drink with Ned later on, if you weren't bothered about going out. You weren't planning on going out tonight, was you?'

'No, I wasn't, so you're all right,' Peggy said, quickly hiding her disappointment. It was true she didn't want to go out though she had hoped to be able to discuss the content of her mother's letter with Elsie and to tell her about the events of the day, once they were alone. But she took a deep breath, accepting that that wasn't going to be possible now.

Elsie began bustling about the room, taking the

used crockery through to the scullery, tidying away her American film magazines and carefully folding the *Manchester Evening News* onto the top of the pile of papers on the armchair. 'I've already put Dennis down in his cot, so he'll be asleep by now, I shouldn't wonder,' Elsie said. 'But if you can just make sure Linda is in bed by seven, that should be all you need to do. Ida's kindly given Linda some of her boys' old picture books. She'll be thrilled when she sees them, so she shouldn't be any bother.'

'Fine,' Peggy said as Elsie slipped into her jacket. 'I won't wait up for you.'

'Was it a nice letter?' Elsie asked as she prepared to leave.

'It was only from my mam.' Peggy tried to sound offhand. 'She just wanted to warn me not to buy any tickets for the panto for her or my brother Colin as they won't be able to make it.' She turned away so Elsie wouldn't see the tears accumulating again as she struggled to keep her voice steady; she couldn't bring herself to say that it was her father who had dug his heels in and wouldn't allow them to come, and her father who was refusing to welcome her at Christmas. Peggy didn't mind babysitting on occasions when she wasn't going out – it had seemed only fair to offer Elsie some of her free time if she was available, and now it had become part of their rental agreement. Elsie, in return had promised to always provide some kind of supper or high tea for Peggy to come home to after a hard day's rehearsal, and normally it worked out well for both of them. But, as Peggy hunted for food in the kitchen after Elsie had left, she felt a flash of anger that, on this occasion, Elsie had left nothing. Peggy looked on all the shelves in Elsie's improvised cool larder to try to find something to eat, but all she could see was a slice of not-too-fresh bread, a started jar of fish paste and an unopened tin of baked beans. She understood that Elsie didn't always feel like cooking and there were times when there wasn't much food available to buy at the corner shop, but she had handed over all her food rationing coupons to Elsie in good faith and so she wasn't able to go out to buy anything more and she was upset to think that on a night like tonight, when she would have appreciated some home comforts, the cupboard was actually bare. Peggy felt aggrieved that she had kept her part of the bargain, helping out with household chores, babysitting the children, and she felt angry at Elsie and let down. She knew it would take some time for her to swallow her hurt, even though she would usually do anything in order to keep the peace.

Chapter 17

Peggy's letter from her mother had stung like a slap in the face. She couldn't get the harsh words out of her mind and she wished she had at least been able to tell Elsie about it and to get some support. Every time she thought about the cruel words she wanted to cry, even though she knew they were really her father's words, but she was upset at the thought of her mother using them. Did she not know how much they would hurt me? Peggy wondered.

It wasn't until the end of the next day that she finally had the opportunity to talk to Elsie about the content of the letter, when they sat down to share supper after Linda had finished her thinly spread jam sandwich and had run upstairs to play.

This time Elsie apologized to Peggy for the meagre supper.

'I haven't been able to find much worth having for several days,' she said. 'There's been hardly any fresh food and only limited stocks of dry goods available at the corner shop,' she complained. 'Everyone's feeling the pinch.'

Peggy shrugged. She wanted to tell Elsie that today food was no longer her main concern. Today, all she could think about was home. But without warning Peggy began to cry, tears streaming, her sobs increasing so that she wondered if she would be able to tell Elsie the full story about her banishment from home. When she did eventually manage to sob out her story Elsie looked shocked, though she couldn't help smiling briefly when Peggy described the other events of the previous day and the mayhem that had resulted from the on-stage prank the rest of the cast had played. Even Peggy began smiling as she relayed the facts although her cheeks flamed as she spoke.

'Yes, even I can begin to see the funny side of that now,' Peggy confessed, 'although I can assure you it didn't feel at all funny at the time.'

'I'm sure it didn't. But it sounds like Jimmy pulled through for you when you most needed him,' Elsie said. 'I wouldn't give up on that young man, if I were you,' she went on. 'I'm sure he means well. Does it make you see him in a different light?'

'Sort of, I suppose,' Peggy admitted, relieved that Elsie had changed the subject. 'And he did stand up to Lawrence when it mattered most.'

Elsie offered her an unironed cotton handkerchief and came over to briefly put her arms around Peggy, hugging her close.

'I know it's tough but it doesn't have to be all doom and gloom you know.' Elsie sounded as if she was speaking as brightly as she could on purpose. 'You said yourself they weren't really your mam's words, so it's not the end of the world, whatever she's said in the letter, when you know she doesn't mean it. And another thing, even if your mam and Colin can't come here to see the pantomime, there's nothing to stop you going to visit them, is there?' Elsie said. 'As long as you time it so your father's not around.'

'But you saw what he said about me not being welcome for Christmas,' Peggy said gloomily.

'I understood that, but what I'm saying is, take no notice. You don't have to wait until Christmas, do you? Why can't you go before that? You can go whenever it suits you, and that can be any time. Like now, before the end of the week – whenever you're due a couple of hours off. Nobody said it has to be for Christmas. I don't think the old man would turn you away from the front door, once you were there, would he?'

Peggy looked at Elsie uncertainly. 'I-I'm not sure.'

'What do you think is the worst that could happen?' Elsie asked.

'I'd be frightened of him physically lashing out at me, he's done that before now, still treating me as if I was a naughty child. I know it sounds like a reasonable suggestion from your side of the table, but I'm not so confident as you,' she said, 'and you don't know my father.' Peggy frowned and lifted her shoulders.

'No, I don't,' Elsie agreed, 'but unfortunately I've known a father who was very much like yours. I don't think my own father would have been any more welcoming if I landed on him unexpectedly.' Elsie shrugged. 'Though I'd like to think he would let me in at least.' Elsie tried to make light of it. 'But I suppose I really can't be 100 per cent sure. The thing is, I'm not suggesting I know all about unwelcoming fathers,' Elsie said with a laugh, 'I was thinking more about how it might be if you were to go and visit your mam and your little brother; you know *they* would be pleased to see you. I remember I tried to keep in touch with as many of my siblings as was possible without my father even knowing. Why don't you go and see your little brother at school? You could meet him at the school gates at the end of the day and walk home with him at least part of the way. I'm sure he'd be pleased to see you.' She paused. 'And your mam, too. You don't have to go to the house, do you? Couldn't you try to see her at work, during a break? It would be better than nothing and if you time it right you won't even miss any rehearsal time.'

Peggy looked up, surprised by Elsie's idea. 'And if you don't want to go alone why don't you ask that nice young man Jimmy to go with you? It might give you Dutch courage. He'd at least be able to help you keep your spirits up and to see the funny side of things if nothing else.' Peggy stared at Elsie as if not believing what she had just suggested, but Elsie wasn't ready to give up. 'I bet he'd go with you if you asked him nicely,' she said. 'It might do your father good to see you turn up with a well-turned-out fella. Let him think you've got a serious boyfriend looking after your interests, that can't do any harm. I know with my old man it was one of the few things that made him stop and think twice.'

Peggy frowned for a moment, then her face cleared as she realized that Elsie's idea made sense and she smiled, wondering if she dared. She had spent all this time trying to avoid Jimmy, but now the more she thought about approaching him to help her, the more the seed of Elsie's idea began to take root.

Chapter 18

Peggy asked Jimmy if he would meet her in the dance rehearsal studio and she waited until they were alone together before she brought up the subject of going home for a visit. Fortunately, she didn't have to wait very long for the others to leave and she took a deep breath before plunging in at what initially felt like the deep end of a swimming pool. She didn't feel the need to explain all the details but she gave him an outline of her family situation and ended with Elsie's suggestion that she pay them a visit before Christmas.

'It's a bus ride out of town in the opposite direction from Coronation Street, followed by a short walk at the other end,' she explained. 'I don't really like asking you, but the thing is that I would appreciate some support and I wondered . . .' Her voice faded. 'I'm sure you can see why.' She gave a nervous laugh. 'It shouldn't take very long, though I'll understand if you say no. It's a bit of a cheek really, asking you to get involved in someone else's family nonsense.'

She backed off before he even spoke and was surprised by his almost eager response. He stretched out his arms and took in a deep breath before jumping several star shapes as if he was limbering up for a fight.

Peggy couldn't help laughing though she was astonished when he said, 'Why not?' as he flexed, then contracted, his arms as if showing off his muscles. 'Flattered to be asked and happy to help if I can. I could do with a break in routine. As you say, it shouldn't take too long and it doesn't even have to break into rehearsal time. We could set off early in the morning and be there and back before anyone realized that we'd gone. And if it helps you, then let's do it.'

They set off very early the next day and arrived at Colin's school before anything was officially open, before the padlock on the gate had even been released, although, strangely, they were not the first to arrive. Peggy was surprised to realize how tense she was – the walk from the bus stop had done nothing to loosen her up. They came to the wooden fence in time to join several mothers and their offspring who were already standing by the locked gates, firmly grasping hold of siblings, or pushing babies in prams as they waited for the caretaker to come and open them. It had been Peggy's job to see Colin to school while she had been living at home but she did not expect her mother to accompany him now. He would no doubt protest that he could go alone, or with his friends now he was growing up.

A steady trickle of youngsters began to arrive and eventually the caretaker came to unlock the gates and let the children into the playground, leaving the parents free to disappear. Peggy felt a sudden panic that she might somehow miss him as she watched them converge into the yard. Then she suddenly spotted him among a gang of young boys who looked as if they had travelled together and who all descended on the gate at once. It had only been a few weeks but Colin looked much taller and thinner than when she had seen him last, although his face didn't look any different. He was busy chatting with his friends and didn't notice Peggy at first, but then he stopped before he went through the gate and stood still, staring up at his sister in disbelief.

Peggy couldn't stop herself throwing open her

arms and taking several steps towards him, as she forgot for a moment that young boys of his age didn't like to be embraced in public. But to her delight, Colin didn't shy away; instead, he ran towards her calling out, 'It's Peggy! It's Peggy!' and he grasped her in a bear-like hug, refusing to let her go. He buried his head in her skirt when Peggy tried to introduce him to Jimmy, refusing to look elsewhere except at his big sister.

'Is it really you, Peg?' Colin seemed to be laughing and crying at the same time as they stood awkwardly clinging together. 'Mam didn't tell me . . .' he said, looking up at her accusingly.

'That's because she doesn't know,' Peggy laughed but Colin suddenly looked anxious and a look of fear crossed his face; his fingers intertwining nervously. 'You can't come to our house, you know.' His little face looked so serious Peggy wanted to pick him up and smother him in reassuring kisses, but she restrained herself when she heard Jimmy's voice naïvely asking, 'Why not?'

'Because Da will kill her, that's why not,' Colin said. His voice was surprisingly strong but he didn't look at Jimmy's face. Neither did he look at Peggy as he said softly, 'I shan't tell our mam I've seen you,' and he detached his hand from hers.

'You can if you like, and you can even tell her about Jimmy, that's up to you, Col,' Peggy said, bending down so she was on a level with her brother's face. 'I'm going to try to see Mam, if only for a few minutes, at work.' Colin's face showed alarm. 'Don't worry, I shan't be coming to the house,' Peggy reassured him. 'And you must only say at home what you feel safe saying. We can't have him coming after you, now can we?'

Colin shook his head.

'The last thing I want is to get you or Mam into trouble, but I thought I'd try my best to set eyes on you, so do tell her I tried, if you can. When I told Jimmy all about you, he wanted to come and meet you too.'

Colin looked as if he didn't totally understand her reasoning but he stepped back, saying nothing. At that moment there was a loud, piercing whistle and all the children in the playground ran about until they had formed several long, straight lines that led from the front entrance marked Juniors.

They were virtually standing to attention, while the teacher who had blown the whistle blew it again. Colin quickly broke rank to give Peggy another hug. 'It's been great to see you, sis, but we're going in now,' he said, hovering as if waiting for one more hug. But as the lines began to move he turned his back on her and moved away into the dark recesses of the school corridor.

'Glad to have seen him?' Jimmy asked as they

walked away. Peggy stared down at her feet and nodded, unable to speak.

'Did it help?' Jimmy asked.

Peggy could only nod again. 'Yes, thanks,' she whispered. It was as if she couldn't bear to say the words out loud.

Chapter 19

Elsie always enjoyed having a drink, particularly if it involved having an evening out at the Rovers. She rarely turned down an invitation and she was grateful whenever Peggy offered to sit in with the children and give her what she thought of as a night of freedom. Elsie was particularly grateful since she had been stepping out with Ned, for it wasn't easy for them to find places where they could be quietly together. But she did wish, sometimes, that she had more privacy in the comfort of her own house.

Elsie would have liked to be able to invite Ned home more often, where just the two of them could be together without setting all the neighbours' tongues wagging. Peggy had shown some real understanding, despite the awkwardness of the situation, and Elsie was grateful. She could see that Peggy did try to give them as much privacy as possible, but even when Peggy stayed in her own room all evening, Elsie was always aware that there was an additional stranger in the house and she could never completely relax. Equally, if she went to the Rovers for a drink, Elsie would find herself looking out for Ned, hoping he might be there so the two of them could share the evening together. Even when she was laughing with other people she would catch herself unconsciously watching the entrance each time the doors opened, as she was tonight.

When she spotted him coming through the double doors, she immediately raised her hand in greeting and stepped forward towards him. But she quickly lowered her hand again, disappointed, when she realized that he wasn't alone. He was, as he so often was when he came to the Rovers, with the slightly older man who he referred to as his friend and business partner, the miserable-faced Vinnie who never seemed to remember her name.

'It's good to see you again, Elsie,' Ned said.

'And you,' Elsie said, gulping down the remains of a gin and tonic. She put her empty glass down on the counter.

'I hope you're not rushing off anywhere on my account? Have you got time for another?'

'Yes, I do, actually, you timed that well. Don't worry. My lodger, Peggy has kindly offered to stop in with my kids for a couple of hours, so no one will be calling the police out looking for me,' Elsie said.

'That's good to hear,' Ned laughed. 'The usual?'

'That will do nicely. Thanks.' Elsie grinned as her empty glass was hastily removed from the counter by Annie Walker and Ned took his place behind the line of regulars waiting to be served. She watched as Vinnie made his way to a table on the far side and Ned indicated that they should join him. Elsie took charge of her freshly poured drink, leaving Ned to pick up the two pints the landlady had also placed on the counter. Vinnie was already sitting at the table, drumming his finger. Elsie gave him a half-smile as she followed Ned to the table, but she was treated to his customary scowl in return.

'Don't worry, he won't be stopping long.' Ned jerked his thumb in Vinnie's direction and tried to sound jocular as he laughed and gave Elsie a wink.

'Just long enough to down a pint,' Vinnie said, his expression deadpan.

'Property hunting is thirsty work,' Ned said, brightly, 'though hopefully we'll soon have something to celebrate.'

'Oh? What's happened to prompt that, then?' Elsie

forced herself to smile as she asked and looked directly at Vinnie although he never raised his eyes from his glass. His expression hadn't changed and Elsie felt as if she was intruding on a private conversation. Ned raised his glass when Vinnie didn't answer. 'You know that Vinnie and me're going into business together?' he asked Elsie, and she nodded.

'I thought you were already partners, right?' Elsie thought it best to clarify.

'Well, we are, sort of, just waiting for everything to be fully set up. It makes sense for us to go in together in a joint venture. Then I can pick his brains, such as they are, and he can filch my money.' Ned sat back and laughed but Vinnie didn't join in and Elsie couldn't be sure whether or not Ned was joking. 'We've already done a few little sidelines together,' Ned said vaguely. He waved his arms about by way of illustration, but far from clarifying the position, Elsie thought he made it sound as though they were involved in dodgy dealings. He didn't elaborate further and she didn't comment.

Elsie was relieved when Vinnie finished his pint. He didn't offer to buy another round and, to Elsie's relief, he also refused a top-up when Ned offered. He stood abruptly. 'I'll see you tomorrow then, Ned,' he said, and roughly pushed his way past Elsie, without apology, almost spilling her gin and tonic into her lap.

'Not a man of many words, your friend,' Elsie said when Vinnie had gone.

Ned shrugged. 'We don't seem to need all that many between the two of us,' he said. 'But he's OK. He takes his time thinking about things before he makes his mind up to act, which is no bad thing, but then he doesn't usually like to talk much about things once a transaction has been signed and sealed. I'm not sure why, but he didn't want to talk about our property search today, though I don't see the harm in telling you, now that he's gone, that we've spent the day seriously looking for some kind of premises for our big venture.'

'And what's that?' Elsie was interested.

'A café, basically,' Ned said.

'And did you find anywhere suitable?'

'I think we may have found something that might be possible; it was once a café but it'll need some work doing before we could use it as that again. We'll need some advice before we make a move, so we weren't in a position to sign on the dotted line today. But we've agreed to go back and check out some of the details one more time before we're prepared for any money to change hands.'

'Where is it?' Elsie felt it was safe, now that Vinnie had gone, to show some genuine interest, although Ned wasn't a great talker either and she began to realize how little she really knew about him.

'It's on the other side of the viaduct,' Ned said and he sat forward, his face suddenly becoming more animated. 'Of course, I'd still like to have a business of my own, one of these days,' he said, 'but Vinnie's persuaded me to go in with him this time and I think he's got a point. A café we can both be involved in might be just what I need right now, till I'm ready to go it alone. And Vinnie seems to think that we'll be able to make enough money for the both of us.'

Elsie suddenly laughed. 'That's exactly the kind of thing my Arnold used to say.'

'And?' Ned asked. 'Did he make it?'

Elsie gave an ironic laugh. 'Sometimes, though I learned not to ask too many questions.' Elsie stubbed her cigarette out in the ash tray.

'Vinnie's been pretty generous so far,' Ned said, 'teaching me all he thinks I need to know. At least if I go in with him I'll not be taking as much of a risk as if I try to go it alone too soon. Hopefully, I'll know when I'm ready to start making my own mistakes,' he went on and then he laughed. Elsie couldn't help but smile warmly at him, admiring his good looks as if she was seeing him for the first time. The irony was that she had been attracted at first by his almost gangster-style appearance and she was still taken by the way his dark hair curled around his ears and flicked away from his coat collar. Conversely, the cowlick that flopped forward onto his forehead gave him a boyish, innocent look. She caught his eye, and their gazes locked for a moment. She tried to pretend not to have him under scrutiny but she couldn't prevent the colour rising to her cheeks as she looked again at his strong-looking hands and neatly trimmed fingernails, which always looked as if they had been scrubbed clean. She had learned about the importance of appearances from Arnold and she couldn't help thinking that it wouldn't take much to smarten Ned up and make him look totally acceptable to everyone else in Weatherfield. The cheap-looking royal blue suit he always wore with a white shirt and a fashionably broad-tongued tie, possibly gave a false impression that he was a bit of a wide boy, but she knew she could soon iron out the creases in the flashy, cheap, material so that she could actually feel proud to have him take her by the arm.

It was several more days before Ned offered to show Elsie the property he and Vinnie had been looking at. 'I presume you'd like to see it?' he said, twirling the keys in his hand.

'Course I would. You don't have to worry I'm going to buy it out from under you or anything.' She gave him a challenging look.

'Quite frankly, I can't work out what Vinnie's afraid of. I'm interested in knowing what you think and I also know you won't tell Vinnie. I don't see the harm, but for some reason he'd be mad at me for showing it to you before any contracts have been signed.'

As they continued walking slowly down Coronation Street, Ned became more animated than Elsie had ever seen him and by the time they reached the viaduct she had learned more about him than she had heard in several previous meetings when he had hardly talked at all. She discovered, for the first time, that the army had rejected him because of his flat feet and, although he had told her before, he assured her several more times that he was not married but lived on his own in a small flat on the other side of Weatherfield.

'It's only a small, rented flat over a furniture shop,' he said. 'But I'll be able to get some decent-looking furniture for a good price and it's as much as I need, when I'm out at work most of the day,' he said. He didn't say any more about what his 'work' entailed but Elsie had always assumed that he had fingers in several different pies. He seemed to like the idea of having several things going on at once, none of which were straightforward, much like her husband, Arnold; and, like Arnold, it soon became apparent that Ned was no stranger to what Elsie called 'under-the-counter dealings'.

Elsie was engrossed in Ned's story and didn't

realize at first that they had passed under the viaduct and Ned had stopped walking. She turned back and looked at him in surprise. He had stopped outside some scruffy-looking premises that looked as if they had once been a café, although when she saw how the windows and door were all boarded-up and papered over with several layers of old posters, she understood why Vinnie might not want anyone to see it yet. The whole place looked dismally uninviting from the outside and Elsie realized, with a sinking heart, that it didn't look any brighter or more seductive when Ned opened the door and switched on the light inside. The single central lightbulb sent undiscernible shadows across the dull-looking space and Ned pulled the blinds down on the windows. But even in the dim light it was still possible to see that overall it was a good-sized room that promised much. As her eyes adjusted to the gloom, Elsie could see that several small tables and chairs had been stacked in the centre of the room and it took no time at all for Elsie's head to quickly fill with ideas as she envisioned how the furniture could be used and the space rearranged in order to make the place come alive.

'What did it used to be?' Elsie asked as she looked around.

'I think it was a milk bar,' Ned said, 'so it shouldn't be difficult to turn it back into some form of café.'

Ned looked very pleased with himself. 'What do you think?'

'I think that's a good idea,' Elsie agreed. 'Though won't it cost a lot to kit it out?'

Ned suddenly looked embarrassed and looked down as he shuffled his feet. 'That's why there's two of us,' he said, though he didn't enlarge and Elsie knew not to ask. 'And that's where living over a furniture shop and having a sympathetic landlord can come in handy,' he went on. 'I reckon he'll offer me a good deal when the time comes to furnish the place.'

Elsie nodded approvingly. 'Sounds good,' she said, 'and I hope you've got connections in other directions too.'

'Such as?'

'Such as being able to get hold of all the foodstuff you'll be needing – that's not always so easy to find right now?'

In the silence that followed Elsie worried that she had asked Ned one awkward question too many about something that was really none of her business. But to her surprise, he grinned at her.

'That's where Vinnie comes in,' he said. 'Contacts. Although I've got a fair few who can supply me with most of what we'll need.'

Elsie noticed that Ned didn't actually use the words 'black market', though she felt they were implied whenever he talked about his friend and what he was bringing to the partnership. She asked no more questions as she silently looked about the room and after a few moments Elsie felt Ned's hands reach out and grasp hers and there was something about the way he rubbed his thumbs across her palms that made her turn in surprise to focus on his face.

'Do I take it these premises would get your seal of approval then, once the place is properly done up?' Ned said.

Elsie looked up at him and smiled.

'They certainly do,' she said. 'They've got a lot going for them – and I must say, I'm flattered you asked my opinion, though I can't believe Vinnie will set much store by it.'

Ned made several noncommittal grunting noises and Elsie had the sense that Ned was looking over her shoulder, staring off into the distance at whatever it was that was behind her. When she turned to see what it was, his gaze seemed to be directed towards a large couch that had been tucked into an alcove at the back of the room. It was half hidden behind a curtain and had been loosely covered with an embroidered velvet throw. 'Now, I wonder what they used that for?' Ned sounded surprised and there was a chuckle in his voice.

'They probably hired it out by the hour, I shouldn't

wonder,' Elsie said and exploded with laughter, not expecting to see Ned rubbing his chin thoughtfully as if he was seriously considering her answer.

'Now there's a thought,' he said, and to Elsie's astonishment he seemed to make a slight jerking motion with his head in the direction of the couch, and she felt an increase in pressure on her arm. Neither spoke and Elsie watched in amazement as, with an impressive flick of his wrist, he pulled the throw to one side. Then, without another word, he covered her lips with his own as he gently guided Elsie down onto the firmly filled cushions.

Chapter 20

It had felt so natural the way they had slipped into a passionate embrace before ending up on the sofa that Elsie couldn't help but wonder how many other young women Ned had recently offered to show around the premises. Not that she could object, for since the day they had first stepped out together Ned had insisted they should not question each other's personal love life, either previous or current. Ned knew about Elsie's marriage to Arnold, of course, that was something that couldn't be avoided, and Elsie believed she was under no illusions about Ned. He swore he hadn't ever been married but she knew with a young man as good-looking as he was, she could hardly expect she was his first romance!

Ned pulled the velvet throw over both of them and Elsie giggled as she snuggled closer to him, enjoying the warmth of his body. She got lost in the memories of her first encounter, which made her feel like a naughty schoolgirl and she shivered with delight.

'Are you OK?' It was several minutes before Ned's voice brought her back into the room and she sat up smartly, silently rebuttoning her blouse as she wrestled with her feelings. Then she stood up, doing her best to brush the creases out of her skirt, though she was not entirely successful. It's not as if I have to feel guilty about anything, she thought. She had long ago pushed such notions out of her mind because she was hurting no one. A girl should be able to enjoy herself once in a while without troubling her conscience. She repeated the refrain to herself – it was something her husband Arnold had taught her. Seize each day and make the most of it; take whatever life has to offer. That was the mantra she tried to live by and that's what she had been trying to tell her lodger as well, although for some reason Peggy seemed to be content doing nothing, letting life wash over her. Elsie didn't understand why she couldn't even allow herself to enjoy being pursued by a presentable and perfectly respectable young man like Jimmy. Elsie certainly wouldn't have let a chance like that go by, and she wasn't going to make such a mistake in relation to Ned; she fancied him and she was going to make the most of his attentions and obvious attraction to her. She would live life now and let the future take care of itself.

Peggy, however, had Elsie only known it, was not as content with her lot as she appeared. She was really keen to change things but the fact was that she didn't know how. She wished she could discuss her difficulties in more detail with Elsie or with one of her new friends from the theatre who she was now getting to know well. But she felt too shy and awkward to say more than she already had, and didn't know where to begin. She had worked hard to give off an air of self-confidence but she now realized that only served as a cover, disguising her underlying feelings. In many ways, as she got to know them better, she realized that she had had a more sheltered upbringing than they had and there were many areas in which she was actually quite ignorant and unworldly, particularly when it came to dealing with young men. Her mother had got as far as warning Peggy to 'be a good girl' and 'not to be free with her favours', as she called it. She had issued constant reminders for Peggy to take care of herself and to prevent an unwanted pregnancy at all costs, but she had offered only vague and limited details about how Peggy should actually address these issues and had offered no guidance on how far it was safe to go.

Peggy had always assumed that, once she reached a certain age, and had moved away from home, everything would suddenly fall into place and the knowledge she lacked about the facts of life would automatically become clear. When she went to work in the theatre and found people like Denise and Nora, not to mention Elsie, who were all close to her in age, and yet appeared to be so much more knowing and confident, she felt this confirmed her belief. She was actually relieved that they seemed to be so much more knowledgeable and worldly-wise than she was as she hoped to be able to follow their example and learn what she needed to know from them. She was happy to look on them as role models and allowed herself to be guided by them. It took her some time to understand they didn't have the answers to everything and there were many things she still needed to work out for herself; such as how best to respond to the kind-hearted Jimmy who seemed to be genuinely interested in her welfare, while at the same time dealing with the deviousness of Lawrence whose motives were at best, questionable.

It took her some time to work out how she should respond to Lawrence's attentions and to understand the power he wielded in terms of the development of her career.

Jimmy's intentions, on the other hand were much easier to comprehend and one night after a particularly late rehearsal, grateful for his company on the unlit pavements, she finally invited him into number 11 for a coffee. Elsie seemed to be pleased at her decision and greeted Jimmy so warmly that Peggy could only wonder why she hadn't asked him in before, particularly since he had accompanied her to Colin's school.

After that first time, she let Jimmy see her home most nights and invited him in for coffee. She found he was very easy to talk to and because she had taken her courage in both hands when she had told him about her difficult home situation and had been glad to have him at her side when she went to visit Colin at his school, she soon found she had no difficulty in conceding that he really was someone she could trust. She had even been prepared to introduce him to her mother that day after visiting Colin, for as she had told her brother she had hoped to locate her mother during her morning break at work. It was unfortunate she had not been able to find her for there had been no further opportunity for Peggy to seek her out. She wondered if Colin had told his mother about her visit, and about Jimmy, for she now knew that she would have liked them to meet, if only to reassure her mother that she really had settled into her new life and was having fun.

Peggy had still been reluctant to go to the cinema with Jimmy but one evening she finally gave in and they went to a second-house showing at the local Luxy picture house. To her relief he didn't suggest they sit in the back row, but when the film action became too tense she found herself automatically clinging on to his arm and hiding her eyes in his jacket, and by the end of the film she was so relaxed in his company that she didn't object when he squeezed her hand comfortingly in his as they strolled home together.

It was a relief for Peggy to be able to talk to Jimmy about something other than work and she began to look forward to going to the cinema with him whenever the films changed, which they frequently did. It provided a wonderful alternative to the extremely hard work that was required at the theatre, where Lawrence expected them all not only to be word perfect but to have all their moves and dance routines down pat as well. He had made some additions to the score and the choreographer had introduced some new sequences so no one could rest on their laurels and Peggy did struggle sometimes to remember all the extra steps.

She was telling Jimmy about this as they were

walking home together one night when she added, without thinking, 'I've been wondering if being an understudy would make it any easier? I wonder if having to learn other parts as well as my own might help me to remember the movements more easily? I was thinking of asking Lawrence about it. What do you think?'

Jimmy stopped in his tracks and flashed the beam of his torch in Peggy's eyes. In the momentary flash of light Peggy could see that his face was creased into a severe frown. She shrugged and turned away before Jimmy could see her blushing.

'I thought it might help because the steps would be different and if I could keep them separate . . .' Peggy began but her voice petered out as she was not sure what she was trying to say. She was sorry she had spoken the words out loud.

'But there already is cover for the main part, and I can't imagine why anyone in their right mind would want to take on Nora's job,' Jimmy said. 'Lawrence knows the panto well and if he had thought it necessary to have any of the other parts covered he would have said so from the start. I think it best if you leave it at that.'

Peggy shrugged, glad that Jimmy couldn't see her face.

'Besides,' Jimmy said, 'have you any idea how much extra work that could involve?'

'To be honest, I was thinking about earning extra money so that I could send it to my mother for Christmas,' she said quickly, although she knew that understudies mightn't get paid extra for covering a major role. She wasn't going to admit that what she had really been dreaming about were the tales of the understudies she had heard of who had been rocketed to instant stardom after they had been forced to take over one of the starring roles at a moment's notice.

'Well, let me tell you right away that you won't earn any extra dosh that way,' Jimmy said with a laugh. 'I thought you'd have known that by now.' Peggy looked away. 'If it's money you're after,' he went on, 'then you'll need to make sure you don't miss any performances, especially on the days around the build-up to Christmas when we'll be doing three shows a day.'

Peggy thought ruefully of her first meagre pay packet that initially she had felt so proud of. It had been a shock to find there wasn't much left after she had paid Elsie what they had agreed for bed and board and taken enough money off for food during the week. She didn't want to tell Jimmy his words had shocked her, for she hadn't really believed that understudies didn't get paid extra, despite the work they had to do. That seemed most unfair but she felt embarrassed now for having mentioned it. It made her sound foolish and uninformed and she wished she could retract her words.

Peggy was getting used to having the children under her feet for much of the time she was at home, except when she firmly shut herself into her own room and refused to answer if Linda knocked. But generally, even when she felt tired, she would do her best to hide her irritation and spend time playing with them, or reading to them. She reckoned she would benefit in the long run as it made for a better atmosphere in the house. Elsie seemed to appreciate her help and Linda was a good little girl on the whole, at least when she was with Peggy. She could be easily distracted by a colouring book and a few crayons or by being allowed to flick through one of the picture magazines filled with portraits of film stars that Elsie usually managed to conjure up. Even the baby, Dennis, once he had been fed and changed, usually settled without too much fuss, so at first Peggy didn't mind offering to stay in and babysit from time to time, allowing Elsie to have the odd night out on her own, but recently she had begun to feel that Elsie was taking her for granted. Peggy felt particularly aggrieved when Elsie didn't fulfil her part of their agreement by providing an evening meal. She didn't expect a hot meal every night, but a few miserable potatoes and some overcooked brussels sprouts with a sliver of spam and not even a slice of bread didn't pass for a meal in Peggy's eyes, not when she had been working all day; and this wasn't the first time it had happened. It was hardly enough to keep body and soul together, never mind keep her fit enough to sing and dance all day; and yet that was all Elsie had been able to offer her recently. Peggy was loath to complain though, because she did understand Elsie's problems bringing up two children on her own, but as time went on Peggy wondered how long she could let it continue without saying anything. When she was alone she practised what she might say, trying to make the words sound like a helpful suggestion rather than a whining complaint.

It was a shame, Peggy thought, for there were so many ways in which Elsie was the perfect landlady; she could be kind and considerate and often would go out of her way to arrange things so that Peggy could also go out to the Rovers of an evening where they would meet up with her friends and neighbours from Coronation Street.

'It's really not a problem,' Elsie said dismissively when Peggy enthusiastically expressed her appreciation for such treats. 'I can remember what it's like being in a strange place and not knowing anyone. But you should bring your friend to join us.

You know, that fellow from the theatre. You should make more use of him to go out more, cos he seems to be really sweet on you. It would be good for you to introduce him to folk, let them get to know him as well as you. I think they'd like that – and that way you won't appear too stand-offish.' Elsie chuckled and nudged her elbow into Peggy's ribs. 'I bet he'd go down well with some of the neighbours I can think of.'

Peggy frowned at first as a picture of Lawrence and his flirtatious smile flashed through her mind, and she turned sharply to look at Elsie. 'There's not one of them wouldn't fall for someone who's young and good-looking,' Elsie said, and Peggy exhaled loudly realizing that Elsie must be talking about Jimmy.

'Really?' Peggy couldn't stop herself asking. 'Do you think they've all taken to Ned?' To her relief, Elsie laughed. Peggy had often wondered what the neighbours made of the young man Elsie seemed so keen on at the moment, though he wasn't someone Peggy had taken to immediately. In fact, she wondered what Elsie saw in him, although she had always been careful never to express an opinion.

'It doesn't matter to me one way or the other,' Elsie said as if reading Peggy's thoughts, 'they don't have to like him. It's not like when you have to take your man home to get your mam and dad's approval.

Though folk round here do love a bit of gossip, especially if it's spiced with a spot of romance. Even some of the men enjoy that kind of tittle-tattle; they seem to thrive on the speculation, almost willing it not to last.'

Elsie tittered but Peggy frowned as she tried to imagine bringing Jimmy to the Rovers and introducing him to the Todds, or to Mrs Ena Sharples and her cronies. She shrugged, not sure why she felt so hesitant. As Elsie said, her Coronation Street neighbours had nothing to do with her theatre friends. But Peggy was always interested to hear Elsie encouraging her to develop her friendship with Jimmy and she was glad she had accepted his recent invitations. He was attractive and she was learning to really trust him; besides which, her friends all seemed to like him and he was popular with the rest of the cast. Maybe it would be a good idea to introduce him to folk at the Rovers. He might go down well with Coronation Street's residents as Elsie was suggesting – and having them approve of her young man wouldn't do any harm to her own standing in the community. She smiled to herself, glad she had already accepted his invitation to the Luxy to see *For Whom the Bell Tolls*. She had been eager to see Ingrid Bergman and Gary Cooper who were two of her all-time favourites and she thought she might have a chance to get to know Jimmy better. She might even agree to sitting with him on the back row, if he insisted, and if they went to the first house then she would suggest they go for a drink at the Rovers afterwards.

Chapter 21

'Are you going to show me the rest of the property?' Elsie asked on her second visit to the proposed café, frowning as she noted the limited number of tables it would take to completely fill the room despite the bay window. It seemed incongruous and a waste of precious space to think of the couch tucked away in the alcove.

'How do you mean?' Ned said

'I mean that I presume there's more to it than this?' Elsie said, hoping she wasn't upsetting him by implying it was so small. Ned reached across to the wall and flicked on a light switch, the dim glow revealing another recessed alcove with several more small tables and an impressive stack of chairs.

'We'll have to get rid of this, though, I'm afraid,' he said, indicating the couch.

'Oh, that's a shame,' Elsie said impulsively. 'It's a bit of a feature – and besides, it's quirky. You could hire it out.' She giggled, acknowledging the sideways glance Ned gave her.

He gave her arm a squeeze. 'Though it will be a shame to see it go.' His gaze held hers momentarily, and he had to clear his throat before he could speak. 'The idea is that we'll clear the rubbish and fit this out so it's a cosy little family-type of café during the day with some nice simple tables and chairs to replace these heavy old things. I told you I live over a furniture shop and my landlord will be happy to supply everything, so long as I've got the readies, if you know what I mean.' He rubbed his thumb across his first two fingers, leaving Elsie in no doubt what he meant. 'That would be the daytime business,' he said.

Elsie looked up at him.

'Oh yes, and what's the nighttime business?' Elsie spoke flippantly, with a deep-throated laugh, but quickly realized Ned was serious.

'Follow me and I'll show you,' he said and he opened a door at the back of the second recess that Elsie hadn't noticed. Ned flicked on a switch revealing a flight of stairs leading down to the basement and he began to descend, inviting Elsie to follow him.

At the bottom he stopped and gave an exaggerated sniff. 'What does it smell like to you?' he asked.

Elsie only took a short breath as a musty smell wafted up the stairs. She was doing her best not to hurt his feelings and wasn't sure how truthful she should be.

'It smells exactly like I would expect a cellar to smell,' she said, giving what she thought was a considered answer and hoped he would see that she was being diplomatic.

Ned shrugged. 'I suppose that's fair enough,' he said, 'because, after all, it *is* a cellar! I reckon we should be able to get it spruced up and respectable without too much effort. We could do most of it ourselves if we have to.'

Elsie gasped, hoping he wasn't including her in the clean-up squad. 'And what does Vinnie think?' she asked, for she could hardly imagine Vinnie wanting to get his hands dirty either.

'Vinnie's not convinced we can ever make it fit for purpose, that's why he's been hesitating over signing the contract and shelling out the deposit money, and my first job will be to prove that we can.'

'I see, and what purpose is that going to be?' Elsie asked.

'A nightclub,' Ned said with a grin. 'I thought it would be a perfect place for us to set up a few gaming tables down here. Entrance would be by invitation only, and we'd start off by inviting a few specially selected friends, offer them a drink or two to come and have some fun. It would be like our own little private club. Word would soon get around and, in the right circles, they'll be queuing up for an invite.'

Elsie was astonished by his forward vision and she was impressed by the way his eyes lit up as he talked about it. That wasn't what she had been thinking of, although she could see how it made sense to Ned. It was just that her imagination hadn't stretched in that direction. But now that she thought about it, serious gamblers and close-to-the-mark businessmen wouldn't be put off by a spot of damp while they did their dodgy dealings. They would hardly notice if the place did smell a bit musty. But Ned hadn't finished.

'There would need to be a few strategic invitations sent to the right people in the first instance, of course, and we'd have to make sure to keep the authorities out of our hair. But that's more Vinnie's territory than mine. He assures me he has favours to call in. The beauty of it is that it wouldn't have to be open every night and we'd choose our opening times carefully. If the heat gets turned up, we have a preplanned strategy for getting rid of any incriminating evidence and switching to running some harmless card games instead until things die down. So long as we keep our ears to the ground, I reckon we can't really lose.' Ned folded his arms across his chest, a satisfied smirk on his lips, and Elsie became aware of his steady scrutiny of her face.

'How would you fancy making some extra pin money?' he asked her, continuing to make eye contact.

Elsie's eyes opened wide. That wasn't a question she had been anticipating.

'Strictly under the table, of course, no questions asked.'

Elsie stared at Ned in astonishment.

'As I say, we won't necessarily open every night, at least not for the serious money; we'll have the regular café that we'll put through the books to keep us ticking over but I can't imagine you'd want to be working there. You'd probably still want to hang on to your own day job?' He paused but not long enough for her to reply, then added, 'If you're interested, I could teach you a few tricks of the trade, like how to deal and how to handle the cards like a professional croupier.' He looked her straight in the eye and winked. 'I bet you'd be a natural,' he said with a grin.

Elsie could see he was serious and she had to admit that her interest was piqued. For one fleeting moment she was so swept away by the potential glamour of it all that she almost forgot that they weren't talking about a fancy casino in the centre of town, but a damp cellar underneath a café by the viaduct in Weatherfield. It took her a few moments to come back to earth, and she shook her head and frowned. Then she laughed. 'We're talking illegal gambling here, I take it?' she said at last.

Ned pondered for a moment. 'It's a fine line, I reckon, at the end of the day. I suppose it might be considered to be technically just on the wrong side of the law, but times are hard enough with no end in sight to this wretched war, so I don't see why people shouldn't be allowed to have a bit of fun.'

Elsie couldn't wait to tell Peggy about Ned's plans for the café and for her possible role in the development of what he planned to call The Basement Club, so the following day she left a note for Peggy to meet her in the Rovers if she arrived home early enough.

The children, it seemed, were at number 3 with Ida Barlow for the evening and when Peggy saw the note she was curious, wondering what could have prompted Elsie to go out to the pub so early.

When she got there, none of the usual crowd had arrived as yet and Elsie was sitting alone at one of the secluded tables tucked away at the back of the public bar. 'I'm really glad you managed to get here early,' she said, 'I was hoping you'd come. I'm meeting Ned a bit later but I thought we might grab a few minutes before he arrived.'

Peggy looked at her, not sure what to expect. 'Here, I got you a drink in,' Elsie said and she pushed a large G and T towards Peggy before launching into her tale about the café. Peggy sat back and listened, fascinated by the animation that had lit up Elsie's face as she revealed the outline of Ned's plans. She talked about him rescuing the building, as well as his offer of possible training that could lead to some rather unusual evening-time employment.

'Isn't it exciting?' Elsie said when she had finished. 'I could quite fancy myself as a bit of a card sharp.' She giggled as she flexed and stretched her fingers as if she were performing a magic trick with an invisible pack of cards.

Peggy felt flattered Elsie had wanted to share such news with her, and she was surprised too, but before she had time to say anything her eyes were drawn to the entrance where she could see Ned was just arriving. As he made straight for their table, Peggy saw, to her dismay, that he was being closely followed by his friend and business partner, Vinnie. She stood up, wondering if that should be her cue to leave, but Elsie waved her back into her seat. 'There's no need to rush off,' Elsie said as she flapped her arms at Peggy. 'At least stay and finish your drink.'

To Peggy's surprise it was Vinnie who spoke next. 'Don't go on our account, darling,' he said as he sat down and he looked sharply at Ned.

'Two pints coming up,' Ned said to him, grinning as he gave a mock salute, then he turned to Elsie. 'How about you two ladies? Need a top-up?' but both Elsie and Peggy shook their head and Ned went over to the bar.

'I take it Elsie has told you about our new venture?' Ned didn't even look at Vinnie, addressing Peggy directly as he came back and set two pint glasses onto the beer mats.

Peggy nodded. 'It certainly sounds very exciting,' she said. 'How long do you think it might take to get it all set up?'

Ned shrugged. 'Hard to say. It's difficult to get hold of stuff right now. You can't depend on the building materials being available when you want them so it could take a while. And then we haven't even signed the lease agreement yet.'

'Why do you ask? Are you after a job as well?' an unfamiliar voice said, and Peggy looked up, surprised to see it was Vinnie who was talking. She turned her head towards him and was unnerved to find that for once he was actually looking at her directly as he spoke. She was the one who looked away first.

'You fancy joining your friend, do you?' Vinnie

said. 'Is that it?' There was an unpleasant grin on his face. 'Maybe we can turn you into a croupier as well. You'll earn more than you get at the stupid pantomime, that's for sure,' and he gave a gravelly laugh.

There was an awkward silence that Ned jumped to fill. 'The place certainly has lots of potential as I'm sure Elsie's told you,' he said. 'Much business to be done there, truckloads of money to be made if we work hard.'

Vinnie had leaned forward now and he lowered his voice as he added, 'Serious money if I have my way. Stick around if you care to find out just how much.'

There was something about the leer on his face and the glint in his eye that held Peggy's attention as she looked at him now.

And whose money was going to back it and make sure that the venture worked? Peggy wondered, but she knew better than to ask the question out loud. Instead, she turned to look again at Ned but his eyes were now on Elsie. Surely he wasn't capable of supporting a project like that by himself? Peggy thought. Then she glanced once more in Vinnie's direction but he had withdrawn again, his eyes hooded and hidden from view.

Peggy cleared her throat and this time she did stand up and remained standing. 'I think I'd best be going home, if you'll excuse me,' she said. 'I'm really pleased to hear about your plans and I wish you all lots of luck.' She looked at Elsie as she said this, and Elsie grinned. 'But I've got an early start in the morning and have some things to prepare.' To her relief, no one made a move to stop her. 'Thanks for the drink, and I'll look forward to seeing the finished product.' She raised her glass to Elsie before finishing the remainder of the gin. 'Enjoy the rest of your evening and I'll see you tomorrow,' she said and, with no further acknowledgement, she practically ran out through the double doors. She slowed down when she reached the pavement outside and was startled by the chill of the evening air. She didn't look where she was going and walked briskly the full length of Coronation Street before turning around and heading back to number 11. The empty hallway echoed as she stepped onto the lino, pausing to retrieve her key from the lock. She wasn't used to coming into an empty house. She hesitated for a moment, automatically glancing behind her as she always used to do at home, as if she expected someone to be following her, then she closed the door carefully, pausing to ponder on just what it was that Elsie might be getting herself involved in.

Chapter 22

Peggy trod cautiously around Lawrence, hoping he would appreciate how hard she was working while she tried to master the new additions to the dance routines. She worked hard so that it wouldn't appear to the others as if she was currying favour and Lawrence wouldn't feel the need to select her for special tutoring any more. She wanted to show him that she was not only making progress but that she would be a worthy member of the company now and after the pantomime was over. She often stayed on late at the theatre and would usually continue to practise specific steps up in her own bedroom at Elsie's. Things at the theatre generally seemed to have settled down and she was pleased to feel she was making good progress, she hoped Lawrence appreciated her efforts as well so he would have no reason to show her up in front of her colleagues. She would get cross with herself on the odd occasions where she got some of the sequences in the wrong order and ended up tripping over her own feet, but she was determined to give the dancing tutor no reason to shout.

Peggy had never completely lived down the events of what she still referred to as her 'dreadful day of humiliation'. The feelings from that experience had been irreversibly seared into her mind and she realized that the memories of the acute discomfort she had felt on that day would probably never go away. But she tried to convince herself that was a good thing, for it literally kept her on her toes. She so wanted to do well, to show Lawrence he was right to have faith in her even though she was still some way off perfect. She knew she had made a great deal of progress and hoped she would continue to do so and that way Lawrence would no longer wish to single her out for special treatment.

She was thinking about this during rehearsal, wondering if perhaps reports about his behaviour had been exaggerated and she didn't need to fear him. Her mind was whirling and she lost concentration for a moment. It was no more than a moment but it was enough to make her miss a step and, before she knew it, she had stumbled, tumbling to the floor and bringing the line of dancers behind her to a crashing halt.

'No! No! No! How many feet have you got, girl?' Lawrence reacted spontaneously, just the way he usually did, and he made no attempt to spare her his anger. Peggy reacted as he shouted the words and slammed his notes down on the table. He was standing, facing the dancers who had fallen in a heap like a collapsed pack of dominoes, looking horrified. They tried to pick themselves up when Lawrence rapped his baton on the top of the piano and indicated that they should start again and there were smirks and self-conscious giggles but no one said a word. They just shook themselves off and began again as if nothing had happened. Peggy's cheeks were burning as she kept her head down and tried her best to concentrate. She was gratified that there were no further accidents and wondered if she should hang back at the end of the session and apologize to her fellow dancers and to Lawrence. But before she could say anything Lawrence beckoned to her to stay behind and she could only watch as the rest of the troupe filed out. To her surprise, he no longer looked angry and as she approached she thought she heard him sigh.

'I allowed myself to be persuaded that you really

had improved,' he said as the last dancer left the stage. 'Jimmy certainly seemed to think so. But it seems he was wrong.' He shook his head, a resigned look on his face. 'I don't know what I'm going to do with you.'

Peggy looked at him, horrified. 'Like what?' She stared at him, disbelieving. 'Oh dear, please don't sack me. It was an accidental trip, I was probably concentrating too hard. It won't happen again, honestly,' she pleaded, her eyes wide. 'Please, give me another chance and I'll try my very, very best,' Peggy implored. 'I can do it, I know I can.'

'I'm sure you have the potential to do it eventually, or you wouldn't have got through the audition, but the problem is, we don't have very much time. If you're to succeed you need to relax so that the movements become automatic. You're far too tense, see?' Peggy suddenly felt his hands on her shoulders and he began roughly massaging her neck. She stiffened involuntarily.

'What did I just say? Let go, for goodness' sake, no wonder you dance as if you had two left feet.' She felt his warm breath in her ear and heard him whisper the word: 'Relax,' as his fingers continued to manipulate her shoulders. It took a few moments for Peggy to be aware that they were the only two people left on the stage. 'I think that, right now, you and I need to do some work together,' Lawrence said, 'if there is to be any hope of you being in that chorus on opening night.'

Peggy noticed that his voice had suddenly become husky. She let out her breath, relieved that it looked as though he wasn't going to sack her. He put a finger under her chin and tilted her face towards him, his eyes burning into hers. 'If you want to stay, then you seriously need to show me how much you want the job and what you're prepared to do to keep it,' he said, and let go of her jaw.

Peggy, surprised by his words, continued to look directly into his face as he forced her to meet his gaze. He had certainly sounded angry when he had first spoken but now she thought she saw the hint of a smile catch at the corners of his lips before he eventually looked away. How many times did she have to prove herself to this man?

'I want the job very badly,' she replied without hesitation. 'It's been my dream for so long. Please don't send me away . . . I want to be an actress and a dancer so much that I'll—'

'Then prove it,' Lawrence cut her off, his voice sharp though his expression was enigmatic. 'Very well,' he said when she didn't respond. 'Meet me downstairs in the rehearsal room in fifteen minutes and be prepared to show me what you can do.'

Peggy took several deep breaths as Lawrence left the stage with a brief, 'Remember, downstairs.

Fifteen minutes. Last chance.' She had initially been upset to think of having to do extra work with him but now she was surprised to realize that what she felt was excited, and that her whole body had begun to tingle. Despite his earlier anger she was being given another chance, was going to work, one to one again, with the great Lawrence Vine – and who knew where it could lead. It was up to her now to make it count. She was doing her best to calm down. Maybe some would say that having to stay behind for extra tutoring was a punishment, the way she'd had to write out meaningless sets of repetitious lines in detention after school. But Peggy thought that maybe this session would turn out to be a privilege. So long as she didn't flaunt it, or boast about it to the others. Maybe she should see it more like having a private session with a famous director, for he would be giving her his sole attention once again, and perhaps that could lead to – no, she had no idea what it could lead to, but surely the possibilities were endless? She needed to see beyond his flirtatiousness. In the theatre, the director had all the power over the cast and if she wanted to get anywhere she had to understand and accept that.

Peggy started singing and dancing her way through the regular chorus routines, determined to show Lawrence how much she did actually know. She didn't stop until Lawrence told her to repeat some of the more difficult sequences.

'You should be able to close your eyes and just feel what your feet are doing,' he said, 'then you need to repeat the exercise as many times as necessary until all the movements become automatic. There's no room for error on a stage that size. You proved that again today. One mistake and the whole bloody chorus piles up on top of you.'

'Yes, I know, and I'm sorry again about what happened this morning.' Peggy took the opportunity to apologize and she twisted her fingers as she spoke. 'I really will try not to let that happen again.'

'Don't try.' Peggy jumped back as Lawrence came up close and pushed his face towards hers. 'Just do it!' he said.

'But I can do a whole lot more than that,' Peggy said quickly taking a step away. 'Would you like me to show you?' and without waiting for him to reply Peggy launched into the role of one of the other characters that she had spent some time practising when she had been thinking about asking to be an understudy. She had learned the lines and some of the songs as well as the moves and she hoped he would be impressed.

Lawrence had been flicking through his notes rather than looking at her, but when she began singing a different song he looked up, astonished, his eyes rivetted until she finally stopped in front of him, panting and out of breath.

'What on earth possessed you to learn all that?' Lawrence asked. 'It's no wonder you can't remember your own part! When did you find the time?'

'I did it a while ago. And you did ask me to show you how much I wanted to stay with the company. I hope that proves to you that I'm serious about the job . . .' Peggy shrugged. 'I thought if I learned some other roles it might help me get a better part.'

Lawrence shook his head. 'There are other ways,' he said, 'or have you not learned that yet?' There was something in his voice that made Peggy feel uncomfortable and she tried not to look at him but he merely laughed. Then a strange silence fell on the room and, for the first time, Peggy was conscious that the two of them were in the dance studio alone, locked away together, underground. She wondered if perhaps in trying to impress him she had gone too far and instead of being flattered by being the focus of his attentions she realized she was actually frightened. What had she been thinking? Wasn't this exactly what she had been warned about? How could she have let herself be manipulated into this position?

The silence was broken by the distant sound of what Peggy realized must be the air-raid siren and she looked about her wildly for the door. 'We're trapped, we must get out!' she cried, forgetting all the air-raid drills they had practised during her first week at the theatre and she was surprised when Lawrence just laughed.

'Where are you trying to get to?' he said. 'Don't you realize we're in the safest place in the building right now? This is probably the best place, even better than the actual air-raid shelter.' He took several steps towards her and, reaching out quickly, gathered her into his arms. Before Peggy could react he was pressing his lips down on hers. The movement was sudden and his embrace all encompassing.

'Not too scared now, I hope?' he murmured. Peggy was trying to wriggle away from him but his strength was formidable.

'Aren't we supposed to gather in a proper air-raid shelter somewhere?' she said. 'They'll be looking for us. Shouldn't we go and look for the others, or they'll miss us? I don't think that anyone knows we're here.'

Peggy felt a moment of panic as she said this, but at that moment the studio door opened and Lawrence smoothly slid away from her, although she could feel the warmth of his hand lingering in the hollow of her back, even as she was flooded with relief when Jimmy Caulfield peered into the room. As he stepped inside and looked about him, Peggy let out the long breath she hadn't even been aware she was holding.

'I saw you come in here earlier,' Jimmy said, 'so I thought I'd just check to see if you were still here and if you had heard the siren. It's only just gone off.' His voice sounded bright, although, given the look on his face, Peggy wondered if it was forced jollity.

'Yes, we did hear it, but thanks for thinking of us,' Lawrence said, sounding anything but grateful. 'We were just about to make our way to the basement shelter. No doubt it will be airier there. But we've been working hard, or at least Peggy has, she'll be glad of a break, I'm sure. I've really been putting her through her paces.' He grinned at Peggy who found it hard to reciprocate. 'Did you know she has ambitions to stay with the company after the panto?' Lawrence asked Jimmy, lowering his voice conspiratorially. 'She fancies going for much bigger, juicier parts than the mere chorus.' Lawrence beamed at Peggy as he said this. 'And I was telling her that such parts aren't always easy to come by.' He shot a meaningful glance in Peggy's direction as he said this, although she wasn't sure she knew how to read it. Peggy didn't dare look at Jimmy now. She knew her cheeks were colouring, and she was grateful when he said, 'Perhaps we really should all go and join the others in the basement shelter, then they won't have to worry about where we are.'

'Good idea,' Peggy said, taking a step towards Jimmy. The siren was still wailing.

'You won't mind if I don't join you? Tell them I'm fine,' Lawrence said, and before Jimmy could reply, Lawrence gave a wave of his hand and swept out of the room, leaving Peggy to stare after him, wondering if she should thank Jimmy for helping her to make what now looked like a lucky escape.

Chapter 23

There were several more air raids that week that thankfully turned out to be false alarms, although Peggy knew that as the planes flew on they would shed their deadly loads on poor folk in other parts of the country. The mechanical wailing of the siren that echoed all about the town meant that other parts of the country would shortly be cruelly ripped apart. It was all very unnerving to realize what was happening throughout the country and Peggy preferred not to be in the house alone when planes were flying past. When she wasn't at the theatre, she took every opportunity to go out, particularly somewhere she could be with other people, somewhere she couldn't be manipulated into an awkward compromising position again by Lawrence and indeed, somewhere she could flee quickly to a shelter, so when Lawrence offered them a few hours off from rehearsals one evening she readily accepted Elsie's invitation to join her for a drink in the Rovers before Lawrence could make any unwanted suggestions of his own.

'I'll be meeting Ned later on,' Elsie said, 'but I thought we could get a round in before he comes and have a chance for some gossip.'

On this occasion it didn't matter when Ned, who was not known for his punctuality, arrived late as this allowed the two women plenty of time to talk about their neighbours and friends and to put the world to rights. Peggy enjoyed their chat time and was glad Elsie had insisted they should make the most of it because when Ned did finally arrive she was dismayed to see his friend Vinnie following in his wake. Peggy could understand why Elsie enjoyed being with Ned for he was personable, good-looking and could be good fun, but she knew Elsie had no time for Vinnie, any more than she did, and she failed to see what qualities Ned admired in Vinnie that made the two such inseparable friends. Vinnie always seemed to look miserable and dour, with an almost permanent expression of anger on his face and the furrowed lines deepened as he snapped or shouted at everyone who tried to engage him in good-natured banter.

Having caught some of the excitement from Elsie about Ned's new venture Peggy wasn't surprised that was all Ned wanted to talk about, and she even accepted him bragging. Elsie had made it sound as though the new café was actually Ned's business and that Vinnie was there to help him out occasionally when additional financial input was required. But the more they talked, the more Peggy began to see that the money, the ideas and the whole basic business actually belonged to Vinnie and it was Vinnie who was graciously allowing Ned to buy into it and do all the hard work and running around. She was surprised to hear Vinnie actually talking about his role in a way she had never heard him talk before and she was surprised to find at times that he was actually speaking to her directly; he even looked her in the eye. But she was shocked that when Elsie excused herself and went off to powder her nose, Vinnie took hold of her hand as he spoke and he actually smiled.

'I can't believe you'd enjoy waitressing, up here,' he said, leaning forwards to make sure she heard, 'but there is more to this than meets the eye.'

Peggy looked at him in astonishment but he was staring down at the table. 'Once your pantomime is over you should think about coming to work in the nightclub downstairs earning some real money at the tables alongside your friend Elsie.' Peggy gave him a quizzical look, not sure if he was serious, but the look on his face sent a cold shiver down her spine.

Chapter 24

As opening night of the pantomime approached, the atmosphere behind the scenes in the theatre changed, and the cast and backroom staff were showing signs of excitement as well as nerves. Would the *Gazette* send a reporter to write a review on one of the press preview nights before they officially opened? That was the burning question on everyone's lips as the anticipation built, or would they wait until the big night itself? Speculation was rife and tempers were fraught as additional rehearsals were called to make sure that everything was going according to plan. It was Peggy's first experience of involvement with a professional theatre and she was concerned that things couldn't possibly be ready in time for opening night. She wasn't convinced, even when Jimmy tried his best to reassure her.

'Believe me,' he said, 'it's always chaotic at this stage of the proceedings. Take no notice when Lawrence threatens to tear his hair out as if this is the worst rehearsal he's ever seen. He always likes to pretend he's never experienced anything like this, even though he's been here before, many times. It's not unusual for him to still make changes to the script, even at this late stage, but he won't bring himself to tell you that this is par for the course.'

It wasn't until Denise, and then Nora, backed Jimmy up that Peggy tentatively began to believe them.

'We're fortunate this time that we're booked in for a longer run than usual so we have time to make any necessary adjustments. Don't forget we've got the theatre from late November through to February this time, so there will be sufficient time to tighten up any loose ends and sharpen up any individual performances once we get going,' Jimmy said.

'And don't forget we don't have to rely solely on the written reviews,' Nora said. 'News will spread by word of mouth once we're underway and it's up to us to make sure all the words in people's mouths are good words.'

'Absolutely,' Jimmy agreed. 'Oral feedback plays an important part in our process and development so it will be very useful if we really do get the good audiences that Lawrence has been predicting. He's usually very good at forecasting such things – and the one thing you can believe is that when Lawrence says we're expecting to have good audiences, we will have. He spends ages studying the sales figures and knows what he's talking about.'

Peggy nodded. She had heard Lawrence saying on several occasions how much their reputation could be enhanced by word of mouth, particularly after the schools had broken up and the audiences seemed to be less fraught.

'When they're on holiday from work and the children are off school, parents are more inclined to book last-minute tickets on the off-chance,' he suggested, 'so there will be lots of additional families buying tickets at the box office on the night. It should add significantly to our healthy run of pre-bookings.'

Some people were prepared to take a chance and go out in the evening despite the ever-present threat of air raids that could interrupt the show at any time, and Lawrence encouraged the company to be optimistic and not just play to the matinee audiences.

'We've got to believe in what we're doing if we want audience numbers to keep increasing,' he insisted positively. 'And we've got to give them what they want so they go away singing all the songs, humming all the tunes and wanting more.'

Peggy found it was impossible not to get caught up in the excitement that was building in anticipation of the big day and she wished with all her heart that she might be able to share it with members of her own family. She had come to realize even more, lately, just how much she missed her mother and her brother and wished desperately that she might find a way to persuade them that it was safe enough for them to come to see her. But since her visit to Colin's school and the unsuccessful attempt to see her mother at work Peggy had heard nothing.

'If you ask me, I think you should just ignore what happened at the factory. It's not as though she was trying to avoid you, she didn't know you were coming, did she?' Jimmy said.

Peggy shook her head. 'I suppose I was afraid she might not want to see me,' she said softly, not really wanting to admit it.

'But the more I think about it,' he said, 'the more I realize you did catch her on the hop, she wasn't expecting to see you.'

'True but—' Peggy began

'But next time you should write to her beforehand. She would be better prepared if you were able to send her something in the post, warning her ahead of time that you intend to visit, in case she has to make any special arrangements.'

'Are you suggesting I should write to her now and try again to see her before Christmas?' Peggy wasn't sure she understood him.

'Why not? That's what I would do if it were my mother and brother,' Jimmy said without hesitation.

Peggy felt a flush of excitement, wondering why she hadn't thought of that herself, and the next day she sent her mother a short note suggesting a day and time for a possible early morning meeting at her mother's place of work and reminding her about the show's opening night. She crossed her fingers in the hope that she might be able to persuade her to defy her husband for once. She put the slip of paper into a plain business envelope and said a quick prayer as she popped it into the pillar box on her way to the theatre. She hoped her father wouldn't be the first in the house to pick up the post from the mat the next morning, and she wondered what chance there might be of her mother bringing Colin to see the show. Her only worry now was how she would contain her excitement until opening night, a thought that only made Jimmy laugh.

'I'm sure you'll manage,' he said. 'You're finding out the hard way that it's not an easy life being in the theatre, and it's certainly not the life for everyone. But if you really love it the way you seem to, then you'll be so good at it that everyone will want to

223

come to see you perform.' That made Peggy smile and she looked at him thoughtfully for a moment. She locked into his gaze and a warmth flooded through her as she nodded, for that's what she hoped for too.

Chapter 25

Elsie was surprised when Ned announced that the street level Coffee Lounge was going to be ready to open before the curtain would be going up at the theatre on Peggy's panto – she would never have believed that all the refurbishing work that was required could be completed so quickly when all she kept hearing about was the shortage of raw materials and the lack of available workers. Of course, she realized later, the work had not all been completed on time, there were still several missing aspects that Ned preferred to gloss over, but sufficient progress had been made to allow the doors to open on the actual date that had been advertised on the posters pinned up in the street. The Basement Club, the name they had unofficially assigned to the newly renovated basement cum nightclub, was also more or less ready, although that wasn't being advertised, relying instead on a more discreet and personal avenue of distribution through a network of private invitations that reached a more exclusive clientele.

Inside the café, curtains and strategically placed screens had been used to close off any aspects of the project that were not yet ready for the public to see. Overall, however, Elsie was impressed by the speed with which the restoration work had been carried out when she was invited by Ned to see the changes that had been made since her previous visit.

'OK, so this is to be the main daytime café and I can see that this will really work,' Elsie said, glancing around the room although she avoided looking at the curtain that partitioned off the old couch. 'But what about the gaming room where all the excitement will be in the evening? How will that be managed? How will the tables be set out for gambling?'

The wooden floor creaked as Ned walked towards the door to the cellar, now covered with the same wallpaper as that on the walls so it was almost invisible. He pushed it open to reveal the flight of stairs and descended into the basement, beckoning Elsie to follow.

'You'll have to use your imagination a bit at the moment because it's not finished yet, but the decoration is done,' Ned said, making no attempt to disguise the pride in his voice. There were now several round tables and chairs scattered about the floor which Elsie thought looked as if they might be better placed in a café than a nightclub.

'Of course, these aren't the finished articles,' Ned said as though reading her mind, 'but they'll do for starters. My landlord is going to find more appropriate furniture for us and he's looking out for some proper gaming tables and anything else that will make it look more like a nightclub than a coffee bar.'

'And what's this?' Elsie stepped towards another door that had also been papered over and she opened it without waiting for permission. 'What's in here?' she asked as she flung open the door and revealed a large storeroom that seemed to stretch underneath the entire length of the café above. The floor-to-ceiling shelves were stacked high with large tins labelled tea; bottles of coffee essence; more packets of sugar than she had seen since the war began, and large cardboard boxes marked with the names of different varieties of biscuits and crackers. That answered her unasked question about where supplies for the daytime café would be coming from, for she recognized the contraband immediately and she wondered if it was Vinnie or Ned who was up to his neck in black marketing, perhaps even theft. The expression on Ned's face suggested that they were probably both involved. Ned watched on as if he was expecting to see a look of horror on Elsie's face but in truth she was neither shocked nor upset by the extent and nature of Ned's enterprises, for she had never been one to judge. For a brief moment, however, she did have a flashback to the time when she had previously encountered such things – when she was first married to Arnold.

'The café is certainly looking very impressive,' Elsie said, aware that Ned was hovering, waiting for her to make some positive comment without being asked. 'I've been telling all my neighbours to go and take a look at the café, not the club.'

Ned beamed. 'That's good, that's what I want to hear, but how about you?' he asked. 'What do you make of it all now that it's nearly done?'

Elsie frowned quizzically. 'The upstairs or the downstairs?' she asked.

'Either. Both.' Ned shrugged his shoulders.

'It's shaping up very nicely,' she said. 'You must have worked hard.'

'And have you given any thought to the job we were talking about? We'll be officially opening the café tomorrow and obviously we've got some staff lined up for that. But what about the club? Still interested in putting in an evening shift once in a while, when that gets going?'

There was a pause, then she said, 'Yes, I'm interested, if you really want me, but to be honest, I didn't think you were serious.'

'Oh, I was serious all right. We haven't worked out any details yet, but as we're going to have a small group of personal friends here on a trial basis tomorrow night, anyway, why not make it your first night? Come down, you can see what we're aiming at and we can talk terms.'

'What does Vinnie have to say?' Elsie asked cautiously.

Ned didn't answer directly. 'You let me worry about Vinnie,' was all he said.

'How do you mean?' Elsie was curious.

'The other night we invited a few close friends for the first time and had a sort of dummy run, to make sure things were ready enough to run smoothly if we invited a few more people as we're both keen to get going.'

'And were they ready?' Elsie asked.

'They were indeed!' Ned beamed. 'Of course, there will be things we have to tweak as we go along but we both reckoned we were ready enough to go ahead with a small number tomorrow night. Of course, we'll be keeping it fairly low-key – you could think of it like a rehearsal – but I can slip you a few bob if you fancy coming here to look beautiful about the place and brighten things up,' he said with a grin. 'I'm afraid you won't be able to tell anyone about what we're doing here, it will have to stay our little secret, but if you'd like to come and see what it's like . . .?' He left the question hanging, but the sum he quoted that he seemed to consider was only a few bob made Elsie draw in a startled breath. 'Tips would be on top of that, of course, once we really get going,' he added quickly, with a wink, then he concentrated his attention on inspecting his finger-nails and appeared not to look at her.

'I suppose there's nothing like starting as you mean to go on.' Elsie's eyes continued to focus on his face, then she laughed. 'But, thank you, I'd like that,' she said finally, shifting her gaze, then she gave a broad grin as she leaned forward eagerly. 'What exactly does the job involve?' she asked. 'We haven't discussed that yet either, have we? Beyond you offering to train me in the art of card dealing and handling two packs at once.'

For the first time Ned looked uncomfortable and he turned away. 'As I say, I've not given the details a great deal of thought,' Ned said, though from the look on his face Elsie didn't believe him; she could tell Vinnie was a planner and she imagined that, secretly, Ned was too. He hesitated before he went on, 'How's about you start off taking people's coats?

Then, if the tables begin to fill up, you can serve the drinks. You never know, you might be able to net a good few bob in tips in time for Christmas.'

Elsie looked unabashed by his comment. 'Better in my pocket than in theirs my husband always used to say.' Elsie's face wore a determined grin and Ned nodded in agreement.

When Ned dropped her off, Elsie didn't look at the time although she had a sense that it was late, but as soon as she got inside the house she went straight upstairs and began rifling through her wardrobe to see if there was anything she might wear in order to take up Ned's invitation. She had every intention of going to the club the following night and was confident she could make herself look as beautiful as Ned had suggested. 'Wear something special,' he had instructed her, and she flicked through her clothes rail, trying to decide what she considered to be her most glamorous outfit.

The following night Elsie dressed slowly and carefully, savouring the excitement of the prospect of her new job and wondering what kind of tips she might be able to expect on top of the generous fee that Ned had suggested he would pay her. Ned hadn't mentioned the sum in front of Vinnie and she wondered if perhaps he wouldn't approve, but she had to admit there was something about the illicit nature of things relating to the club that thrilled her and made her want to know more about what was really going on between Ned and Vinnie behind the scenes. She was unsure how much to tell Peggy about the developments in the basement, but she couldn't help sounding a little boastful describing Ned's generous offer, and feeling a little smug when Peggy looked suitably impressed.

'When will you be handing in your notice at the factory?' Peggy asked. 'You can hardly keep two jobs going, can you?'

'I'm not sure it will actually come to that as we're only talking about the odd evening, initially at any rate, but there's no rush and no reason why I can't do both.' Elsie tried to sound offhand. She didn't want to admit that leaving her old job had not been her first thought when Ned had approached her about the club. Before she took such a step she would need some solid evidence that the new job would cover all her needs and expenses. But then, she reasoned, why should she give up her job at the factory? Ned hadn't asked her to, had he?

Elsie arrived early at the club on what she thought of as opening night and, although she understood why, couldn't help feeling disappointed that there was no razzmatazz to greet her or the first clients either. As instructed by Ned, she approached the basement through the back alley that ran behind the café and, mindful of the blackout, traced the silhouette of the building with the fine ray of her penlight torch.

'Who's there?' a hoarse voice whispered and Elsie jumped back, snapping off her own torch as a beam from a stronger light was aimed directly at her eyes.

'It's Elsie Tanner,' she whispered back, relieved to have recognized Vinnie's face. 'I've come to work here tonight. What are you doing?' she asked without thinking.

'I'm watching out for rozzers, or nosy parkers – they're all the same to me,' Vinnie said edgily. 'You're lucky I didn't knock your block off, creeping around like that.'

'Charming!' Elsie muttered. 'Didn't Ned tell you I was coming in to do a night's work?'

'He may have mentioned it,' Vinnie mumbled.

'Well then, if you'd be so kind as to shine that light on the door instead of my face, I'll get out of your way as fast as possible.'

Ned seemed to have been waiting on the other side of the door for he appeared as soon as Vinnie lifted the latch and pulled the door open. He seemed to be jumpy and on edge and he let out a long slow breath as he slammed it smartly shut behind her.

There weren't as many punters as Elsie had imagined there might be, despite Vinnie's boast that he and Ned had spread the word as far as they dared among their friends and acquaintances, but once a steady trickle of mostly men began to filter through, Elsie was kept busy in the cloakroom. Then, as Ned had suggested, she switched to the bar, ensuring everyone was kept constantly supplied with drinks while Ned and Vinnie encouraged them to keep upping the stakes and dipping their hands deep into their pockets.

It wasn't until Elsie finally began to relax that she realized she was actually enjoying herself, flirting lightly as she kept up a constant stream of banter to accompany the drinks that she served with a smile. Some of the punters flirted back and they were fun, although too many of them were only interested in the cards, studiously focusing on the game in hand. They didn't seem to notice the pretty barmaid who was desperately trying to attract their attention. But as the evening wore on she was gratified to see Ned giving her a brief thumbs up, a sign that everything was going well, and even Vinnie gave her a nod of approval, accompanied by a reassuring pat and squeeze on the bottom.

Elsie had worked hard and she was exhausted. She had been on her feet all night and she was grateful when the punters began to leave, even though it meant she was back on cloakroom duty. Ned came to join her, to shake people's hands, thank them for coming and to encourage them to come back once the club started opening more regularly. Vinnie, it seemed, had no time for such niceties for by the end of the evening, without explanation, his face had hardened into an angry-looking scowl and Elsie thought it best to ignore him.

It was very late and Elsie, assuming that Ned would be seeing her home, claimed her own coat and made her way to the office to tell him she was ready to go. But before she reached it she was brought up short by the sound of angry voices – Vinnie and Ned were locked in a private battle. She stopped with her hand on the door handle, unwilling to interrupt, and much as she was tempted to listen, she took a step backwards. It had been a long day and now her nerves were tingling because of the anger she could hear, but all she could do now, in case her intentions were misconstrued, was to back away from the door before she was caught red-handed. Instead, she went back to the club room and made a start on cleaning up, going from table to table, emptying the overflowing ashtrays and collecting the glasses so she could wash them in the makeshift bar. When the two men finally emerged, Ned didn't say a word, just clasped Elsie's arm by the elbow and guided her out up the stairs and through the doors of the café above. Elsie looked about her, her eyes alighting on the drawn curtain at the back of the room and she let out a sigh. There would be no quick tumble on the old sofa tonight.

It was well after midnight when Ned left her on the front doorstep of number 11 Coronation Street. She didn't invite him in for a nightcap as she sometimes did, and Ned himself tipped his cap in a farewell gesture and made no move to come inside. She was pleased she had asked Ida Barlow to babysit rather than any of the young schoolgirls she sometimes approached but she was surprised to find that Ida had already gone home and it was Peggy who was sitting alone as Elsie practically fell inside the front door. Peggy stood up quickly when Elsie came in, and she put her hands out to steady her.

'Oh my goodness, I don't remember when I last felt so tired!' Elsie exclaimed, kicking off her high-heeled shoes. She flopped down onto the old sofa cushions and rubbed ruefully at what looked like the beginnings of a bunion.

'I'm surprised you're up so late when you're so close to opening night,' Elsie said to Peggy. 'What time did Ida go? Is everything all right?'

'Everything's fine. It was our final rehearsal and we were having such a god-awful time Lawrence insisted we stayed until we got it right, that's all,' Peggy said miserably. She put her head in her hands and it took some time before she looked at Elsie again. When she did, she sounded thoroughly miserable. 'Everything that could go wrong, did go wrong,' she said at last. 'Tempers were short and everyone was shouting at everyone else.' Peggy stood up. 'But here, you must be wiped if you've been working all this while. Let me get you a cup of tea – it's a freshly brewed pot.'

'Ta, love, that would be great. I've not had the greatest of nights myself,' Elsie said as she gratefully accepted the cup from Peggy and sat down at the table.

'Why's that? Wasn't it fun? I thought it was going to be exciting. What did you have to do?' Peggy bombarded her with questions which Elsie neatly sidestepped. 'I suppose it seemed to be going well enough from Ned's point of view,' she said eventually, though she hesitated thinking of Vinnie's sour face and the shouting match she had happened upon. She took a deep breath. 'I can't afford not to do it, but truth be told, I'm beginning to wonder just what I've got myself into.'

Chapter 26

Peggy hadn't yet had the time to visit either the café or the basement nightclub as her own opening night was almost upon them and following the disastrous dress rehearsal, on Lawrence's orders, she spent every spare moment with the rest of the cast at the theatre. When she was at home, she did her best to listen sympathetically to Elsie's stories, even though she wasn't clear about the extent of her involvement with either of the two young men.

'I'd love to come and see the club for myself,' she told Elsie, 'and I will if ever I get such a thing as a proper day off,' she promised, 'but for the moment I can't see beyond the curtain being raised on our opening night.'

As that day drew nearer, so the tensions behind the scenes at the theatre rose and tempers shortened and Peggy became even more aware that she wasn't the only one getting worked up and anxious. Everyone in the company seemed to be going about with jangled nerves. It was as if they were in a constant state of high alert, even though the bombers and the air-raid alerts were few and far between at the moment and the imminent threat of having to clear the stage and the auditorium was unlikely. But Peggy was conscious of even the slightest change in people's mood as it affected the general atmosphere both on stage and off. People seemed to accept a more or less permanent state now of feeling jumpy. If an aeroplane flew overhead, regardless of the direction of its flight path, everyone suddenly looked scared, poised as if they were ready to make an immediate dash for the shelter.

Opening nights on any stage had always been special as far as Peggy was concerned, even in the world of amateur dramatics, and she could see that the preview and press nights on the professional stage meant just as much because they provided an opportunity for any last-minute adjustments to be made. The tension and excitement was building during the final days before the full opening and Peggy was grateful to be able to spend most of her time at the theatre. It was good to be able to share her feelings and vent her emotions with others in the company who shared them, people that she now considered to be her friends.

'Come and have a look,' Denise whispered on the first preview night when they were expecting a full audience, and despite warnings and instructions to the contrary from Lawrence and Jimmy, she dragged Peggy across the stage by the hand so that they could sneak a peek at the entering crowds through a chink in the heavily draped curtains as, family by family, the audience packed into the theatre. Peggy could only see a small section of the front stalls through the tiny gap so she wasn't sure what she expected to find, but she was very excited when she caught sight of Elsie Tanner arm in arm with Ida Barlow, lining up behind a young usherette as they waited to be shown to their seats. Elsie had insisted they bought their own tickets and Peggy was touched to see the two of them in the crowd, knowing it wasn't easy for Elsie, in particular, to pinch a couple of hours out of her fully booked working day and it seemed they had both made a special effort to be there.

'I'll definitely come to see it, probably more than once, but I'll not promise when,' Elsie had warned Peggy. 'It's all right for me and Ida to come at night but I've promised that I'll bring Linda one afternoon once she breaks up from nursery.'

Seeing Elsie at the first performance touched Peggy deeply and it made her wonder if perhaps her own mother might have made special arrangements as a surprise and would actually be there with Colin. She tugged at the curtain and looked out into the audience even harder and for a few moments felt a wave of optimism and hope. But then Denise tugged at her hand, indicating Lawrence was angrily gesticulating for them to leave the stage immediately and Peggy realized she would have to accept that having her own family magically appear was really too much to ask.

Chapter 27

Elsie was surprised how easily her life slipped into a new routine to accommodate the antisocial hours of her new job. She had always been determined to make the most of any opportunities that came her way and she was delighted that she had been able to grab the chance to earn some extra cash. Now that the refurbishment work on the club had almost been completed and word slowly began to spread, the trickle of regular customers – mostly men – gradually increased as they enjoyed long evenings of illicit gambling. Elsie herself had never been much of a gambler but that didn't stop her from wanting to work at the club, which held a certain fascination for her. She had learned from her husband what little she did know about the most popular card games and she was attracted by the thrill of it all. She was looking forward to Ned making good his offer to teach her some card-handling skills so, in preparation, Elsie attended all the games evenings as she was desperate to earn the kind of money Ned had talked about. So far she had been disappointed; the money in the envelopes when he actually paid her was far short of the fee he had tempted her with before the club opened. In fact, it barely made up for the extra she had to pay to secure a reliable babysitter, someone who could stay late on club nights, enabling her and Ned to have a little personal time together after hours when they could take advantage of the privacy that was offered by the sofa that had not yet been removed from the alcove in the café upstairs.

When she was working, Elsie concentrated on making the most of what skills she already had and spent her time flirting and making up to the regular punters, prompting them to be generous with their tips. They seemed to be mostly compulsive gamblers, the kind who were willing to place bets on anything, including the proverbial two flies crawling up a wall, and from the way they handled their cards there was no doubt they were all hardened gamesters with families to support, probably too old to be called up for the war effort but trying desperately to improve their lot. Given the weight of the commitments and responsibilities that rested on their shoulders, Elsie never ceased to be amazed at how easily they could be parted from their money – even someone like Ned, who superficially at least, seemed to be so sensible, although she did question at times how he had come to be so involved with someone like Vinnie.

The longer those two worked together, the more Elsie became aware of the behind-the-scenes discord between them. They were frequently caught up in arguments that seemed to flare up out of nothing, or at least nothing that she had ever been a party to, and when these occurred she tried, as far as possible, to avoid going into the office they shared in one of the back rooms. She never had completely understood what had drawn them to work together or the nature of their working partnership and Ned had never explained, but from the way he had spoken she had always assumed that Vinnie had bought some financial stake in what was essentially Ned's business. However, it was now becoming clear to Elsie that Vinnie played a more important role than she had at first realized and was more involved in the day-to-day running of the business than she had been led to believe.

Ned had never been one to talk much about his affairs, but her suspicions were confirmed one night when she and Ned were alone together. They had both had a rather large amount to drink and Ned was becoming unusually talkative. He had suggested a quick tumble on the sofa upstairs and afterwards, for once, seemed to let down his guard. Before they left, he invited her into the office where he handed her a small envelope.

'I'm sorry there's no notes in there,' he said, his words slightly slurred as he handed over a packet of loose change. 'But they seem to be in short supply.' Ned grinned. 'I've come a bit unstuck in my calculations and I've hardly earned any myself this week, certainly not enough to pay off Vinnie what I owe him and if I don't pay up soon he's going to throw me out on my ear.'

Elsie raised her eyebrows questioningly though she didn't say anything. 'He says it's taking me too long to get the money together for what we agreed was to be my share of this place,' Ned went on. 'He doesn't think I'm serious about wanting to buy in.' Ned shrugged in a helpless gesture.

'What will he do instead if you go?' Elsie finally spoke up.

'He'll get someone else in who's actually got the readies. He's warned me once before, but this time he's even given me a last-chance deadline. It's amazing how it's the last people you'd expect who can turn on you.' Ned shook his head. 'I thought we had an agreement but now he seems to think it's OK for him to change the terms – just like that.' He clicked his fingers in the air. 'He says he wants his money now or he'll get someone else to buy in, because on his own he doesn't have enough to make the business viable.'

Elsie looked at him in astonishment, not surprised when he didn't meet her gaze. Ned turned away as he continued to speak and Elsie was shocked to hear how much he had promised to put in, in order to buy himself a share.

'The trouble is,' Ned said, 'Vinnie's not only talking about the cards and the tables in the club, he's threatening to cut me out of any future business, including what profits he makes on the black market stuff we've got stashed, even though I paid up front towards that when he bought the stuff. We'd agreed to share that, cos I'd already given him what money I had – all my savings. But now he's changing the rules. He's threatening to sell off the café and I wouldn't put it past him to lay claim to all the money he gets for it, even though I did contribute to the original deposit we put down.' Ned looked exasperated and drummed his fingers on the small mahogany desk. 'And he'll no doubt take any profit we might make on the foodstuff as he sells it on the black market.'

'So much for the partnership,' Elsie said crossly.

'Huh!' Ned sneered. 'So much indeed!' He gave a hollow laugh and looked at her as if he were resigned. 'I put all my savings into that café and I paid half towards the stuff we were going to sell under the counter so I'm entitled to a cut.' His voice faded as he gave a huge sigh and cupped his face in his hands in a gesture of hopelessness.

Elsie opened her mouth to speak but then changed her mind when Ned went on, 'As if the situation wasn't bad enough, on top of everything else I then did a very stupid thing.' His voice was barely above a whisper now and Elsie had to strain to hear him. 'I thought maybe I could win some extra money quickly so I could make up the shortfall and I went to one of those smart casinos in town, but things didn't go to plan. It was great to start with, and yes, I won some. I was feeling really lucky, doing very well by the end of the evening. I notched up half of what I needed in one night. But then I got too cocky.' He raised his head and pulled a face. 'Went back the next night to see if I could double my money, keep the lucky streak going. Then I had second thoughts . . . Trouble was, I bumped into an old mate of mine outside the club and when I told him what I was at, he convinced me I was doing the right thing and to keep going. "Strike while the iron's hot," he said and it didn't take much to persuade me. I was on a winning run, or so I thought. Blew the lot on one round,' he said hoarsely and shook his head slowly from side to side, 'and I lost.' He took a deep breath.

'The trouble is that's left me worse off than I was before. I begged for some short-term credit but it doesn't really help. They gave me an IOU that said that I promised to pay back by next week . . .' Elsie's hand flew to her mouth, he looked so utterly beaten. 'I don't expect Vinnie to have any sympathy,' Ned said forlornly. 'He'll just say I had no business gambling in the first place. And I suppose he's right, cos now I've got a gambling debt on top of what I already owe him.' Ned sighed. 'I should have known better.'

'Don't you think he'll understand if you tell him everything you've just told me?' Elsie asked. 'Have you tried talking to him? Maybe he'll be more lenient than you think.' But her words sounded hollow, even to her own ears, and the look on Ned's face told its own story.

'If I want to be a part of his business then I owe the man a lot of money, Elsie,' Ned said hesitantly, his voice sober and serious.

Elsie frowned. 'Are you saying you won't be able to get enough together even to meet Vinnie's dead-line?' she asked.

Ned shook his head. 'Probably not.'

'But the club has hardly been open for more than

two minutes,' Elsie said, exasperated. 'Surely he must have realized what an impossible situation he's put you in?'

Ned laughed. 'If he does, he's not sharing it with me.'

'He must know you need more time.' Elsie threw her hands in the air, even more puzzled now as to why Ned had got so embroiled with Vinnie in the first place. She'd always feared he wasn't to be trusted. 'Maybe you should approach him again,' she suggested, 'spell it out for him, maybe you can make him understand.' But even as she said the words she could see that Ned didn't believe her.

Ned hesitated. 'I'd promised him enough money to make this place viable, Elsie. I really thought I was going to be his full partner. But I gambled on it and I was wrong.'

Elsie frowned. 'What will happen if . . .?' she asked although she didn't complete the question.

Ned answered as though she had. 'He'll just get someone else in, someone who already has the money in his hand. And before you even ask, he certainly won't return any of the money that I've already put in. I know, it doesn't feel fair but I can hardly complain to the police or go after him through the courts, now can I?'

Chapter 28

After the incident in the rehearsal room, Peggy did her best to avoid Lawrence, trying not to come into one-to-one contact with him despite his attempts to get her on her own. In the build-up to the previews she had managed to avoid meeting him at all, apart from the last-minute rehearsals that required the full cast, so she was dismayed when he sent for her at the end of the second night's preview. She was about to leave with the others when he asked her if she would see him in his office before she went home and she could hardly refuse. The first thing she noticed when she entered the room was a chunky whisky glass on his desk and she didn't know what to make of it when she saw that he had another one in his hand that he was holding out towards her. She made a negative gesture and shook her head as she hovered uncertainly, close to the door.

'I just wanted to tell you how much I've enjoyed your performances during these previews,' she thought he said, though his words were not entirely clear. 'I know how anxious you were in the build-up and I thought I should let you know that you've made the grade as far as I'm concerned.'

Peggy gave an uncertain smile. Nice as it was to hear his praise she didn't feel she could completely trust him and she couldn't believe that was all he wanted to say. She shifted her weight uncomfortably from one foot to the other, wondering what he really wanted. He paused for breath, and when he began with the word, 'However,' Peggy braced herself for what might come next, but before he could complete his next sentence there was a knock at the door and the welcome face of Jimmy peered in.

Peggy was surprised to see his eyes light up when he saw her and, to Lawrence's obvious consternation, he stepped inside the room.

'Ah, the very person I've been looking for,' Jimmy said quickly before Lawrence could say anything. 'I'm really sorry to interrupt, Lawrence, but I'm afraid Wardrobe are urgently looking for Peggy; said they must catch her before going-home time.' He ostentatiously looked at his wrist watch. 'Which, according to my reckoning, was about ten minutes ago,' Jimmy grinned. 'Something about an urgent costume adjustment,' Jimmy said when Lawrence looked puzzled. 'Could the rest of your meeting possibly be put off until tomorrow? They really need to line up any changes now that will be needed for tomorrow's matinee performance. So, if it's all the same to you, I'll whisk Peggy away now, if I may.'

Lawrence's frown deepened while Peggy was wondering how Jimmy had known where to find her. But there was no point in dwelling on that now – she was just grateful for his intervention, although it wasn't the first time he had been on hand to rescue her from a potentially difficult situation involving Lawrence.

'Thanks for coming to tell me,' Peggy said, flashing a smile at Jimmy. 'I can nip down there right now if that's all right with you,' she said, turning to Lawrence but she slipped out of the door before he could say no. She pretended not to hear him when he called after her to be sure to come back to his office first thing in the morning before the Notes session that he had called for the entire cast.

Peggy hurried back to the dressing room where the wardrobe mistress removed the row of pins that had been lined up in her mouth and, looking relieved to see her, began refitting one of Peggy's costumes. Peggy wasn't convinced that the situation was as much of an emergency as Jimmy had indicated – she was sure it could have waited until the morning – but she gratefully accepted Jimmy's obvious concern regarding Lawrence. There wasn't much she could say as she slipped back into her costume and patiently stood still while the wardrobe mistress cut and pinned and made several adjustments that would make the rather tight number of required costume changes much easier to manage.

Peggy sighed. She appreciated that Jimmy was looking out for her and she intended to thank him properly tomorrow, but even he must realize that he couldn't always guarantee to be there for her in keeping Lawrence at arm's length. She stared at her reflection in one of the brightly illuminated mirrors and smiled. The fitting finished, the wardrobe mistress left and Peggy got dressed.

'Can I walk you home?' Peggy jumped, when she heard Jimmy's voice. She had turned off the illuminated mirrors and in the darkened dressing room she couldn't see him at first. She couldn't make out his face but she fancifully thought he sounded as if he was smiling and she didn't feel she could refuse his offer.

'You know, you have a way of always popping up at the right moment,' she said jokily. 'I bet you were a jack-in-the-box in a former life? Or maybe a policeman?'

Jimmy laughed. 'Just a caring friend who happens to be staying not far from you,' Jimmy said and he picked up her jacket from the back of one of the chairs and held it while she slipped her arms into the wide sleeves.

'I don't know if you realize how often you've managed to save me from Lawrence's advances, but I want to tell you how extremely grateful I am for your concern. Do you think Lawrence has noticed,' Peggy asked.

Jimmy laughed. 'You make it sound like I've done it on purpose,' he said, his face taking on an innocent look.

'And didn't you?' Peggy laughed. 'I'm not sure I believe in coincidences.' Then her face clouded. 'The only problem is, do you think my job could be in jeopardy? What might he be capable of if he doesn't get his way eventually?' Without warning, Peggy's voice suddenly cracked. 'And I don't know who I could complain to if that did happen. I don't imagine the police or the theatre management would be interested in listening. *I'd* be the one to lose my job, not him, and that's a scary thought. It's quite a shock to realize that he has so much power.' Peggy shivered involuntarily. She had hoped that by expressing her concerns out loud Jimmy might be able to allay her fears, but to her dismay he didn't disagree.

Chapter 29

Once Elsie had settled into her new job at the club and business picked up, she really began to enjoy it, volunteering to work more than one evening a week. She had no objection to flirting with the customers and she looked forward to the occasions when Ned was able to spare the time to teach her more about handling decks of cards. She was a quick learner and, as word spread and the room was filled with eager customers, she felt she would be able to hold her own at one of the tables should she be called upon. She was learning the language, referring to the sessions as private parties and never using the words gambling or betting. In the meantime, to Ned's relief, they were busy enough for Vinnie to realize he wouldn't be able to manage the whole operation alone and that it would be best to let Ned stay on while he paid off his debt.

There was a strange atmosphere in the club that seemed to keep the participants on a high level of alert; it was a mixture of fever and excitement coming face to face with the thrill that surrounded the carrying out of illegal acts and the fear of the consequences of being caught. Sometimes money changed hands so quickly it was difficult to believe there was a war on and it felt as if they were wrapped up in their own special cocoon. At the end of each session it fell to Elsie to tidy up the playing room once the punters had gone and she would help to close the bar while she waited for Ned and Vinnie to cash up and lock the proceedings away in the sturdy old safe.

She never ceased to be amazed at the number of discarded cigarette packs that she found scattered about the floor and it seemed there were never enough ashtrays, but she was surprised one night as she reached down to release something she saw caught up in the cushions on the sofa, to find a well-stuffed business envelope. It had no name or address and, as she peered inside she was shocked to see it was filled with banknotes. Mostly they were the war time blue and orange one-pound notes but they were together with some brown ten shillings and some larger plain-coloured notes that were only printed on one side which she realized were five pound notes, a denomination she had only ever seen Arnold handle occasionally. The whole package amounted to more money than she was used to seeing at one go and she racked her brains trying to think who it might belong to. She remembered seeing a silver-haired gentleman sitting at this table and he'd been handling a package this size but she had thought he had eventually stuffed it into his inside jacket pocket. She did recall that he was the worse for wear and didn't really know what he was doing, so it was possible he could have missed his target, but she had no proof and it was unlikely that someone as drunk as he was would be able to remember what had happened. Elsie looked around but there was no one else about, no one had come back looking for their envelope, and she stared down, unsure what she should do with it. At that moment she heard voices as a door opened and Vinnie emerged from the office. Without thinking, Elsie stuffed the envelope into her dress pocket and fastened her cardigan which crossed over at the waist, covering it up. By the time she thought about what she was doing it was too late to tell Vinnie about it without incriminating herself. Initially, she hadn't meant to keep it but she now realized that the longer she waited, the more difficult it would become to declare it until it was too late to do anything except to take it home and put it somewhere out of harm's way until she'd decided on the best action to take.

Elsie ran upstairs as soon as she arrived home and, relieved to find that Peggy wasn't home yet, stuffed the envelope in what she considered to be the safest place in the house, under Linda's mattress, in her daughter's room where Peggy slept. She had previously used the space to keep private letters and any odd bits and pieces she didn't know what to do with, so it was well hidden, and it wasn't until several days later that Ned made reference to it.

Elsie had been suffering from a particularly heavy cold and Ned had suggested that she should take a night off from the club and go to bed early with a hot drink. She had such a pounding headache that, unusually for her, she gratefully followed his advice. It was two days later before she saw him again and she was shocked to see that he had a black eye.

'Well, you chose the right time to be off, you did,' were his first words before she had a chance to comment.

'Why's that, then?' She raised her eyebrows questioningly.

'Cos all hell was let loose in here, that's why,' Ned said. 'It was a good job you weren't here, given some of the language that was flying about; it would have made your hair curl, as my old man always says.'

'I'd have thought you'd have realized by now that

rude or crude language is all the same to me – and it certainly doesn't bother me – but it looks like there was more than loose words flying about.'

Ned touched his blackened cheek gingerly and Elsie giggled as he said, seriously, 'I'm afraid there were some fisticuffs too, though me and Vinnie did manage to dodge most of them.'

'What was it about?' Elsie asked.

'One of our – shall we say more *elderly* customers? – apparently lost an envelope that he claimed had lots of money in it. Money that he said he had come with. I wasn't sure whether or not to believe him and I know Vinnie certainly didn't.'

Elsie felt the colour rise to her cheeks while she wondered what she should say. But before she could say anything, Vinnie appeared, sporting a heavily bruised cheek and Elsie became aware that he was carefully scrutinising her face. He was staring at her directly as he said, 'Accused me and Ned of stealing his money. Insisted that he lost it on these premises, so he reckons we're responsible for paying him back.'

It was not like Elsie to be lost for words but Vinnie's mouth had a mean twist and she felt a cold shiver run down her spine as he continued to stare at her accusingly. She wasn't normally one to lie but this time she turned away, scratching her head. Then, with a hardened look, she declared that she knew nothing about it.

Chapter 30

Peggy was floating on cloud nine. Despite Lawrence's constant urging for the cast to do better, according to the reviews in the local *Gazette* the show the reporter had seen on one of the preview nights was 'up to the usual high standard of Weatherfield's Yuletide entertainment – one not to be missed'. Word was obviously spreading and young families were flocking in sizeable numbers to the Majestic. In addition, there had been the excitement of receiving her mother's response to Peggy's suggestion of a meeting time and place. Jimmy had been right, it had been worth pursuing. She had pulled the scrappy piece of paper out of her pocket so many times now that she remembered the words by heart. *I am really sorry that we won't be able to come to your opening night but I've managed to persuade your father to let you come home for Christmas dinner.* The next few words were smudged with what Peggy liked to think were her mother's tears, followed by, *Good luck with the panto, Lots of love from Mam.* The disappointment of having no one from her family there on any of the preview nights was already beginning to fade, having been partially assuaged by Elsie's appearance with Ida Barlow, and by the excitement of receiving an invitation to Christmas dinner. She accepted now that her mother and Colin would not be magically appearing and instead looked forward to seeing them on Christmas Day. She was prepared to settle for that and was beginning to relax and enjoy the performances. It was hard work for all of them and Peggy was usually too tired to do anything at the end of each long day other than accept Jimmy's invitations to walk her home, but on the actual opening night Lawrence insisted that there should be a small party in the dressing room after the performance to acknowledge their hard work and to wish them joy and success for the rest of the run.

Things continued to run smoothly, the cash tills at the box office ringing as regularly as Big Ben chimed until the week before Christmas when a different kind of excitement began to build as the holiday grew nearer and most of the cast were looking forward to spending Christmas itself with their loved ones. But then different tensions began to creep in. Throughout the week there had been regular morning performances as well as matinees and evenings and as the weekend drew closer people were beginning to show signs of exhaustion, their tempers growing shorter by the day.

It was Friday, with not long to go before the curtain would go up for the third and final time that day and several of the company were snapping at each other while they carried out their superstitious rituals as they did before every performance. Lawrence was behind the scenes, fussing about several props that seemed to have gone missing and nagging at Peggy to find them immediately as they were essential for the opening scene in the market square. The stage manager was also behind the scenes, doing one of his impromptu inspections of the scenery, when there was a sudden loud noise like a clap of thunder and the whole stage seemed to quiver. Peggy looked up from the props she was sorting and was horrified to see at least half of the wooden flats that formed part of the background set of the market scene come crashing to the ground in slow motion.

Peggy's first thought was that it wasn't real because it looked more like something out of a Buster Keaton film where the whole side of a building would fall, narrowly missing the star's head, which would then appear, miraculously intact, through an open window. But after a moment of shock she realized that this wasn't some carefully orchestrated manoeuvre that was meant to amuse and entertain, but an accident, a potential disaster, that had actually knocked out several of the cast and stagehands as the painted panels tumbled to the ground. In their wake, the air was instantly filled with clouds of dust, causing an outburst of coughing among those who had been standing nearby and a cacophony of expletives, screams of pain and shouts for help. All those who had not been in the immediate vicinity rushed onto the stage as the truth dawned about what had happened and there were heroic attempts to rescue anyone unfortunate enough to have been trapped underneath the collapsing set.

When the dust settled, Peggy could see nothing but confusion, people wandering about in a daze. Lawrence was nowhere to be seen and it was Jimmy who was doing his best to inject some order into the chaos and calling for an ambulance to be sent for. Amidst the pandemonium it became obvious that several cast members had been hurt and many were pinned underneath the flats. As the noise gradually subsided, Peggy was able to see that one of the casualties was Millie, who had been playing the part of the Giant, and it seemed at first glance that it was the Giant's house, situated at the top of the fast-growing beanstalk, that had collapsed, bringing the rest of the set with it. Peggy drew a breath in sharply as she spotted Millie waving her arms through the cut-out window, as if she was drowning, and she climbed over the fallen scenery to see if there was any way she could help.

'Peggy, please be careful!' It was Jimmy who shouted a warning. 'The rest of that treehouse looks unsafe and the pieces are far too heavy for you to lift.'

Peggy looked across helplessly, realizing Jimmy was right, for Millie was wedged underneath what had been a precarious-looking structure at the best of times. It had once had a balcony spanning the distance across a double window but the whole structure was now in pieces that were strewn haphazardly across the stage.

'Hang on, Millie, help is on its way,' Peggy called out and she crossed her fingers as she said it, hoping that was true. But her attention was drawn to the side of the stage where the remains of the curtains were hanging unsteadily as she had spotted Daphne trapped by the curtain rails and tangled in the abundant black material. She had last seen the principal boy only seconds before the crash, standing in the wings talking to Lawrence. Peggy was shocked to see that the beautiful young star now looked a sorry sight with her head covered in blood and she prayed that the ambulance would arrive soon.

Fortunately, her prayers were answered and it was only minutes later that she heard the clanging of bells and realized, with relief, that a fire engine as well as an ambulance had been despatched at the same time, an action that could considerably hasten the rescue process. The firemen wasted no time in freeing those who were trapped and Peggy could only watch, impressed by the speed with which the injured were assessed by the ambulance people and shipped off to hospital.

The remaining cast and crew who had been lucky enough to escape injury hovered by the stage as the emergency vehicles pulled away, uncertain what to do until Jimmy appeared and, to everyone's relief, calmly took charge of the situation. Clipboard in hand, he stood at the front of the stage, inviting those who were left to gather in the front stalls of the auditorium so that he could tick off their names on his roster.

'Unfortunately,' he said, 'it seems that Lawrence was injured and he's gone off to hospital. I'll keep you informed about everyone's progress as I get news and, as to what will happen next . . . once I know who's still available we can begin to make some decisions about resuming. Naturally, we want to cancel as few shows as possible. I've already talked to our stage manager, Fred, about rebuilding some of the set, but the Giant's house will certainly have to be redesigned, and, as you can hear, some work in that direction has already begun.' He turned to indicate the carpenters and joiners behind him who were already sorting out what remained of the old set and beginning to restore whatever they could. Jimmy had begun his talk in what Peggy called his conciliatory voice that varied between calming and comforting, and she could see that it was already having a positive effect on his audience, all of whom had been disturbed and upset by the accident.

'In the meantime,' he continued, 'it's been agreed that I will go down to the hospital a little later with Fred so that we can see for ourselves the extent of people's injuries and discuss with the doctors how soon they might be able to come back to work. The stage crew will spend the rest of the day working on the set and later today we should be in a position to assess the overall situation and consider the best way to proceed. Sadly, there is no question about tonight,' he said. 'Difficult as it is, this evening's performance will be cancelled. But with any luck we may be back in business by tomorrow night.'

There were loud murmurings as people began discussing the situation among themselves and Jimmy held his hand up for silence. 'Of course, I may have to do some juggling with the cast, so please bear with me, but it will depend on what we find at the hospital.'

Peggy was impressed that Jimmy had wasted no time prevaricating and she was pleased to hear him make no bones about overriding Lawrence's mantra that 'the show must go on'. This was one instance when clearly it wouldn't. Jimmy at least seemed to be taking a sensible and pragmatic approach, and all her friends agreed. The level of conversation died down as Jimmy paused to clear his throat.

'Before we break up,' he said, waving his clipboard, 'I'd like to suggest that we have another cast meeting tonight, so we can report back about our findings at the hospital, and discuss our plans for the immediate future. Shall we say eight o'clock sharp in the stalls? And you'd better bring your scripts with you in case I have to make some changes. At worst, some of you may have to learn a new part overnight.' He grinned as he said that and the room buzzed once more as everyone speculated about what changes might occur.

Peggy didn't go home after the meeting. Jimmy had disappeared as soon as the crowd broke up and Denise suggested they should all take the time off, the small group coming to her digs and she invited Peggy to join them.

'I don't know about you,' Nora said, 'but I feel

pretty shaken up by the whole incident and a few hours off is just what I need. A nice cup of tea in town wouldn't go amiss,' she added, while the others nodded in agreement. It was a chilly but bright December afternoon with the sky clouding over as the early evening darkness gathered. 'At least it's not snowing, though I had been hoping for a white Christmas,' Nora added and they all laughed. The boys had declined to join them but Peggy, Nora and Denise caught the next bus into town to treat themselves to an afternoon of window-gazing in Manchester before it became too dark to see the Christmas displays in the department store windows.

They had all been upset by the accident and while it felt good to get out for a breath of fresh air, they soon realized it wasn't going to be a particularly jolly trip as they were all feeling somewhat subdued. Peggy was relieved they had made a pact not to talk about the morning's events and no one mentioned Daphne's name for they all understood the implications of what it could mean for Nora if the principal boy's injuries were actually as bad as they had seemed.

By the time they returned to the theatre, most of the cast were already assembled in the front seats of the stalls and Jimmy came out of the wings onto the stage almost as soon as the girls had taken their places. He looked as though he had had a long and difficult day and Peggy felt concerned that the dark patches beneath his eyes signalled the extent of his tiredness. As he looked down into the stalls, she made a point of meeting his gaze and she gave him an encouraging smile.

'Is there anyone here knows of anybody missing, apart from those who were injured?' Jimmy asked the audience. Three names were identified.

'Well, we'll have to begin without them,' Jimmy said, irritation creeping in to his voice, 'there's too much on the agenda for us to wait any longer. You can fill them in with the details. The good news is that we have decided that it *will* be possible for us to put on an evening performance tomorrow.'

A cheer went up and Jimmy had to raise his voice in order to be heard. 'I've been told the set won't be ready in time for a matinee, but the crew think they can get it together by the evening.' The voices quietened. 'I'm afraid you'll have to put up with me standing in as director for the next little while as Lawrence's injuries were fairly extensive and the hospital are insisting on keeping him in for a few days, under observation.'

There was a collective sigh that could have been interpreted in different ways, then a buzz of conversation, punctuated by pockets of self-conscious giggles, seemed to ripple around the room. 'Lastly, what I suppose is the worst news of the night is that

Daphne has concussion,' Jimmy said then and this time there was a general gasp. 'However, before we all get too depressed, many of you will already know that we are in the very fortunate position of having an understudy for this most important role. Nora!' he said as he spotted her on the front row and he gestured for her to stand up. 'For those of you who don't already know, Nora is Daphne's understudy and is primed and ready to take over the principal role. Maybe she should be at home now brushing up on her lines.'

Everyone laughed. Peggy felt sorry for Nora as she watched her friend's cheeks change from pink to scarlet for she knew this was the first official notice Nora had received that she would be standing in for Daphne. As if reading Peggy's mind, Jimmy came to the edge of the stage and, crouching down, spoke directly to Nora in a soft voice. 'Sorry about the quip, come and see me before you go home tonight, Nora, so we can sort out the details.' Then he stood up and turned back to his clipboard. 'Finally,' he once more addressed the room at large, 'apart from general cuts and bruises and quite a few headaches among chorus members and backstage crew, the only other major casualty was Millie who was playing the part of the Giant. Rather ironic that it was her house in the treetops that came crashing down, but she sadly suffered a broken shoulder as a result.' A sigh went round once more but Jimmy continued, 'Unfortunately, we don't have a ready-made understudy for that role and there are several ways we could handle that problem. But I haven't come to any conclusions yet. I'll let you know as soon as possible and I'm calling for a full rehearsal in the morning at nine o'clock sharp in case there needs to be some last-minute adjustments to the script. That way we can make sure we're up to scratch in time for the evening's performance.' He hesitated for a moment, then he said jokily, in his best Porky Pig voice, 'That's all, folks.' He grinned widely, then with a brief wave of his hand he turned abruptly and left the stage.

Peggy stood for a few moments staring at the empty stage then watched Nora collecting her things until she felt Denise nudge her with a good-natured elbow in the ribs. 'Great chance there for you now, eh, Nora?' Denise said. 'Get your name up in lights. It shows, if you only wait long enough – though I'm really sorry for Daphne – a great opportunity comes along for you.' She looked at the watch on her wrist. 'And I don't want to spoil the fun cos I know you've got to see Jimmy, but if Peggy and I get a move on we can catch the last house at the Luxy.'

'Don't let me get in the way,' Nora said jokingly, lifting her nose in the air. 'I'll just go off to prepare for the biggest night of my life!' and she began to edge out of the row of seats. But when she reached the aisle, Peggy called out to her, 'No, Nora, don't go, wait for me, I'm coming with you! Sorry, Denise, but I can't go to the flicks right now.' She turned to her friend who had stopped in surprise, then she looked across to Nora. 'Don't worry, I'm not after your job,' she assured her. 'You'll make a much better principal boy than me. I'm going to see if I can be the Giant!' She was aware that both Denise and Nora were staring at her now but she had made up her mind. 'Come on!' she said, linking her arm through Nora's. 'Let's go and see if we can change the course of history!'

Chapter 31

Jimmy was sitting behind the smaller desk in the room that he and Lawrence had designated as their office and he looked surprised when Peggy walked in as Nora left. 'I hoped you might have a minute,' Peggy said, 'although I'll understand if you'd rather I leave it till the morning.'

'Leave what?' Jimmy looked puzzled. 'At least tell me what this is about.'

'It's about the Giant's role.' Peggy thought she should come straight to the point. 'I don't know if you were considering me for the role but think I could do it and I wanted to know if you would let me take it on.'

Now Jimmy looked dumbfounded. 'What makes

you think you could do it? Not that it's a big job—' he stopped while he chuckled at his own joke, 'but you've never had a solo part, have you?'

'No,' she admitted, 'but you might remember there was a time when I was trying to impress Lawrence . . .' She spoke the words softly, as though she herself didn't want to be reminded. 'Anyway, I thought it might help my career to become an understudy and I learned practically the whole script; the individual songs, the dance routines – *everything*, not just the chorus.' She felt the heat in her cheeks. 'It sounds odd now, but the point is I do know most of the Giant's part and I wouldn't have to read from the script. If I spent a bit of time on it tonight I could try it out at rehearsal tomorrow.'

'Well, well,' Jimmy said. 'Now that does sound promising.' He glanced up at the large clock on the wall and rubbed his eyes which by now were rimmed with red. 'There's not a great deal of time left tonight,' he said, 'and it's been rather a long day, but if you think you can do it I'd say let's give it a try. Come to the theatre first thing in the morning, I'll get the choreographer to put you through your paces, and we'll see what you can do. Then the only other thing that we'll need to do will be to alert Janet in Wardrobe and get her to make up a new Giant's costume. As it is, Millie's would probably have been too big for you, besides hers getting damaged in all the kerfuffle.' He stretched his arms above his head and yawned and Peggy felt sorry for him – she didn't like to say that she was suddenly finding renewed energy.

'But you'll have to excuse me right now,' Jimmy said, 'I'm feeling dead on my feet.' He stood up and removed his jacket from the back of the chair. 'I'd be perfectly happy if you'd like me to see you home, but I'm afraid our departure would have to be imminent because I'm whacked.'

Peggy smiled and held up her hands. 'Ready when you are,' she said.

Chapter 32

Peggy was surprised how quickly the songs and dance movements came back to her and she started work as soon as she got home. Elsie was as excited as she was when she told her exactly how it had all happened and she offered to help her go over some of the lines. Peggy hardly slept a wink that night as the words and music were pounding away in her head and in the morning she wasn't surprised to hear Elsie singing some of the songs as well.

Peggy appeared at the theatre well before the rehearsal time and she was delighted when the dancing instructor approved her taking over the role. 'You've come a long way, Peggy, from not being able to untangle your feet, to this,' she laughed. And

Peggy was thrilled when Jimmy added his, 'Well done!' later that morning. 'All that practising paid off and not a casting couch in sight,' he said when he pulled her aside to tell her she had got the role. 'It's only a shame that Lawrence isn't here to see it.'

Amazingly, the set had been restored and the cast were in a state of heightened tension when Jimmy popped into the dressing rooms that evening to wish them all luck. 'Under the circumstances I hardly want to say the usual, "break a leg",' he said, 'but know that I wish you well, and I'm sure Lawrence is rooting for you too.'

After the last call for overture and beginners, Peggy heard Jimmy's voice coming over the Tannoy, apologizing to the audience who were now filling the auditorium for the unexpected cancellations and announcing the changes to tonight's cast. When Peggy heard him announcing her name and that she would be taking on the role of the Giant, she couldn't stop herself bursting into tears.

It took some moments for her to regain her composure before making her entrance on stage and for the rest of the evening Peggy felt as if she was in a magical daze. It might not have been the most coveted of roles within the company, and was certainly not the role she would have chosen for herself, but Peggy would happily settle for it for the time being. She was excited about having any kind of solo part and now it was important for her to do justice to the faith Jimmy seemed to have in her. She must ensure she was favourably noticed by the audience and by any reviewing press. She didn't seriously expect to find anything written about her in the national press but she was sure the show would get some kind of notice the following day in the *Weatherfield Gazette*. But she didn't want to think about it yet. And when she walked home after the show, she still had the encore songs ringing in her ears, and the congratulations of the rest of the cast and crew commending the efforts of both her and Nora, who had proved to be a sensation, standing in for Daphne.

'No question, you and Nora saved the day,' Jimmy said as he walked Peggy home. 'Wait till Lawrence hears about it. If they do write it up in the papers it'll be great publicity for the show, and you know what they say about publicity.'

Peggy didn't know but was too wrapped up in her own thoughts to worry about it.

Elsie was waiting up for her when she got home and she brewed a pot of fresh tea while she encouraged Peggy to tell her how the evening had gone.

'That's wonderful news,' Elsie said. 'It's only a shame not one of your family or friends were there to see it. But never mind, we can go to the Rovers tomorrow night to celebrate, and I personally will make sure everyone knows it was you as managed to turn things around!'

The next day the cast assembled so Jimmy could bring them up to date with the latest developments. Before he arrived the choreographer was blocking out some changes she wanted to make and some new moves she wanted to add when Jimmy appeared at the back of the stalls in the empty auditorium and marched triumphantly down the centre aisle waving a well-thumbed copy of the *Weatherfield Gazette*.

'Sorry to interrupt,' he said, 'but I really think you need to see this.' He climbed onto the stage and invited them to come and look. The first words Peggy caught were the headline, 'Giant Saves the Day'. Jimmy beckoned her and Nora to come forward and held his hands up for silence. He began to read the text out loud. '*Understudy Nora Johns proved to be a star in her own right,*' he read, '*as she sang and danced her heart out in a flawless performance, standing in for the injured star, Daphne Dawson. Indeed, she claimed her right to stardom, rescuing what could have been a disastrous night. Although we all wish Miss Dawson well and hope for a speedy recovery after the freak accident, it would indeed be a shame to extinguish Miss Johns' own shining light so soon and this critic, at least, predicts that we will be hearing more of Nora Johns. But it was Margaret de Vere, stepping up from the chorus ranks, who stole the show last night, striding in at the last moment, in her oversized boots, to play a formidable Giant.'*

Here, Jimmy paused and looked up, grinning broadly at Peggy, as he made eye contact. '*If ever there was an up-and-coming star with a natural gift for comedy,*' he read on, '*it is this young lady who brought a freshness and charm to what can sometimes prove to be a pedestrian role. Mark this name readers, Margaret de Vere, for we will definitely be seeing more of her in the future.*' Jimmy stopped as Peggy gasped and he smiled down at her as several of the cast spontaneously applauded both her and Nora. Peggy's eyes were glistening and she didn't know what to say, so she clasped Nora's hand and gave her friend a hug while the rest of the cast and crew crowded around the grinning pair, patting them on the back and loudly congratulating them both.

'And I'm afraid you two will have to do it all over again tonight and through all of tomorrow's performances,' Jimmy said, 'and until further notice if you think you can bear it.'

Nora and Peggy smiled at him and then at each other.

'I think we could manage that,' Nora grinned as Peggy nodded vigorously. 'And let me just say I'm in no hurry to give the part back,' Nora said and Peggy enthusiastically agreed.

Chapter 33

'Have you seen this?' Elsie couldn't wait to show Peggy her own copy of the *Weatherfield Gazette*.

'I know,' Peggy admitted somewhat bashfully, 'Jimmy brought it to show us.'

'You should be showing it to all the folk round here, in case they don't realize it's you.'

Peggy laughed.

'In fact, I think that's exactly what we'll do tonight,' Elsie said. 'It's high time we went for a celebratory drink and now it seems we've got two things to drink to.'

Peggy looked at her quizzically.

'Not only are you a full-blown professional actress

but apparently you're also something I never had you pegged as – a comedienne no less!'

That made Peggy laugh. 'Trust you to make the most of it,' she said, but she didn't protest when Elsie marched her off to the pub later that night.

The Rovers Return was crowded and, as they entered, Peggy was greeted by a loud cheer. They had to fight their way to the bar where they found two glasses of port and lemon were waiting for them. It seemed everyone had already read the report in the paper and they were all clamouring for more details about the accident and the promotion, each one desperate to be among the first to offer their congratulations. Peggy was glad to have Elsie by her side to steer her through, although she couldn't help feeling a little embarrassed by Elsie's boastfulness with regard to her success.

'But you must tell everybody, Peggy,' Elsie said. 'Or they'll never know. Tell them that I'm not exaggerating. You've earned that part and you've got it at least until the end of the run and who knows what will happen after that. My point is, folks,' Elsie was on her soap box again, 'there's no excuse for anyone in this neighbourhood not to go and see the panto. I'm taking our Linda next week, even though I've seen it once. I'm telling you, it's a really good show. Everyone in the street should go and see it,' Elsie managed to say every time there was a momentary lull in the conversation. 'It was very enjoyable when I saw it at the beginning, and now it has our very own Peggy as the star attraction, well!' She held her hands out. 'What more can I say?'

Peggy's cheeks had become hot and she turned away just as Mrs Sharples grasped hold of her hand. 'Don't mind her,' she said, nodding towards Elsie. 'There's nowt wrong with a spot of bragging, especially if someone else is willing to do it for you. There's no harm in her telling them just how good you are, they need to know if you want them all to buy tickets.'

Several people from the neighbourhood insisted on buying her and Elsie drinks after that and Peggy was surprised how many she managed to fit in before closing time. But as they finally drew a line and decided to head home, Peggy's head was beginning to feel as if it were stuffed with cotton wool. In an attempt to clear it she tried singing softly to herself, going through all the tunes she remembered from the show, goading Elsie to join in and smothering with giggles the words of those she couldn't remember. Peggy was so engrossed in retrieving all the tunes that she didn't notice the silhouetted figure that stepped out from the shadows until it was too late, and she heard Elsie cry out in shocked horror and pain.

Chapter 34

Peggy could make out the outline of the man though he was wearing a balaclava so she couldn't see his face. He was almost twice the size of Elsie and had had no difficulty in knocking her to the ground – and despite them both crying out there was no one on the street at that moment to come to their rescue.

'You stole my money, you bitch, and I want it back!' the man shouted while pummelling Elsie with his fists. 'I know it was you, so don't think I'm going to let you get away with it, you and your flirty eyes. I want every last penny back!' He spat the words out and Peggy was terrified that he might be drunk enough to really harm Elsie as he hit her again. Then she heard Elsie's sobs turn into an astonished shout of surprise as he whipped off his balaclava and Peggy saw her friend's face freeze in recognition.

'Yes, it's me,' she heard him hiss at Elsie. 'Now you know you'll have to give me my money back or I'll come after you. See, I know where you live.'

Peggy drew in her breath sharply as she thought she too recognized the man but she had no time to dwell on that as he was aiming a deliberately vicious kick to the side of Elsie's head that caused both Elsie and Peggy to cry out for him to stop. Peggy was doing her best to pull him off Elsie, although she had too slight a figure to have any impact, but now their screams had attracted the attention of the neighbours and several front doors were flung open, the stocky figure of Albert Tatlock emerging from one of them as he came rushing out onto the pavement with Ida Barlow following closely in his wake. Albert's outstretched arms seemed to be punching nothing but air in the pitch blackness until Peggy heard a thud and a man groaning when Albert eventually made contact with his target, striking the attacker hard on the back of his head. As the blow connected, the man, who had been swinging his arms wildly, swayed slightly on his feet as he tried to stand straight. For a few seconds his face was caught in the moonlight, long enough for Peggy to realize that Elsie's attacker was none other than Vinnie, the so-called friend and partner of Elsie's boyfriend, Ned.

He held Peggy's gaze only briefly, looking waveringly uncertain, but then he jerked into action and set off racing down the street as if he were being chased by wild animals.

'He looked a bit familiar, do you know him, Elsie?' Albert Tatlock asked as he put out a firm hand to help Elsie struggle to her feet.

'Yes,' Elsie could only whisper. 'I do. I'd always thought he wasn't the sort I'd want to get tangled up with on a dark night, and now I know I was right.'

Peggy shuddered when she looked at Elsie's face where the bruises were already beginning to show, but she didn't say anything.

'Should I waste my breath chasing after him?' Albert said, while he inspected his own bruised knuckles. Ida had now joined them, breathless at all the excitement.

'No, leave him alone, but thanks for the rescue,' Elsie said. 'You've saved me from an even worse battering and we know where he hangs out.'

'A place you'd be best to avoid,' Albert said, but that only made Elsie smile as she slowly shook her head.

'Never mind that, right now you're coming to my house,' Ida said. 'I'm going straight in to put the kettle on – a cup of hot sweet tea is what's called for right now.' Ida grasped hold of Elsie's arm and gently steered her in the direction of the front door, calling over her shoulder to Peggy as she went, 'Come on, love, you must come too, it's been a shock enough for you an' all.'

'I think we could all do with a brew, if not summat stronger,' Albert said, 'while we decide about calling in the police.'

'Police?' Elsie was aghast. 'I don't want to get involved with the police, and I don't think he would appreciate that, either.' She jerked her thumb in the direction her attacker had taken. 'Then he really would try to kill me.'

Albert frowned. 'This wasn't a random attack, was it?' he said. 'It sounded like he was after something specific and that he'll be back to make sure he gets it.'

'That's the only thing I'm afraid of.' Now Elsie shuddered and put her hand to her head as she did so. 'Crikey, I bet I'll have one big headache by the morning.'

'But you'll have to get the police involved, cos you know he'll be back, don't you? And you do know what money he was talking about, don't you?' Peggy asked, and her suspicions were confirmed when Elsie didn't answer.

'I think he's right,' Peggy said when Albert Tatlock had finally seen them safely to their own front door.

'You've got to involve the police or you'll never want to put your face out of doors.'

'I don't scare that easily,' Elsie said defiantly, although Peggy did wonder whether she was just putting on a brave front.

'I didn't want to push it when Albert brought it up,' Peggy said, 'because I could see you weren't keen, but you could be in danger if you don't report what happened tonight.'

'But I can't.' Elsie's face reflected her determination. 'Don't you understand?'

'No, I don't,' Peggy said. 'Perhaps you'd better tell me why, cos from where I'm standing I reckon he'll not give up till he gets what he wants.'

Elsie looked away.

Several seconds elapsed before Peggy asked, 'Are you going to tell me what this is about? Or are you going to leave me guessing? What is going on? If you don't tell me I can't help.' And when Elsie still didn't reply, Peggy added, softly, 'Is it to do with the large envelope you've got hidden under my mattress?' Elsie looked shocked as Peggy spoke the words out loud.

'How do you know about that?' she asked, an alarmed expression on her face.

'Honestly, I wasn't trying to spy on you. I was looking for somewhere safe to put my mother's letters,' Peggy said.

'Perhaps we need to sit down,' Elsie said, pulling two chairs out at the table. 'This might take a little while,' and she began to explain how she had come by the money-filled envelope. 'So, you see, strictly speaking it's no more his money than mine and no doubt the punter who brought it into the club in the first place was claiming that it was his that he had won elsewhere.' Elsie made a tutting sound. 'Trust Vinnie to try to bag it as his own! But the point is that it wasn't mine to take either, though I'll be blowed if I hand it over to the likes of him.'

'I can understand why you don't want to talk about it,' Peggy said. 'It did feel like a helluva lot of money.'

Elsie exhaled loudly. 'It *is* a lot of money,' she admitted, 'though I didn't actually steal it. The problem is, I don't know what to do with it. If I give it back, Vinnie will know immediately that it was me as removed it, whereas at the moment he's only guessing, but if I keep it I can't spend it.' She shook her head. 'I wish I hadn't been so stupid as to pick it up in the first place. I don't know what I was thinking of. I should have left it for the cleaners to find.'

'Perhaps you should just chuck it in the river,' Peggy said, trying to lighten the mood with a false laugh.

'Believe me, that did cross my mind at one time,' Elsie said, a serious look clouding her face, 'and I might have actually done it if it hadn't been such a large amount.'

Chapter 35

Peggy tossed and turned during what was left of the night, upset by what had transpired and concerned for Elsie, wondering if she was sleeping any more soundly. The answer came in the morning. Although she could see her landlady was doing her best to keep up a jolly front, Peggy was aware that the dark circles around Elsie's eyes were more than mere signs of sleeplessness. She said nothing when Elsie commandeered the hall mirror as she attempted to cover the telltale black-and-blue rings with layer upon layer of make-up.

'I could let you have some of my panstick,' Peggy offered, 'but I'm afraid it's at the theatre at the moment. I can bring it home for you tonight.'

'Thanks, that would be helpful,' Elsie said. 'My stuff isn't really dark enough.' She turned to Peggy and grinned. 'Can't let that beast ruin my best asset.'

Peggy was thinking about this as she set off for the theatre, mulling over the dreadful events of the previous day. She was so deep in thought that she didn't hear approaching footsteps and she wasn't aware of anyone coming up behind her until she felt a tap on the shoulder and spun around, body tensed, arms raised, as if prepared to ward off any onslaught. To her immense relief it was Jimmy she came face to face with, and he looked startled as he put his hands up ready to defend himself.

'Whoa! Hold on,' he said, skipping back a few steps. 'What did you think I was going to do to you?'

Peggy apologized instantly. 'Sorry if I'm a bit jumpy this morning. There is a reason . . .' And she found her story about Elsie pouring out before she was able to stop it.

'Gosh! I'm so sorry,' Jimmy said. 'That all sounds pretty shocking.'

'Sorry to have blurted it all out like that, but I'm afraid it was shocking,' Peggy said.

'Did you report it to the police?' Jimmy wanted to know.

Peggy had to look away as she shook her head.

'This club your friend works at, what kind of place is it?' Jimmy asked.

Peggy felt her face flush to think that Jimmy had put his finger on the heart of the matter so quickly. 'It's not been open very long,' she said, 'but I'm sorry to say it's an illicit gambling joint run by someone she knows.'

'Not that that should make any difference,' Jimmy said. 'Nobody should have to be afraid of being beaten up in the streets of Weatherfield.'

'I agree, but as you can guess, she was hardly in a position to go to the police,' Peggy said.

'No, I understand that.' Jimmy rubbed his chin. 'So, what is she going to do? It sounds like this Vinnie could be a real threat.'

'He is.' Peggy brushed her sleeve across her eyes, not wanting Jimmy to see her distress. 'Look, I'm sorry, I didn't mean to swamp you with Elsie's problems like that.' Peggy struggled to keep her voice steady. 'It's hardly your concern.'

'No, but I'm glad you've told me cos it's obviously affecting you too and there may be some way I can help.' He pulled a crumpled but clean white handkerchief from his pocket and handed it to her.

Peggy smiled at his gesture as she gratefully accepted it and, pausing in front of the theatre, dabbed at her eyes which had suddenly misted over. They climbed the steps up to the main entrance and

Jimmy held open one of the heavy double doors for Peggy to enter. She turned to look at him, suddenly feeling very grateful for his presence. 'When you come up with an idea for what Elsie might do with the money, and get Vinnie off her back, let me know,' Peggy said with a weak smile.

Jimmy looked thoughtful. 'Maybe you should look to Jack and his beanstalk for inspiration,' Jimmy said flippantly. 'This Vinnie might fancy himself as a giant when he's really nothing more than a common thug who needs chopping down to size,' and he held the door while Peggy disappeared inside.

Chapter 36

Peggy couldn't help admiring Elsie's indomitable spirit as she boldly added layers of Peggy's panstick on top of her usual make-up. It also had a transforming effect on her appearance as the black-and-blue bruises were brushed out of sight.

'Party night tonight?' Peggy asked. 'Aren't you afraid to go to the club? Won't he be there? Shouldn't you stay at home?'

'What, and let the bugger win?' Elsie protested defiantly. 'There'll be too many people about, and I don't believe he'd try anything in front of Ned. You know, most of these bullies are really cowards at heart. So long as I don't let him get me on my own, I'm sure I'll be all right.'

'Tell me something,' Peggy was unable to suppress a thought that had been lurking all day, 'I've been meaning to ask if you ever have Sunday night parties at the club?'

Elsie laughed. 'Yes, of course,' she said. 'We've got some Sundays marked on the calendar. In fact, we've got one coming up next week. Why do you ask? Want me to get you an invite?' Elsie laughed. 'I never had you pegged as a gambler.'

'I might fancy a night out,' Peggy said. 'I'll let you know because I might possibly have an idea . . .'

Peggy didn't want to say anything further. She was not willing to share her thoughts with anyone other than Jimmy and she grabbed the opportunity for them to have a coffee together between shows.

'I've been having some thoughts about helping Elsie and I'd love you to tell me what you think,' she said as soon as they sat down, and she quickly outlined her plan. Jimmy listened attentively but to her dismay he was frowning by the time she had finished.

'I don't know whether you realize it, but from what you've told me so far about this man any one of us could get into a lot of trouble having any connection with him at all,' Jimmy said. Peggy was disappointed. She knew he was right, though she didn't want to admit it, but she couldn't go ahead with her plan without him.

'I know it's a lot to ask.' Peggy refused to let go. 'And I realize Elsie means nothing to you, but she has been very good to me and I feel I have to help her in any way I can. She could be badly hurt, or even killed, and that's not something I would want on my conscience for the rest of my days.' Peggy looked at him through lowered eyelids and gave him what she hoped was a winning smile. Then she put her hand over his. 'If not for Elsie, will you do it for me?' she said, looking at him directly now. She kept her hand over his, and held it there until Jimmy finally cleared his throat and said, 'OK, then. Just for you.'

Peggy avoided Elsie as much as possible during the following week, not wanting to jeopardise the plans she had made with Jimmy, and she didn't want to tip her off until the last possible minute. On Sunday morning she made two large parcels of what looked like bundles of costumes she had brought home from the theatre and, without further explanation, announced she would be taking them across to Jimmy at his digs.

The doorbell gave a shrill single ring when she pressed it and Peggy stood for a moment on the newly whitened step, self-consciously clutching her packages.

'Can I help you?' Peggy was surprised when an older woman answered the door and was relieved when she heard footsteps on the stairs and saw Jimmy peering over the woman's shoulder.

'Don't mind Mrs Jones,' Jimmy said when the woman had disappeared into her own flat. 'She's the landlady here and she feels it's her right to vet everyone's visitors.'

Peggy followed him up two flights of stairs, saying, 'Does that mean you had to tell her why I'm here?' Peggy was anxious to know.

'Not at all,' Jimmy reassured her, 'you don't have to worry about that. If it had come to it I wouldn't have felt compelled to tell her the whole truth. Not something I would normally do, I hasten to add,' he said as he closed the door of his flat and relieved Peggy of the packages.

Peggy grinned up at him. 'Me neither,' she said, 'though needs must.'

'Now, do you need a stiff drink?' Jimmy asked. 'Cos I know I do. Would rum and Coke be all right? It's all I've got, apart from a bottle of bitter.'

'It's a bit early for me but under the circumstances I'll join you and rum and Coke would be fine,' Peggy said hastily, not wanting to admit that she had never tried it.

'I haven't told anyone about our plans for this evening, by the way,' Jimmy said as he flipped open the top of a bottle of beer and handed her a tall glass with a small measure of rum and a bottle of Coke.

'No, that's good,' Peggy said. 'Neither have I, though of course I had to warn Elsie before I left the house. We'll have more chance of pulling it off if nobody else knows.'

They sat in silence, sipping their drinks, until Jimmy looked at his watch and put his glass down on a small side table. 'I took your parcel into the bedroom,' he said, 'you can be private in there. I'll stay in here and you can let me know as soon as you're ready. I think it's about time to get started.'

Peggy was grateful for the full-size mirror embedded into the door of the dark wood wardrobe and when she was satisfied that even her own mother wouldn't recognize her she knocked on the bedroom door and shouted that she was ready. Jimmy came in almost immediately and Peggy was delighted to see he had fully entered into the proposed spirit of the evening, for he certainly looked the part.

'Well, it's a good job you told her, cos I don't think your friend Elsie will recognize either of us,' he said, pulling gently on the long red curls that hung from the crown of Peggy's wig, then he placed his arms on her shoulders and eyed her up and down.

'I think we both could fool our families,' he said with a grin. 'Now, there's just one more thing to do, so let's do it before I change my mind.' He shut the door firmly and led the way downstairs. He paused by the phone box in the hall to feed in some coins and Peggy watched with mounting trepidation as he dialled a number quickly, pressed button A and gave his message. Then he took Peggy by the hand and squeezed her fingers. 'Let's go!' he said. 'The scene has been set and it's too late to undo it all now.'

Chapter 37

When they reached the club, Peggy gave the special knock she had inveigled out of Elsie and muttered the password of the week that Elsie had told them to use. Peggy took off her coat, confident that the combination of her wig and slightly unfashionable clothes would be enough to disguise her true identity. Elsie's face remained impassive as she took their coats without a flicker of recognition and showed them to a table where Vinnie was already seated, a pack of cards laid out in front of him, ready for the poker games that were to follow. Peggy felt a cold shiver down her spine as she took her place beside Jimmy, clinging to his arm, looking up at him every now and then with flirtatious eyes as she had seen

Marlene Dietrich do in true gangster-moll style, putting all her acting skills to the test. It was all a charade – only her fear was real.

When Vinnie began to deal, Peggy held her breath, not relaxing until she was sure Jimmy really did seem to know how to play and she was happy no one watching him would guess he was here under false pretences. The game continued smoothly for some time, Peggy not daring to look at Jimmy's cards, until, without warning, he flung his entire hand onto the table, disturbing the pot of money that had been accumulating in the middle.

'I've had enough of this!' Jimmy shouted, and he glared accusingly at Vinnie, yelling, 'This game has been crooked since the opening deal and I want my money back!' Jimmy then stood up in such a dramatic way that he caught everyone by surprise. Even Peggy wondered if he would go so far as to overturn the table with all the money as she had seen John Wayne do in several cowboy films, but she was impressed when he stood his ground, glaring at Vinnie. To her surprise, Jimmy was joined by the other players at the table who, unscripted, also stood up and threw their cards into the centre, shouting, 'This man's right! This game's been crooked right from the start.'

Peggy could see the anger on Vinnie's face, watching as the blood crept up his neck until his whole face and head were suffused. 'Are you accusing me of cheating?' Vinnie snarled, hastily attempting to gather the money together before anyone else moved towards it. He stuffed the notes into his pockets. 'If the cap fits,' someone muttered but not loud enough for Vinnie to hear, which was just as well for he looked as if he was ready to throw a punch.

Peggy was clinging desperately now to Jimmy's arm, wondering if they were going to be strong enough to carry on playing their roles, when there was a hammering on the door and a deep voice shouted, 'Police – open up this door!' and everyone in the room stood as frozen as if in a game of statues.

Now Vinnie's face was drained of colour. 'Who the hell tipped off the rozzers?' he demanded to know but no one answered, heads turning this way and that as panic set in. There was more banging and shouting until Ned reluctantly opened the door, letting in a cold blast of air together with three burly policemen who came storming into the room with raised truncheons.

'Well, there's interesting! Our tip-off was right. A bunch of gamblers, no less,' the oldest-looking copper, who had three stripes on each arm, said. He looked about the room as if trying to memorize each individual face. 'What? No one tell you fellers it's illegal?'

'It's his fault!' someone declared. 'He's the one what started this gambling lark,' he went on, pointing at Vinnie.

'An' he's the one what's got a crooked game going,' another voice grumbled. 'It's not even straight down the line.'

The police sergeant laughed at that. 'Worried he's been cheating, are you?' he said. 'I think you've got more things to worry about than that, right now, but I take your point. We'll take him on a little trip so we can sort out a few things at our place.' He walked over to where Vinnie was still sitting, his pockets bulging with notes, and grabbed hold of him by the shoulder. 'Yes, you, young man. Why don't you come with us for a nice ride into town? I think we have a lot to talk about.'

Peggy was surprised that the policeman, occupied with Vinnie, didn't seem to notice the rest of the card players quietly slipping out of the door and disappearing into the night. They only seemed interested that Vinnie had been caught red-handed with his pockets stuffed full of illicit takings. They didn't even try to stop Ned when he left the room, muttering something about getting the keys from his office, and took Elsie with him. They did listen, however, when Jimmy stepped forward and addressed the sergeant.

'I don't know if it helps you,' Jimmy said 'but it

was us who called you with the tip-off.' He put his arm round Peggy. 'We're both appearing at the Majestic in the Christmas panto, by the way, but we thought you should know what was going on.' Both he and Peggy pulled off their wigs and the policemen stared at them, wide-eyed.

The sergeant laughed. 'Well, I'll be damned,' he said as he slapped his thigh. 'At least someone had some common sense. May I say that was very public spirited of you, sir, and I thank you. If everyone thought like you our job would be a lot easier.' And with that he instructed one of the constables to handcuff Vinnie and they marched him out to their waiting car.

Chapter 38

'You never did say where on earth you got such awful clothes,' Elsie said. 'Talk about trying to look like a gangster's moll, you looked more like a fully blown madam!' She cackled with laughter. 'Even Ned didn't recognize you.'

Peggy joined in her laughter, and catching a glimpse of Jimmy's face was pleased to see he was amused as well. 'That was the idea, not much point in dressing up otherwise.'

'Talking of which, where did you get the whole idea to go to the club in fancy dress?' Elsie wanted to know.

'I don't know, exactly, though it may have been from something Jimmy said about Jack being cheated in the panto. It did get me thinking when I was scratching around for inspiration.' She held her hands out. 'But what does that matter now, it worked, didn't it?'

'It certainly did.' Jimmy joined in the conversation.

It was several days after the dramatic events had played out at the club and Peggy, Jimmy and Elsie were sitting at Elsie's table, once more going over the dramatic events of that memorable Sunday.

'I know you gave me a hint that you would be up to something, and thank goodness you did or I might have blown your cover, but I didn't imagine you'd try to pull anything like that,' Elsie said. 'And I'm sure you'll be pleased to hear that Ned really had no idea.'

'We've got a lot to thank the wardrobe mistress at the theatre for, I know that. She was extremely helpful,' Peggy said. 'Although she was the one to blame for picking out that wig with those dreadful red ringlets.' Peggy covered her face with her hands at the memory.

'But she was right,' Elsie said. 'Cos in the end you both really looked the part and once you were fully made-up I don't think even your own mothers would have known you.'

'I know. It's a long time since I've had so much hair as the wig was blessed with,' Jimmy said. 'Only problem was I wanted to scratch my head all the time.'

'The main thing is that it fooled who it needed to fool,' Peggy said, 'and Jimmy was great in the part, like when he actually accused Vinnie of cheating – I know my heart was pounding when he did that. Vinnie really looked as if he wanted to punch you.'

'Don't remind me. I felt I was on shaky ground as I wasn't sure whether the evidence would stand up,' Jimmy said.

'Thank goodness for those other men,' Peggy said, 'whoever they were.'

'Who would have thought that the punters would turn on Vinnie so quickly like that?' Elsie said. 'It felt like they had been waiting some time for an opportunity to have a go at him and your outburst had given them the courage to stand up to him.'

Jimmy grinned. 'Hidden acting talents,' he said, hooking his thumbs under his jacket lapels. 'Maybe I should ask Lawrence for a part in his next production?'

Peggy looked at Jimmy sitting across the table and, putting her hand over his, gave his fingers a squeeze. 'He can joke,' she said to Elsie, 'but I couldn't have done it without him. He really helped me to stay in character. There were bits of it where I even enjoyed myself, knowing it might help you get out of a very difficult situation if only we could expose Vinnie's crimes. It helped, too, knowing Vinnie was about to get his comeuppance and it was very good of Jimmy to join in.' She smiled at him again. 'He didn't hesitate as soon as I explained the situation.'

'Glad to be of service,' Jimmy said, nodding his head as if in deference. 'Truth be told, I was flattered when you asked me,' he said. Peggy looked up coyly, and she actually felt a warm glow when she saw that he was continuing to smile in her direction.

'I must admit I didn't imagine the police would arrest Vinnie on the spot,' Peggy said. 'They really seemed serious about clamping down on gambling, but it also seems they're particularly keen on catching those they consider to be the ringleaders, and Vinnie certainly matches that description.'

Elsie nodded. 'According to Ned they've got him on extortion charges as well as illegal gambling,' she said, adding, 'And Ned reckons that he himself was lucky not to be arrested at the same time.'

'I suppose the same goes for the punters too,' Peggy said.

'Ned felt the police seemed quite clear about who was leading the operation,' Elsie said 'Apparently, they've had dealings with him before, and as we all know, anything to do with extortion could certainly be laid at Vinnie's door.' She sat back, looking thoughtful, then turned to Peggy. 'But from my point of view, the best of it is that they've also charged Vinnie with theft; he's accused of stealing hundreds of pounds that appeared to have been "lost" by one of his own customers.'

'Really?' Peggy let out an involuntary shriek and clapped her hands as she looked at Elsie. 'I'm delighted to hear it, as that was the whole point of the exercise,' she said smugly. 'If they really think Vinnie took it then they won't waste time accusing you.'

Elsie looked delighted. 'I understand from Ned,' she said, 'that the man who had lost the envelope had already been convinced earlier in the evening that Vinnie was a cheat and an out-and-out rogue, so he had no difficulty in persuading himself that Vinnie must have stolen his envelope with the money too. And he had no trouble being convinced to press charges to that effect and to give a statement with convincing evidence against Vinnie.' Elsie paused, a look of satisfaction on her face. Her eyes twinkled as she said, 'The joke of it is that I've still got the money!' She looked at Peggy. 'As you know, I couldn't decide what to do with it so I'm afraid the envelope stuffed with pound notes and fivers is still where it was, under the mattress, where Peggy has been keeping it warm every night.' She laughed, though Peggy could see that Jimmy looked uncomfortable.

'Peggy did tell me about that,' Jimmy said. 'So, what will you do with it now?'

Chapter 39

After Peggy and Jimmy had left for the theatre to prepare for the evening performance, Elsie found it difficult to stir herself, although she knew that unless she did something about it, the whole night would stretch ahead of her. She felt very flat after all the excitement of the past few days although she didn't usually let that get her down and she poured a fresh cup of tea and lit a cigarette as she sank down on the sofa while she tried to work out what she should do. She was surprised when the doorbell rang and she went to the front door cautiously, wondering who could be calling at this hour. She glanced at the hall mirror and plumped up her hair with her fingers then set a welcoming smile in place in case it was one of her friends as she opened the door only a crack to check out her unexpected visitor.

'Why, Ned!' She didn't try to disguise her surprise and she glanced on either side of him to be sure he had come alone. 'What are you doing here? I wasn't expecting you tonight, although funnily enough I was just thinking about you.'

'Nice thoughts, I hope,' he said, putting his foot over the threshold. 'Can I come in?'

She stood back from the door though she only left just enough room for him to enter, and closed the door smartly to make sure he wasn't being followed. 'What's brought you here at this hour? Is there any more news?' she asked as she led the way into the living room. She thought back to her conversation with her previous guests, her mind whirling.

'Only that Vinnie is now actually in prison, awaiting trial on charges of theft and assault. I suppose it was only a matter of time. He was doing some pretty mean things, even to his friends. My big mistake was to trust him with all my savings.' He rubbed his chin ruefully.

'It's always easy to be wise after the event,' Elsie consoled him. 'But that's how life gets you sometimes, you couldn't have known.' She sighed. 'Have a seat. The kettle's not long since boiled if you fancy making a brew while I just nip upstairs to fetch something.'

When she came back down again, she took a deep

breath and headed for the kitchen. Before she had time to change her mind she handed Ned the large brown envelope she had been clutching. He looked at it curiously.

'What's this?' he asked.

'Why don't you open it and find out?' she teased and she watched his face carefully.

He stopped what he was doing and frowned, as if not understanding. 'It's the missing money,' she explained, 'only it's not missing any longer. And before you say anything, I didn't steal it. I want you to know that. I found it stuffed behind one of the sofas at the club one night. Someone must have parked it there for safekeeping and forgotten where they'd put it. Or else it could have fallen out of their pocket, I suppose,' she said, but Ned didn't seem to be listening. He was examining the contents of the envelope and looked amazed as he mentally added up the money.

'I've never counted it,' she said, 'though anyone can see it's a lot.'

'And this is really the money Vinnie's been accused of stealing?'

'The same,' Elsie said. She was watching his face as his lips curled.

'Hmm. I can't help feeling that prison is no more than he deserves for all the rotten things he's done,' he spat the words out like venom. 'But it's ironic that actually stealing this money from one of his own punters isn't one of them. All I can say is: may he rot in hell for what he's put us all through. But why are you giving it to me? I never had anything to do with it. If he accused anyone, it was you, Elsie.'

'I know that,' Elsie said, 'and I also know he stole from you in lots of other ways, so it seems perfectly fitting to me that the police think he stole it – and I reckon we should leave it that way. I feel you deserve to have it to help you get going again – only without him, this time. I know he took all your life savings and it seems to me he's squandered everything you gave him.'

'That's true,' Ned agreed. 'But he's already had some punishment. The police have not only closed down the club but the council have refused to give permission for the remainder of the café renovations to go ahead.'

'I didn't know that, but I can't say I'm surprised,' Elsie said, and it was all she could do not to rub her hands together in glee. 'Then this will help you get a fresh start,' she said, pointing to the envelope. 'I know you reckon you've got off lightly in all this as far as not being arrested is concerned, but you've lost what little money you did have.' She paused before she added, 'And I'm sorry to have to tell you but you're about to lose something else.'

'What's left to lose?' Ned sounded bitter and Elsie

almost changed her mind, but she was concerned about what could happen if she didn't go through with it. She had thought long and hard about what she was about to say and in her heart Elsie knew now was the time for her to seize the moment before it was too late.

'Me,' she said eventually. 'I'm afraid you're about to lose me.' Elsie lowered her eyes as well as her voice; she couldn't look at him as she delivered what she was sure would feel like a final blow, and she wasn't surprised when she heard him swear.

'What the bloody hell? Why?' and she realized she couldn't really answer him. 'Didn't we have fun?' he asked.

'Yes, we had fun, it isn't that,' she whispered, a smile coming to her lips as she thought back to their tumbles on the sofa in the café upstairs despite its dilapidated state, 'but I'm afraid it's over. Put it down to me spending too much time living on the edge,' she tried to joke but gave up when she looked at his stricken face. 'I suppose there was some promise of glamour at the beginning – but maybe I'm just not cut out for that kind of life.'

When Peggy got home from the theatre she found Elsie sitting in the dark with only the dying embers of the coal fire still sparking in the grate. Jimmy had walked her home as usual but he hadn't come inside and she was concerned to see that Elsie had actually fallen asleep in the chair. As she opened the kitchen door Elsie was startled awake.

'Is everything all right, Elsie?' Peggy was concerned.

Elsie stood up and stretched. 'As all right as it might be,' she said and she told Peggy some of the details about Ned's visit.

'That's a shame – are you sure you won't regret it?' Peggy asked,

'Yes, it is a shame, but let's face it, there was no future in it.'

'Did he agree?'

'I didn't give him the chance to,' Elsie conceded. 'On the plus side, he was very pleased to get the money.' She looked over at Peggy. 'I know what you're thinking, and yes, he wasn't all bad, but he did cost me a lot, one way or another, for all the trouble he caused, with that so-called friend of his, Vinnie, not to mention all the extra babysitting I had to shell out for. I've come to the conclusion that all I wanted really was to have a good time and I think he wanted something more serious.'

'What did he say? How did it end?' Peggy wanted to know.

'He said thank you and then he went on his way,' Elsie said. 'He promised to keep in touch, but who knows?' She shrugged. 'The world is a big place, and as the saying goes, there are plenty more fish in the sea. Vinnie is safely locked away and he'll probably never know what happened to that money. I bet you one day I'll hear that Ned has moved on too – only this time he'll be leaving me behind.

Chapter 40

When Daphne Dawson returned to the theatre and declared she was fit enough to continue as the principal boy, at least until the end of the run, Peggy felt sorry for Nora as she was effectively nudged back onto the understudy sidelines once more and had to take her place back in the chorus.

'It's a shame but at least the audience got to see your legs,' Peggy consoled her friend, 'which is more than they see of me when I'm tucked into the Giant's costume.'

'But you at least get a chance to make up your own antics and make the audience laugh,' Nora said, laughing now, 'whereas I remain pretty anonymous.'

'I suppose that's one way of looking at it,' Peggy said.

'But you don't have to apologize on my behalf,' Nora added. 'In this business it seems to me you have to grab hold of any kind of break you can get, and that goes for any solo piece that makes you stand out from the crowd.'

Lawrence, though, had been kept in hospital because of some serious complications that had developed with his broken leg that would require further surgery. But as Denise pointed out, 'He doesn't have to hurry back, does he? Jimmy's doing a great job standing in as director, and I for one don't miss Lawrence.'

Peggy silently agreed. In Lawrence's absence she felt more able to relax. She didn't have to worry that someone was breathing down her neck all the time and if Jimmy gave her critical feedback on her performance his manner was empathic and never brutal. Peggy was actually surprised how much more 'at home' she now felt when she was on the stage and when she began to feel as though she had always been a part of the theatre she knew her acting career had been well and truly launched.

Things settled down in the theatre and thanks to all the additional publicity, the panto continued to do well. Ticket sales were up, and they continued to get the occasional mention in the social pages of the local *Gazette*, reminding readers what live theatre was bringing to their lives and how much it was lifting everyone's spirits, even in the darkest of hours.

It seemed like no time at all before Christmas was upon them and everyone was talking excitedly about their forthcoming break.

'It will be great to have an extra day off,' Denise said to Peggy when they were in the dressing room together, then she stretched and yawned. 'I don't know about you, but my mother says she's determined to pamper me and I intend to eat and sleep my way through them, only taking time off to open my presents. I'm still like a kid when it comes to things like that.'

'Two whole days?' Peggy asked as if only just registering what that meant.

'You *are* going home, I presume?' Denise asked, frowning slightly.

'Yes, of course,' Peggy said quickly, not wanting to admit that there had ever been any doubt. Since receiving the note, she had had a card from her mother wishing her luck and from Colin, too. He had sent her a hand-made one with his own naïve drawing on the front of a house and a family with two children that he had wax-crayoned in garish reds and greens. She proudly displayed both cards on the mantelpiece in her bedroom, shedding a fresh tear each time she looked at them and clasping them close to her chest as she reread them a dozen times.

Notices were distributed about the town announcing that the theatre would be closing early on Christmas Eve, as the management had decided there should be no evening performance, and there was a frantic rush to clear as much as possible from the stage as soon as the final curtain came down on the afternoon matinee. Carpenters rushed back and forth checking the set, the wardrobe mistress gathered the more extravagant costumes to store them away safely until they were needed again, and Peggy did her best to ensure that all the props were returned to their starting places, ready for the first performance after the break. The cast and crew were all in high spirits and there was already a party atmosphere about the place so it took some time for people to assemble when Jimmy tried to call them all together and the high buzz of the conversation level didn't reduce until he unhooked the microphone and stepped forward to the front of the stage, announcing, 'Testing, testing, one, two, three!'

'Before everyone disperses,' Jimmy said, 'I want to wish you all well and a very happy Christmas. Now, I know most of you will be leaving Weatherfield for a couple of days, but I would like to suggest that as it's Christmas Eve those of us who will be staying in town tonight should meet up to have one last drink together before the holiday. I feel we deserve it. We need to celebrate our amazingly successful season and congratulate ourselves for the way we conquered all adversity – and I do mean adversity!'

A huge cheer went up, accompanied by shouts of, 'Here! Here!' and loud ululating noises.

Then Jimmy went on: 'And where better to meet than the Rovers Return, the pub on Coronation Street many of you are already familiar with.' Another cheer. 'Who's ready for a party?' Jimmy's cry was greeted by a third loud cheer and those who had gone down into the auditorium and were standing in the stalls climbed back up the stairs onto the apron front to rejoin the others. Peggy had been about to leave the stage when she felt Jimmy grasp hold of her arm. 'Will I see you later?' he asked.

'Oh, no, you probably won't, Jimmy,' Peggy said, suddenly feeling torn. 'Elsie was hinting she's likely to need a babysitter and I've sort of promised I would help. She relies on me if she can't find anyone else. I imagine she'll be going to the Rovers to meet her mates so you'll be bound to see her there, but if she needs me to stay with the kids I can't let her down.'

'Of course not, though it's a shame from my point of view.' Jimmy looked genuinely disappointed. 'And of course, I won't see you tomorrow either, you're off home, I take it?'

'That's right,' she said. 'Very early in the morning. And that's all thanks to you suggesting I should give her some warning of a time and day. What better than Christmas Day?'

'Indeed. That's wonderful news,' Jimmy said though a sad look crossed his face even as he tried to smile.

'There might not be that much to eat,' she said, 'but at least we can all be together.'

'How are you going to get there?' Jimmy asked.

'There's a bus I can get first thing in the morning.'

Jimmy smiled now and almost coyly put his arm round her shoulders. He briefly pulled her towards him so that her head was momentarily leaning against his chest. He gave her a squeeze and grinned as he looked down, and for a few moments Peggy felt breathless. 'I hope you have a lovely time with your family – I'm so pleased they've come up trumps,' he said, and Peggy felt her throat tighten and her eyes mist over at his genuine delight.

'Thanks, I hope so too, though I've got mixed feelings as you might imagine, but I'm looking forward to seeing Mam and Colin, if nobody else,' she said, struggling to keep her voice under control as she thought about the inevitable confrontation with her father.

'Have a good time!' 'See you next week!' The cacophony grew louder as everyone began to shout at once and when someone stepped between her and Jimmy, Peggy used it as her cue to disappear.

As soon as Peggy put her key in the door her suspicions were confirmed that Elsie wasn't home, although these days once it was dark it wasn't always easy to tell. She was heading for the kitchen where she knew she could confidently make a full blackout before switching on the light, when she realized she had stepped on an envelope that had dropped onto the floor by the letterbox. She picked it up and was surprised to see it was addressed to her; then came fear as she recognized the handwriting. She took a deep breath and ripped open the top of the envelope as quickly as she could. Her mouth went dry as she read the contents which filled not more than half of the single sheet of paper inside. As usual her mother kept her note brief and to the point.

> *Sorry to have to cancel at the last minute,* Peggy read, *but I've had an accident and am in bed. I slipped and broke my wrist and can't have visitors so you can't come tomorrow. Don't worry about me, I'll be fine once I've had a bit of rest. You have a nice time with your friends instead,*
> *Love from Mam.*

PS I'm sure you'll be better off in the long run. Your father found out we'd met you behind his back.

Peggy gasped. Slipped and broken her wrist! Who was she kidding? But there it was in black and white. She felt a faint throbbing behind her eyes. She knew that the words were shorthand for something more like: 'Your father had a few too many and laid into me' but she could hardly call her mother a liar and there was nothing she could do. It was the kind of thing that happened from time to time in the Brown household, though nobody talked about it. Such accidents were never spoken about, even by those who bore witness. Peggy had been sworn to secrecy about what went on in the house for as long as she could remember and she had been warned repeatedly of the dire consequences that would follow if she ever spoke out of turn. It was something she had grown up with and had never questioned and certainly had never challenged and her first thought, even now, was what story she might tell Elsie rather than admit to the truth. How could she tell anyone when she felt so ashamed, when she felt so guilty even though she knew logically that it wasn't her fault? Her throat felt constricted and she wanted to shout out at the injustice of it all. Her mother had been used as a punching bag, and she and Colin were once more being made to suffer – all she could do was to gulp for breath and swallow her anger.

Peggy was surprised when Elsie finally came home to see that neither of the children were with her. 'Change of plan!' Elsie announced, and she shook her hands freely with such exaggerated pleasure that Peggy had to laugh.

'I presumed they were all tucked up in bed by now, what have you done with them?' she asked.

'They *are* tucked up, at Ida Barlow's,' Elsie said. 'When Linda said she wanted to go to Ida's house to sleep it worked out well, cos of course Dennis went too. Linda was very excited about being with Ida's boys and I don't know why, but they always seem to like having her about.' She grinned at Peggy. 'That lets you off the hook tonight, I thought you'd be pleased to know.'

Peggy managed a weak smile though her mind was swirling, still thinking about her mother's letter, but before she could tell Elsie her sad tale, Elsie spoke up first. 'So, as you're not going off to your mam's till the morning, I thought you might like to come with me to the pub for an hour or so,' she said.

'Oh!' Peggy didn't know whether to laugh or cry at the kind thought. She was grateful to be included in Elsie's plans, at least for tonight, even if it did mean she would have to put on a brave face all evening. She wasn't sure she wanted to go but it did seem churlish to refuse and she could put off thinking about what she should do on Christmas Day until the morning.

'Having Linda out of the house for a few hours will give me a chance to wrap up her presents, without her trying to look over my shoulder all the time,' Elsie said. 'I'm sure she'll nag to come back dead early in the morning wanting to open them all, but Ida said she'd be up early with the boys in any case, so it wouldn't be a problem.'

'I can wrap mine up too,' Peggy said, 'and I'll put them with yours.'

'That's very sweet of you to have bothered,' Elsie said. 'You really didn't have to buy them anything, you know. War or no war, they'll hardly go short.'

'I know, but I wanted to,' Peggy said, thinking about Linda and how she had talked of nothing else throughout the whole week. 'In fact, I'll go and get them now,' she said, and she moved toward the stairs, remembering how, despite everything, the build-up to Christmas had always been one of the most exciting events of the year when she was young, everyone doing their best not to let her father spoil their fun. The memories of Christmases past were among some of the best of her childhood. 'I've only bought little things,' she went on, 'there's not much in the shops to buy at the moment. But I can remember when I was Linda's age how I felt about getting presents, any presents, especially ones that were wrapped up nicely with a bow.'

She paused, feeling a catch in her throat as she thought ahead, with dread, about having to spend Christmas Day alone and she ran up the stairs before the trickle she could feel running down her cheeks turned into a flood.

Chapter 41

The dank street was as dark as she had come to expect while the country was still at war and Peggy and Elsie walked along Coronation Street to the pub, picking their way carefully so as not to slip on the damp cobbles. The whole neighbourhood was lit only by a smattering of stars and the sliver of moon that shone out from behind the clouds and Peggy switched on her torch for a few moments when she sensed some obstruction ahead on the pavement. Ever fearful of falling, they managed to skirt carefully around a large, newly dug hole that took up most of the pavement but their actions were admonished by a gruff voice shouting at them from across the street.

'Turn that damn thing off! Do you want to make it easy for them German bombers by showing them where we are? Don't you know by now the Jerries make no concessions for Christmas?'

Peggy quickly switched off the light, while Elsie shouted back, 'Sorry, Mr Tatlock,' and Peggy was put in mind of the posters that had been pinned up around the town, warning the public to be extra vigilant and not to lower their guard just because it was Christmas.

They trundled on in what was now pitch-black and when they made it safely to the pub Peggy flung open the double doors in relief, allowing a warm draught of air to blast out in their faces. The air brought with it the sounds of someone thumping on an old piano – Mrs Ena Sharples, in her element, playing her favourite carols which people were happy to join in with gusto.

'Typical!' Elsie made a tutting noise. 'Can't keep her down for long, though I suppose you can't blame the old goat. She can't wait to get the hymn-singing going at the best of times and Christmas is the only time no one objects.' She chuckled. 'Not even me. Some of them carols have such nice tunes even I don't mind joining in the odd song or two when I can remember the words.' At that moment the singing swelled and the air was filled with soprano voices soaring above the continuous drone that was the hubbub of the general conversation.

As they stepped inside the pub, Peggy looked about her in astonishment for it was like stepping into another world. 'My goodness,' she said, 'they've really gone to town with their decorations. They've done an amazing job.'

Elsie nodded her agreement. It was as though Annie Walker had been determined not to allow any signs of austerity to creep in and spoil their Christmas. Long paper chains criss-crossed the walls and ceiling, encompassing the whole of the bar area and they had been interspersed with strips of tinsel that glittered as they twisted on the warm currents of air and caught the light. In one corner of the bar a hugely intrusive fire extinguisher had been draped with strings of tinsel, and on the countertop there was a small Christmas tree adorned with colourful unlit candles and sparkling baubles. Small, neatly wrapped parcels hung from the lower branches, although from the way they bobbed about it seemed the bright but flimsy wrapping paper contained nothing more than empty boxes. Fresh holly with an abundance of bright red berries was draped over the upper arms of the tree and at the top was a sparkling fairy clutching a wand and hanging on to a brightly glittering star. A fire sparked and crackled in the grate, making the whole scene look homely and warming, although in reality the burning coals only threw out heat to those who were standing close by, like the painted wooden figures of Mary and Joseph and their baby son who had been laid out in the nativity tableau at the far end of the bar. The whole scene looked like a Christmas card and Peggy couldn't help contrasting it with the simple decorations Elsie had created at home in her effort to make the house look a bit special for Linda.

The pub was already crowded, filled with far more people than might be found there on a regular Friday night and drinks were being passed from hand to hand as there was little room for bar staff to circulate. Peggy, following in Elsie's wake, was pleased to be greeted by Elsie's friends, mostly people she had met on previous visits and she was suffused with a surprisingly warm glow as people welcomed her with a hug and even Mrs Sharples' two cronies standing by the piano gave her a friendly wave.

She heard someone call her name and she looked up to see Jimmy standing with some of the chorus and several members of the backstage crew. She had forgotten that the remainder of the company had arranged to meet in the pub, but they all looked so pleased to see her she could only smile and introduce as many of them as possible to Elsie.

Jimmy was beaming at her and it didn't take long before Peggy saw him battling through the crowd and thrusting a tall glass into her hands. 'I take it the usual is OK?' he said and Peggy had to blink rapidly to clear the mist from her eyes. She raised the glass to him in thanks and he nodded his acknowledgement, then tapped the side of his glass with a metal spoon that was lying on the counter. At first no one seemed to take any notice and it wasn't until Annie Walker rapped on the countertop with her knuckles and called for some hush that people did quieten down. Jimmy cleared his throat.

'Mrs Walker and fellow drinkers,' he began, 'my name is Jimmy Caulfield. Some of you might know me already as I'm currently the director of the Weatherfield panto and if you've been to the theatre already to see our marvellous show you may have seen me flitting about behind the scenes. Now, I would like to say a few words, and I promise what I have to say won't take long, but I'm sure you won't mind if I hijack a few minutes of your drinking time to raise a toast to my colleagues.'

There was more table banging until Annie Walker intervened once more, only this time she raised her hand for silence and when everyone calmed down she came forward to speak.

'Not at all, Mr Caulfield,' Annie Walker responded warmly. 'I'm sure no one will mind, and this is a very special evening. But please, I'm going to ask you to indulge me before you say anything further.'

She gave him a gracious smile before saying, 'I know I speak on behalf of myself and the staff but I'm sure all the local residents will join us when we say that we welcome you and, indeed, all thespians to Weatherfield, to Coronation Street and especially to the Rovers. You have done us a great honour by reviving our very own pantomime tradition at a time when so many of us were in the doldrums and we have appreciated being given something to smile about.' She turned to Jimmy. 'So, thank you from all of us; we hope this may be the start of a new Weatherfield tradition, and we look forward to welcoming you all again soon. Now please, do continue with your toast.'

'Thank you,' Jimmy acknowledged her greeting. 'Believe me. It's a pleasure to be here and I know that so many of your customers have already supported us by coming to see our show.' A loud shout and a cheer went up. 'And to those who haven't yet managed to see us performing, then may I urge you to do so in the New Year before our current contract runs out.' There was much laughter followed by another cheer. 'But in the meantime I would like to propose a toast to the company and to one or two of the artistes in particular. One is Peggy here,' he put up his arm to indicate where she was standing next to him, 'or should I say Margaret de Vere, otherwise known as the Giant who is a relative newcomer to the stage; another is the more seasoned veteran Nora Johns who isn't here tonight as she's zoomed off already to spend Christmas with her family. I'm singling them out as they were the ones who led the way in saving the day when we suffered that unfortunate accident on stage and it seemed possible that we might have to close down.

'However, I really need to thank all of the company as they rushed in with their help and support. The cast were amazing, and the backstage crew worked tirelessly to rebuild and restore our set. Thanks to all of them, we survived. So, a huge thank you to you all.' He paused while he looked around the room. 'And finally, I must add a tribute to our director, Lawrence Vine, who unfortunately is still in hospital recovering from his injuries from that fateful day. We wish him a speedy recovery. Without him and his vision for reviving the theatrical tradition here in Weatherfield, there would have been no show in the first place. May I invite everyone here tonight to raise your glasses and join in our toast, to Peggy, Nora and Lawrence and the whole company.'

'To Peggy, Nora and Lawrence and the whole company!' people shouted. Peggy stood rooted to the spot, filled with embarrassment. That was something she had not expected and she didn't know what to say or where to look, but another voice had joined in again as Annie Walker seemed determined to have the last word.

'And make sure you and your company come back next year,' she shouted above the melee, raising her glass in Jimmy's direction, and everyone raised their glasses and followed suit.

Peggy felt a hand slide across her shoulders and glanced up at Jimmy, but before she could say anything he leaned towards her and kissed her fully on the lips. She was so surprised that she automatically tried to take a step back but found it impossible without stepping on somebody's feet. Before she could move, Jimmy leaned in towards her once more and she felt the warmth of his mouth on hers as he kissed her again. This time her body responded and Peggy felt the heat rise up to her neck and into the roots of her hair.

'Sorry about that,' Jimmy said but his face was wreathed in smiles and he didn't look a bit sorry. 'I hadn't expected you to be here, but it is Christmas Eve and you must understand that I had to do it.' He held his hands up in a gesture of surrender and indicated with his eyes that she should look up. When she did, she realized she had been standing underneath a healthy-looking sprig of mistletoe with its plump white berries. Those who were standing close to Peggy cheered and broke into spontaneous applause, causing her another round of embarrassment. But Jimmy himself gave her the thumbs-up sign. 'It was the least I could do, and was no more than you deserve,' he whispered in her ear and with the warmth of his breath on her face Peggy could feel her heart beginning to pound and the nerve endings in her limbs seeming to fire off in all directions. But far from being embarrassed, she couldn't stop smiling at the lingering memory of the comforting moistness of his lips on hers and she felt the tingling sensation ripple once more through her entire body.

'Merry Christmas, Margaret de Vere,' he said. 'This is no doubt the start of what I hope will be a great career. May this only be the beginning and may you land many more plum roles; as the song goes, may all your Christmases be white.'

Peggy giggled and realized the drink had gone straight to her head, but Jimmy was looking serious. 'I must admit it was touch and go whether you and Nora really could hold the fort without people demanding their money back.' He gave a sly grin. 'And I can admit now there were times when I thought the show would never be able to complete its run,' he said, 'but somehow we've made it through to the end of the year with rave reviews and I no longer have any concerns about being able to fulfil our contract.'

What was left of the evening flew by and it seemed like no time at all before Annie Walker was calling time and Peggy reluctantly bundled herself up into her coat, winding her thick scarf several times around her neck.

'It's at times like this I'm grateful I don't have far to go,' she said though her teeth were chattering uncontrollably by the time they stopped by the front door of number 11. Elsie had gone on ahead to check on the children at Ida's and Jimmy had insisted on accompanying Peggy home.

'You must be exhausted,' Jimmy said, 'I know I am, it's been a long day at the end of a tricky period with rather more obstacles along the way than we bargained for, although we do seem to have clambered our way through or around most of them.'

Peggy's eyes filled with tears. 'From where I'm standing that sounds like an understatement,' she said, wondering if she should tell him about her cancelled arrangements for tomorrow.

'It probably is, but as the old saying goes, the show must go on, and this show just did. I think we can all be very proud of ourselves. And you especially – your first year in panto and you landed an important role without having to resort to the casting couch or give in to the director's bullying. You were able to land that part all by yourself and your professional acting career is now officially launched!' He put his finger under her chin and tilted her face towards him, and this time she offered her lips to be kissed.

She knew that by now her face must be the brightest of pinks but she didn't mind, knowing Jimmy couldn't see it in the inky blackness. She thought back to how Jimmy had helped steer her through some of the show's more difficult moments, and a wave of gratitude washed over her.

'Maybe next year, by which time you'll have more standing in the company, you'll be able to aim even higher than a character with a fancy costume and a plywood house in the treetops.'

Peggy laughed. 'Kind of you to say,' she said, 'but next year seems like a long way away. I feel as if I'm only just getting started with my first solo role, even though you were talking about me trying to get an even bigger and better part.' She didn't want to tell him how delighted she was just to be considered one of the company. 'I used to be scared I'd be overshadowed and all my talents would be overlooked when there were people like Nora and Denise ahead of me in the pecking order,' she said. 'I thought I wouldn't stand a chance if we were all competing for the same roles, but now I'm not so scared as they've both told me they don't intend returning to Weatherfield.'

Jimmy looked surprised and Peggy hoped she hadn't spoken out of turn.

'Where do they want to go?' he asked.

'They've been talking about going south, by which I assume they mean London, where there'll be far more acting opportunities,' she said.

'True enough, though there will be far more competition. And you?' Jimmy asked. 'Wouldn't you want to try your luck with them?'

'Not necessarily.' She didn't want to tell him she was tempted – just to get as far away from home as possible.

'Well, you might be able to avoid having to work with Lawrence again if you don't want to,' he said, giving her an enigmatic look.

'Oh? And how's that?'

'How would you feel about working with me?'

Peggy looked at him, wishing she had more light to read his face.

'I feel I've done my apprenticeship and I'm seriously thinking of starting my own company,' he said. 'A company where I'll be the director and I'll choose my own cast and crew.'

'That sounds good!' Peggy felt like hugging him and wishing him luck.

'Of course, I won't be able to guarantee I'll always give you the plum part, but I can say I would always consider you and invite you to audition.'

Peggy caught her breath. Impossible dreams? She sighed. Dreams did sometimes come true. She suddenly felt the chill of the wind and shivered – that was, no doubt, a conversation for another time.

'Well!' Jimmy said, pulling his coat more tightly around him, and he rubbed his hands together to keep warm, 'I mustn't keep you from your beauty sleep if you're going off very early in the morning.'

It was on the tip of her tongue to tell him, but something held her back and she felt too embarrassed to give him more than a noncommittal smile, a smile that he probably couldn't see, and she felt rather than saw his eyes in the darkness, trying to scrutinise her face. 'I'll bid you goodnight, then,' Jimmy said. 'I wish you a Merry Christmas once again and I hope you enjoy yourself tomorrow.' He touched his fingers to his cap in a mock salute and by the time she felt able to respond Peggy realized that Jimmy was actually walking away, shouting, 'Merry Christmas!' And that the sound of his footsteps was receding into the night.

Chapter 42

When Peggy woke up on Christmas morning her head was pounding and she lay back on the pillows, trying hard not to move, thinking about the previous night. She wasn't used to drinking so much and although she had felt no ill effects at the time, she knew she would have to find some aspirin if she were to get through the day. But rather than suffering the ignominy of having to confess to Elsie that she would not be going to her mother's for Christmas dinner, she decided to stay in bed and let the rest of the day pass her by. Elsie would be taking the children to the Mission of Glad Tidings, where the Coronation Street committee had organized a communal Christmas lunch that all the local residents had contributed to. It had been agreed that everyone would pool their resources, including their food rationing coupons, and that they would each bring whatever food items they could spare for all the residents to share.

Peggy had assumed she would be long gone on her way to see her mother by the time the party was to start, and hadn't considered asking for an invitation, but it was too late now. It was just unfortunate that things hadn't worked out as planned but she knew she couldn't face the thought of having to tell the whole street that her mother had rejected her and she had nowhere to go. She convinced herself it would be better to stay in her room until she heard Elsie and the children go out, then she could slip downstairs for an hour or two as she would have the house to herself. By the time she had to explain and tell Elsie her story the day would be almost over. Pleased she had at least arrived at an acceptable solution, she pulled the blanket over her head and curled up tightly in a ball, willing her banging headache to leave her alone.

She lay there for a while, wondering what time it was, until she could no longer speculate. She finally plucked up courage and turned over gingerly to peer at the luminous dial on her alarm clock that stood on the small bedside table. It told her it was only seven thirty and she wondered how long she would have to wait till she would have the house to herself. Once she had established the time, she tried to sit up briefly so he could peep out through the crack in the curtains to check on the weather, but she immediately regretted the sudden movement. Luckily, she could see at a glance that Jimmy's wish for a white Christmas had not been granted. The pavements, however, were covered with a glistening film of light drizzle that seemed to hang in the air below the murky grey sky and showed no signs of breaking up. Peggy groaned and gently sank back down again. The house was quiet and she lay there for some time, wondering how much longer she could tolerate the pain that had now shifted behind her eyes. She could hear no movement downstairs and wondered where Elsie was; perhaps she had gone to fetch the children from number 3? Linda and Kenneth Barlow were bound to be up early to start tearing open their presents.

The pain in her head was becoming intolerable and Peggy knew she had to find the aspirin. Her bare feet were cold and she could feel the outline of the insoles as she tried, unsuccessfully, to slide her feet into her shoes but she knew she couldn't bend to put on her socks without making her headache worse. She pulled the flimsy cotton dressing gown her mother had once given her for her birthday over her winceyette nightdress and steeled herself to go downstairs as quickly and quietly as she could. She could only pray that she might get back up again without bumping into Elsie.

She was sitting on the child-sized stool at the end of the bed, peering into the small mirror that hung on the wall at Linda's height, when there was a sudden commotion and the clattering of leather soles on the wooden floor of the tiny landing at the top of the stairs, and the bedroom door was flung open. The noise was followed by a loud scream as Linda came tumbling into the room, fell on the bed and stared at Peggy, a horrified look on her face. Peggy felt as if her head was about to split in two but her immediate concern was Linda.

'What on earth's the matter?' Peggy said, grasping hold of the little girl's hand and lifting it to touch her face. 'You look like you've seen a ghost, but it's me, it's only Peggy.' She tried to sound calming and reassuring, aware that Linda was scrutinizing her face.

'I . . . I didn't think you were here,' Linda said, her voice trembling. 'Mummy said you'd gone away,' she added uncertainly, her lower lip quivering. 'She said you were going to see your mummy.' Peggy tickled her fingers down the child's arm until she was holding her hand.

'Yes, I was supposed to be going away to my mother's,' she said, keeping her voice as soft and gentle as she could, 'but, as you can see, I didn't get there.' Peggy did her best imitation of a cheerful smile and she squeezed the girl's fingers gently as if to reassure her she was real. 'I'm very sorry if I gave you a fright.' She tried to laugh but Linda kept staring.

'Are you going away now?' Linda asked, her voice and her demeanour almost returning to her usual confident self.

'I . . . I'm not quite sure what I'm going to do,' Peggy said, but Linda wasn't listening, she was too busy peering inside Peggy's bag that was lying open on the floor.

'When are you going?' Linda demanded. 'You're such a slowcoach,' she added with a giggle, 'you haven't even finished packing yet! Can I stay and watch you? I saw my mummy packing a bag once and you have to fold everything like this . . .' And she picked up Peggy's blouse and tried to fold it into a square.

Peggy stood up but felt dizzy at the sudden movement and had to sit down again on the edge of the bed. Linda came and sat down beside her for a moment or two before she started bouncing up and down on the well-worn mattress until Peggy had to beg her to stop. Linda jumped up then, and grabbing hold of Peggy's pillow, began to make kissing noises while smoothing her hand over the pink pillow case.

Then Linda held it away from her and spoke to it as if it were a doll, or even a real person.

'Oh, but I've missed you,' Linda said, holding the pillow in front of her. 'Have you missed me?' she asked. 'I hope you've been nice to my friend Peggy. I might have left you for a little while but I'll be coming back soon.' She looked up at Peggy, a serious expression on her face now. 'When you go to see your mummy, my mummy says I can sleep in my bed so it doesn't get too lonely,' and she continued to stroke the pillow and bury her face in it.

'That sounds like a good idea.' Peggy didn't know what else to say but it didn't matter because Linda's attention had already strayed and she was looking into Peggy's half-filled bag once more. She put her hand deep inside but seemed disappointed in what she found there and she pulled her hand out in disgust.

'Why aren't you taking any presents with you for your mummy?' Linda asked, staring at Peggy accusingly. She stood up then and put her hands on her hips, taking up an Elsie-like stance, tapping her foot as if she was getting impatient waiting for an answer. Peggy couldn't help smiling.

'Don't you love your mummy?' Linda wanted to know. 'I love my mummy and she says she loves me. That's why I've made her a special picture she can put up on her bedroom wall, next to all those film stars.' Linda barely paused for breath before she plunged on, 'And she's got me lots and lots of presents.' She lowered her voice and put her finger to her lips. 'I'm not supposed to know but I've seen them in the fireplace at the bottom of the chimney. Santa must have left them there. I told Mummy what I wanted Santa to bring but she says he might not be able to carry them all at once so I may have to wait. In any case, I'm not allowed to open any of them yet. Not until the big finger is on the twelve and the little finger is on the nine on the mantelpiece clock because that's when it's really morning. Will your mummy have lots of presents that Santa left for you? She will if she loves you, you know.'

An unbidden lump that rose in Peggy's throat suddenly stopped her from responding, but Linda didn't seem to notice. 'Have you got a present for your brother?' she asked now. 'I've got one for Dennis. Mummy says he's too little so I shouldn't bother, but I'm going to give him one of my books. It's too babyish for me now.' She paused for a moment, then burst into a fit of giggles. 'I hope Santa got everything for everyone fitted in his sack – and didn't get stuck inside anyone's chimney!' She made a gurgling sound while Peggy took the opportunity to swallow the lump that hadn't budged from her throat. She felt a wetness on her cheeks and brushed the sudden stream of tears away with her hand, hoping that Linda hadn't noticed.

Linda turned her large, innocent-looking eyes in Peggy's direction. 'How old is your brother? Is he bigger than me? Show me,' she said and she jumped off the bed and stood beside the tape measure that had been pinned onto the door. 'Is he this big?' Linda put her hand on the top of her head and tried to look at the tape's marking at the same time. She twisted herself into such contortions that it was impossible to ignore her. Despite herself, Peggy burst out laughing as she stood up, amazed to find her headache had begun to recede. She indicated a mark on the door that was high above Linda's head. 'Oh, he's a big boy,' Linda exclaimed. 'What's his name again?'

'Colin,' Peggy said.

'I like that name,' Linda said. 'There's a boy in my nursery class called Colin. Maybe it's your brother,' she said with the immovable logic of a three-year-old.

'Now you're being silly,' Peggy said and Linda laughed out loud and ran downstairs. Peggy shook her head. She felt as though she had been caught up in a whirlwind and she was about to close the door when she heard Elsie ask Linda, 'I thought you'd gone back to the Barlows'. Where on earth have you been?'

'I've been talking to Peggy in my room. She was crying.'

'Now, Linda, you must stop this.' Elsie sounded cross. 'What have I told you about telling fibs?'

'I'm not telling fibs,' she heard Linda insist, and she could imagine the scowl on the little girl's face.

'Then who were you really talking to? Your imaginary friend again? Cos that in my book is just as bad as telling lies. Either way, you're making things up. Now tell me what you were really doing. Talking to your pillow or whatever it is you chat with up there? I thought I told you to stop that nonsense now that you're getting to be a big girl.'

'I only spoke to my pillow a little bit,' Peggy heard Linda say. 'I was really talking to Peggy.' But that response made Elsie even more cross and Peggy heard her emitting a loud, exasperated sigh. At the same time the sound of a smart slap echoed up the stairs, followed by a yelp.

'What was that for?' Linda wailed.

'It was a reminder to stop telling fibs!' Elsie said crossly. 'Honestly, you make up such stories I'm worried you're actually beginning to believe them. I told you, Peggy's gone away so you could hardly be talking to her in your bedroom, now could you?'

'But I was!' Linda sounded defiant now as she tried to talk over her tears, and Peggy, breathing heavily, had to close the bedroom door quickly. But almost immediately she heard an urgent-sounding knock that she thought must be Linda and she only had seconds to decide what to say. She couldn't stand by and let the little girl take the blame when she was really the innocent party. Peggy knew she would have to come clean and explain everything to Elsie. She grabbed her cardigan that had been slung carelessly over a chair and opened the door, prepared to go downstairs, but it wasn't Linda, it was Elsie who was standing there, open-mouthed, with Linda tugging at her skirt behind her.

'What are you doing here?' Elsie sounded astonished. 'I thought you were long since gone and I was just telling Linda off for telling porkies.'

'I know and I'm sorry, I was coming down to explain that you shouldn't take it out on her cos it's all my fault, really.'

To Peggy's relief, Elsie's face relaxed. 'Well, why don't you come down now? We can have a cup of tea and you can tell me what's happened.'

Chapter 43

'So long as you're sure you're not ill or anything,' was Elsie's first comment as they sat down at the table. Linda had propped open a picture book and was pretending to read it, although Peggy knew she was really listening.

'No, I'm fine,' Peggy assured her, and she told Elsie the story of the letters and her mother's broken wrist.

'But why didn't you say anything?' Elsie sounded incredulous. 'I'd have understood.'

Peggy shrugged. 'I don't know really, but I was so upset and ashamed of my father's behaviour and that my own mother was shutting me out like that . . .' She hesitated. 'I can't begin to tell you how it made me feel. She didn't seem to be considering my feelings at all. And I felt I couldn't tell anybody. I suppose I just didn't want to admit she'd actually told me not to come.'

'But what were you going to do here all day? Sit and be miserable on your own?'

'I dunno,' Peggy admitted. 'I didn't really think it through. I reckoned, if the worst came to the worst, I could always stay in bed all day. I certainly didn't want to spoil your day – you've all been planning it for ages. You didn't need me tagging along.'

'Yes, but you wouldn't be tagging along. You must know folk round here by now, they'll always make room for one more, especially if it's someone they know and like, and they would be very happy to include you in their plans at any time, I know they would. My goodness, they supported the panto, didn't they? And don't they always go out of their way to make you feel at home in the Rovers?' Elsie was doing her best to help, but her comments just caused Peggy's tears to flow faster. 'And what about Jimmy?' Elsie tried a different tack. 'What's he up to today? Couldn't you have arranged to spend the day with him?'

'He was so pleased to think he'd helped Mam and me to patch things up that I couldn't bring myself to tell him when it all fell through,' Peggy said.

'Besides, I think his landlady had invited him to join in the lunch at the Mission when she heard he was likely to be on his own.'

'And what made you think *your* landlady wouldn't invite you if she'd have known?' Elsie sounded offended. 'Do you honestly think I'd have left you to spend the day alone if I'd have known the whole story?'

Peggy shrugged. 'I'm sorry, I suppose I really wasn't thinking.' She shook her head from side to side.

'You know we're all taking something from our own larders for everyone to share, so what's the difference if we take summat extra? We're all suffering from the same rationing, so no one will have anything special to offer, but I'm sure we can make whatever we bring stretch to one more sandwich so we can feed one more mouth.' She laughed. 'I'd have thought you'd made enough friends around here to know by now that we wouldn't have left you out in the cold. In this house, and most likely next door as well, you're as good as one of the family.'

At this point Elsie paused long enough to find a newly ironed handkerchief that she passed to Peggy to stem the flow of tears that continued to erupt.

'So that's settled, then,' Elsie said. 'Do we have a new agreement?'

'What's that?' Peggy looked at her, confused.

'No more bloody secrets, that's what!' Elsie said, with a laugh.

'I don't know how to thank you.' Now Peggy had something to wipe her eyes she was glad she wasn't smearing make-up across her cheeks.

'Don't thank me,' Elsie said, 'it's Linda you should be thanking, and I have to apologize for not believing her.'

'I think maybe she deserves to open her presents now, don't you?' Peggy said and she nudged Linda who stopped pretending to read and closed her book faster than greased lightning.

'Why don't you go and fetch the first parcel?' Elsie encouraged her, and Peggy watched as a delighted Linda began sorting through the pile of little packages that she was convinced had been dumped in the hearth by Santa. Well, Peggy thought, the morning may have got off to a rather bumpy start, but as far as I'm concerned it can only get better from here.

Her thoughts were interrupted by a squeal of laughter as Linda pulled the paper off one of the little parcels and sat staring at its contents.

'What's this, Mummy?' Linda picked up the small orange-coloured ball gingerly and frowned as she examined it, uncertain what to do with it. She tried squeezing it and then rolled it along the table, but it didn't go very far and she threw it in Elsie's direction.

'No, it's not a ball!' Elsie caught it but made no attempt to throw it back.

'What is it, then?' Linda was curious.

'It's something good to eat,' Elsie said, and Linda frowned as she tried to take a bite out of it.

'Not like that!' This time Peggy couldn't stop laughing and it was all she could do to stop Linda from sinking her teeth into the orange rind. 'You have to take the skin off first and you eat all the soft juicy bit that's inside. It's called an orange, although I suppose you've not seen one before. I only remember them faintly from when I was a child myself.'

'I don't think Linda's ever seen one,' Elsie said, 'and I can't tell you how difficult it was to find that one, but I was determined we would have at least one to share between us this Christmas.'

Linda slowly worked her way through the pile of little packages, revealing such items as a small colouring book and some brightly coloured crayons, a fairy story book for Elsie to read to her, and some woolly gloves that Elsie had found on the local market. Peggy had added to the pile with a bright hand-knitted scarf she had made out of an old jumper she had unpicked. Linda loved it immediately and once she had tried it on she didn't want to take it off.

Linda had just presented Elsie with her specially

hand-drawn picture of a two-child family who lived together in a large house when there was a knock at the front door.

'It must be Ida,' Elsie said, smiling as she got up to open it. 'I told her I'd got a little something for the boys.' But when she opened the door her eyes widened in shock. 'Peggy, it's someone for you,' she called out, then said, 'Do come in,' to the newcomers. And before Peggy could get to the hallway to see who it was, Elsie had ushered her mother and brother into the kitchen.

'I couldn't let Christmas come and go without seeing you,' her mother said after everyone had hugged and been introduced, 'and I couldn't work out how else I could give you these . . .' She handed Peggy a soft package, then she eased herself into the chair Peggy pulled out for her and rested her plastered wrist and sling on the table. 'Colin here was all for coming on his own if I couldn't have come, he was that desperate to see you, Peg, but I felt easier in my mind bringing him myself.' Her face was drawn and gaunt but she managed a brief smile.

'I'm pleased you could both make it,' Elsie said. 'I'm delighted Peggy has her own family here for Christmas and you're very welcome, but I must tell you that we're off out soon, to our Coronation Street Christmas dinner.'

Mrs Brown's face dropped and her eyes blanked in obvious pain.

Elsie smiled widely. 'But of course you must come with us! Peggy is one of us, now.'

Peggy clapped her hands together, feeling like a child again. 'Oh, you must come,' she said enthusiastically, 'if you think it will be all right, Elsie?' Then she giggled. 'We'll be taking over this party soon,' she said.

'Why don't I go and raid the larder, see what else we can take to help feed us all?' Elsie said, and she left the Browns to catch up on their news.

They picked up the Barlow family as they set off for the Mission, and when they arrived found Ena Sharples was already belting out tunes on the piano while her friends Minnie Caldwell and Martha Longhurst were encouraging everyone to join in and sing along. Annie Walker, the landlady from the Rovers, seemed to have taken on the mantle of being in charge of laying the tables. When the original party had turned into a sit down meal it was agreed that everyone would benefit from the space provided by the Mission hall and Annie Walker had given in gracefully when they decided to change the venue. But she had still volunteered to take on the responsibility of sorting out the food.

Peggy was surprised to find several extra places

had already been laid out for her and her family. 'We always do that,' Annie Walker said confidentially when Peggy introduced her mother, 'to make people feel welcome. In my experience there are always some late cancellations as well as a few last-minute extra guests who need to be catered for, and we do like everyone to feel included right from the start.' Peggy thanked Annie, although she was only half listening as her eyes were busily scanning the room, eagerly looking out for Jimmy. Now she no longer had to keep it a secret she couldn't wait to tell him her news.

'So, you're the mysterious young man from the theatre,' Mrs Brown said, when Peggy eventually introduced the assistant director and that made Jimmy laugh.

'I don't know about mysterious,' he said 'but I'm certainly from the theatre where your daughter has been acting in the panto.'

'Then you must be the kind young man Colin told me about when you took our Peg to see him at school.'

'Yes, I suppose I am,' Jimmy said with a laugh and he made a dismissive gesture with his hand.

Mrs Brown lowered her voice. 'Well, you might not want everyone to know but I need to tell you how delighted I was to get those pantomime tickets you sent and I'm pleased to be able to thank you in person for them. It was such a surprise, and it was very generous of you and we'll be there, broken wrist or no broken wrist. I'm looking forward to it and so's Colin, as you might imagine. We're counting off the days and I might even be rid of this thing by then,' she said, indicating the sling, and she tentatively lifted her plastered wrist although she had to lower it again quickly.

Jimmy beamed. 'It's nothing,' he said. 'I look forward to seeing you then. And I hope you'll be able to see Peggy in lots of other productions as well, once the panto season is over. I've got all sorts of plans,' he went on, his eyes twinkling.

'Oh, is she going to be in lots of other things too?' Mrs Brown asked eagerly.

Peggy couldn't believe her mother was talking so openly.

'She will if I have my way,' Jimmy said.

'Well, if she gets any more theatre work in Weatherfield in the future she won't have to worry about getting digs,' Elsie said. 'A bed at number 11 will always be waiting for her; it will be her home away from home.'

'Oh, you'll be seeing a lot more of her from now on, you mark my words,' Jimmy said, 'she's going places that one, she's going to be a star.'

Peggy only caught the tail end of their conversation and she felt her cheeks flame as she approached.

She didn't like to interrupt, but her heart had warmed to hear Jimmy's encouraging words. Fresh tears welled when she realized that, without her knowledge but as good as his word, he had sent two tickets for the panto directly to her mam. She felt quite overwhelmed, wondering how she would ever be able to thank him enough.

As Elsie had predicted, Peggy and her family were warmly welcomed at the Mission hall and places had already been laid out for them all to sit together. Peggy had just settled her mother into a chair beside her – Colin had disappeared, having been taken under the wing of Annie Walker's boisterous son Billy – when there was a shout and a call to order.

'Ladies and gentlemen!' It was Annie Walker, who seemed to fall into the MC role almost naturally at such well-populated functions. 'Ladies and gentlemen . . . no, what I really should say is: good friends and neighbours, it seems I've got the pleasure of welcoming you all here,' Annie began. She looked around the room and there was a ripple of laughter. 'Glasses of wine and bottles of beer are now available on the table over there,' she pointed, 'so please make sure you go and help yourselves or shout out if you need some help.' There was a general flurry of activity as everyone rushed to fill their glasses and then Annie came forward again. 'I will now ask you all to kindly raise your glasses,' she said, leading the way by lifting hers. 'Now we can wish everyone a very Merry Christmas and may the new year bring the peace we all long for.' Everyone drank and then Annie raised her glass again. 'And now I suggest we drink to old friends and new beginnings.'

'To old friends and new beginnings!' the shout went up together with the raised glasses, and Peggy found herself laughing and crying at the same time.

Acknowledgements

It is only on completion of a new book when the work of everyone involved is finished that there is finally time for the author to sit back and reflect on the entire process from initial conception of the idea to the final production of the book itself. It is only then that the author can consider and recognize the valuable part played by everyone, the professional team and all those who have been involved in the process, for without them there would have been no book.

The production of a book is no mean feat at any time and is not something a writer can tackle alone. Each writer treads their own path in their own way through the sticky treacle of characters and plot, but at the end of that journey when I wrote the magic words 'The End', I was finally able to sit back and reflect on the process, to consider the contributions made by those who had guided me along the way and to acknowledge the debt that I owed to the various individuals involved.

Thanks on this occasion therefore go to my wonderful editor Kate Bradley, Publishing Director at HarperCollins, for her help and guidance, and to my always-at-the-end-of-the-phone agent, Kate Nash, for all her support. I would like to thank my friends and family, who supported me through the difficult bits, in particular Rita and Miriam, Hanna Klein, Kathryn Finlay, my professional colleagues Ann Parker and Jannet Wright, and my fellow romantic writers Sue Moorcroft and Pia Fenton (Christina Courtney) for their help and understanding. Special thanks also go to actor Sunny Ormonde for setting me straight about the theatrical world.

Thanks also to Dominic Khouri and the team at ITV for their invaluable help and advice on the world of *Coronation Street*.

Maggie Sullivan

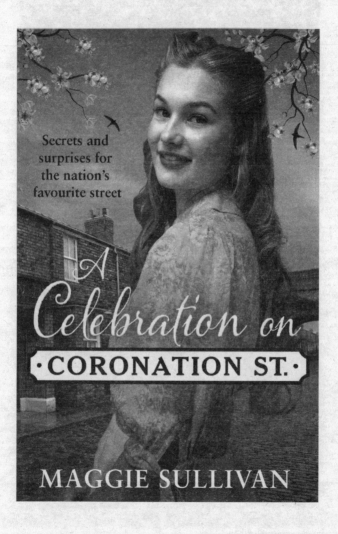

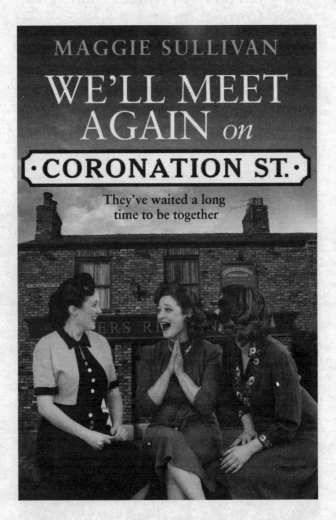

MAGGIE SULLIVAN

WE'LL MEET AGAIN *on*

·CORONATION ST.·

They've waited a long
time to be together